Leaving Yesler

Leaving Yesler

a novel by
Peter Bacho

Pleasure Boat Studio: A Literary Press
New York, NY

Leaving Yesler
©2010 by Peter Bacho

ISBN 978-1-929355-57-0

Library of Congress Cataloging-in-Publication Data
    Bacho, Peter.
    Leaving Yesler / by Peter Bacho.
        p.   cm.
    Summary: Bobby, a sensitive seventeen-year-old living in the projects of
Seattle in 1968, copes with his mother's death from cancer and his brother's
death in Vietnam, and tries to determine his own identity in the midst of
many challenges.
    ISBN 978-1-929355-57-0 (alk. paper)
    [1. Coming of age—Fiction.   2. Grief—Fiction.   3. Filipino
Americans—Fiction.   4. Racially mixed people—Fiction.   5. Seattle
(Wash.)—History—20th century—Fiction.]   I. Title.

PZ7.B132174Le 2010
[Fic]—dc22   2009038945

Design by Susan Ramundo
Cover by Rick Landry

The author wishes to acknowledge PNWA's 2005 anthology *The Pen and the Key*,
which published two chapters of this novel in celebration of its 50th anniversary.

Pleasure Boat Studio is a proud subscriber to the Green Press Initiative. This
program encourages the use of 100% post-consumer recycled paper with
environmentally friendly inks for all printing projects in an effort to reduce
the book industry's economic and social impact. With the cooperation of our
printing company, we are pleased to offer this book
as a Green Press book.

Pleasure Boat Studio books are available through the following:
SPD (Small Press Distribution) Tel. 800-869-7553, Fax 510-524-0852
Partners/West Tel. 425-227-8486, Fax 425-204-2448
Baker & Taylor Tel. 800-775-1100, Fax 800-775-7480
Ingram Tel. 615-793-5000, Fax 615-287-5429
Amazon.com and **bn.com**

and through

PLEASURE BOAT STUDIO: A LITERARY PRESS
www.pleasureboatstudio.com
201 West 89th Street
New York, NY 10024
Contact **Jack Estes**
Fax: 888-810-5308
Email: *pleasboat@nyc.rr.com*

to mary and to an old community that no longer exists

Chapter One

Bobby Vincente thought that after his mother died a year ago, things couldn't have gotten worse—but they did. For the last two months, he'd been wandering in a fog after getting news that Paulie wasn't coming back from Vietnam.

Time stopped immediately, his sense of it becoming a confusing mix of out-of-body dreams and unconnected fragments of memory. There was the cold, blustery day of the funeral. He remembered, or thought he did, the flag-draped coffin; Taps being played; his father, Antonio, mouth open, staring at nothing.

Then he remembered, or thought he did, hearing someone say that the casket had to stay closed. Paulie, the voice whispered, was in too many pieces. There wasn't enough of him left for the undertaker to put back together.

But that couldn't have been. For a moment, Bobbie saw Paulie through the corner of his eye. He was whole and standing next to him, his arms and legs intact. He gently put his hand on his younger brother's shoulder and told him not to cry, please don't cry, that no number of tears would change what happened.

Besides, Paulie snarled, it was embarrassing. No brother of his should be caught dead crying.

Bad for the rep, especially in Yesler Terrace, he said, where surviving depended on rep. "You're soft," Paulie whispered. "Don't matter to me; just don't let your enemies see."

Bobbie, head still bowed, nodded and mumbled, "Okay." He turned to his brother, a wan smile his sign of understanding. But this time all he saw was his father, standing stock still with his eyes closed, lost in the fissures of his ruptured heart.

Bobbie was just as lost, Paulie's unexpected appearance notwithstanding. He began wondering if he'd seen his brother at all. Maybe it was just a daytime dream, like the night dreams in which Paulie routinely appeared, cracking jokes and offering advice.

But seeing Paulie in a dream was one thing, seeing him during the day and someplace he shouldn't have been was another. Bobby wondered if his sorrow was finally making him crazy and that his unbroken sadness, his worries about the future and a boat full of other unspecified concerns, had nudged him over the edge.

Today was no different, another messed-up day in the mush. He had skipped his afternoon classes at Taft High in Seattle and caught a bus downtown, revisiting the seedy places he and Paulie used to prowl, always at his brother's insistence. Now it was a ritual, a habit—his way of killing time and remembering. On First Avenue, he toured the pawn shops, then the adult bookstores—making sure to lower the brim of his dark blue baseball cap to look older and more mysterious than seventeen. He fooled enough clerks to last most of the afternoon, before a bug-eyed, cranky graybeard—probably the owner—told him to buy something or get the hell out.

Bobby shrugged. In truth, the ladies in leather bored him. He glanced at his watch—twenty to five, close to the time Dad expected him home. Just as well, he figured, as he walked out of the store without saying a word.

On his way home, he walked by a tavern Paulie had taken him to before he went overseas. Paulie, two years older by a day, was in uniform when he and Bobby walked into the joint. Paulie lowered his voice and told a burly bartender with U.S. Navy tattoos on his forearms that this was his last night stateside, and that even though he wasn't 21, he was old enough to die for his country. The least his ungrateful fellow Americans could do was to serve him a Bud in a frosted mug in this, his indifferent hometown.

Preferably on the house, he added with a wink.

"And don't forget my buddy here," Paulie said, pointing to his brother.

"He's leavin' next week."

Bobby grunted on cue. "Gotta stop them commies," he mumbled and watched as Paulie's latest Oscar-caliber performance summoned a patriotic parade of beers—all on the house. Same, too, with the cheeseburgers and fries that followed.

"Land of the free," Paulie whispered to his brother.

That was Paulie, who seemed to have been born with a swagger—and the physical skills to back it up. Try as he might, Bobby could never quite match his brother's blood-chilling stare and quick fists.

But the differences didn't end there. Built-like-a-beer-keg Paulie was dark, just like Dad, and he had oversized knuckles on his thick hands. Just like Dad.

Despite being younger, Bobby was slightly taller—and much thinner. But the trait that caught neighbors' attention was the color of his skin. He was much lighter than Paulie, which was hard to figure since Dad was the color of old mahogany and Mom was part black.

High-Yella, some of the kids in their housing project called him, usually behind his back but sometimes to his face.

Bobby was cool with the other Filipino kids—most of them were mixes of some kind anyway, with Filipino fathers and fill-in-the-blank mothers. No problem there.

But a few of the black boys would sometimes call him out over that, and he'd always show up, whether he wanted to or not. They became bolder after black became beautiful, and he wasn't black enough. When Stokely and others raised the closed-fist sign and snarled revolution, they thrilled a generation of young black people. But Bobby just watched.

Sure, he could do it, but only in private. Otherwise, he felt like a fake, a one-drop-of-blood pretender. The truth was, he wasn't especially angry—or at least not enough to take it to the streets. He didn't—couldn't—see the world in black and white.

His looks led Bobby to his share of scuffles. But he managed to avoid many more battles because his would-be predators knew full well they'd have Paulie to deal with later.

That's what Cortez had to learn the hard way two years before. Cortez—first name or last, no one knew—was a juvy-hall veteran who conked his hair like the other thugs and declared himself to be an up-and-coming gangster, the baddest young brother in Yesler Terrace or any other project. One day, he snuck up on Bobby, called out his name and sucker punched him when he turned around.

As he slumped to the sidewalk, Bobby could hear laughter from more than one source. "High-yella punk," Cortez snorted as he and his pals fished through Bobby's pockets for loose change. Bobby struggled to rise, but couldn't because Cortez had placed a size-ten high-top Converse squarely on the side of his neck.

"Little boy, if I was you, I'd stay right where you are," Cortez snarled before turning to walk away.

It took Paulie a couple of days to catch up with his brother's attacker, but when he did he wanted to make sure Cortez would always remember their meeting. A friend told him that Cortez and his buddies sometimes hung out at a convenience store a block east of the Terrace. For at least a couple of hours, they'd cluster near the store entrance, talk loud, drink port from paper cups, and use the pay phone to buy and sell drugs.

According to his source, Cortez always began his Friday nights like this. He and his friends would eventually leave—between eight and nine—but would often stop by Cortez's apartment before disappearing into the night. Paulie smiled. That meant they'd be walking up one of the narrow, dimly lit paths that honeycombed the projects.

On such a path one Friday night Paulie jumped out from the shadows and used a 28-ounce Louisville Slugger saved from his Little League days to break Cortez's left shoulder and one of his legs. Paulie chose the ultra-light bat because he knew there was a chance he'd have to slug more than one target. But Cortez's too-high friends, upon hearing their leader scream something about his leg, fled in different directions, leaving Cortez crumpled on the ground to face his fate.

"That's for Bobby. Remember his name," Paulie said evenly, as he turned to walk away. "And if you call the cops, or come after him, brotha man, I know where you live."

The girls, though, found Bobby handsome. More than a few said he was "pretty"—a description that bestowed on its bearer a mixed blessing on the street. Angie, a Filipino-Indian girl, spent her day teasing her thick, black hair so that a handful of strands always defied gravity, standing up and curling at the ends. She lived two units down and told him one day that he looked like Smokey—as in Smokey Robinson—and ooh,

Baby, Baby, her folks were at work so could he please come over and croon to her some falsetto lyrics of love?

He declined the invitation—and several others—because he wasn't interested. He may have been the only boy in the Terrace to have ever turned Angie down. But he just wasn't interested.

He'd heard the whispers—that he was *that way*—but he ignored them. He didn't dislike Angie or the other girls he knew, but he wasn't fond of what it took to get and keep them—the late-night creeping, the loud-talking, fist-throwing, territory-establishing rituals that other boys did.

Silly, he thought, too much mess—way too much, especially for the young women, whose main value seemed to be their skill at making their less-than-faithful lovers feel good about themselves. He'd seen it happen too many times. They would be the ones left holding diapered surprises and having even less chance of changing their lives and leaving Yesler. It happened to Angie, who gave birth to twins a year or so ago. No sign of the kids since. Word had it they were with an aunt in Tacoma or sucked up by the state.

And now she was ready to risk it all again. Bobby thought she was foolish, but not that different from a lot of the other Yesler girls he knew.

"Get over here, girl," Bobby had heard streetwise Romeos snarl at Angie and other young women often enough. But it wasn't just the words that stung his ears, it was the universal tone, like a master summoning his beaten-down dog. If that was all he wanted, he'd have gone to the pound and adopted a beagle or some telegenic Lassie lookalike.

Bobby expected more, or maybe it was less—he wasn't sure. He figured that having a girlfriend should be simpler and fairer—two people meeting, talking, finding out they liked each other, deciding to be together, deciding to be apart.

That's why entertaining Angie was the furthest thing from his mind. He knew how she'd expect him to be, and that just wasn't him. Besides, he had other things to worry about, like how he looked, which bothered him because it led him to questions he didn't want to ask.

Mom said Paulie's looks and attitude reminded her of Dad before the war. Bobby once summoned the nerve to ask her who he reminded her of.

She smiled and kissed his cheek. "An artist, Baby," she said.

Mom was right. Bobby loved to sing and write and sketch and, money permitting, paint pictures of scenes not seen in the projects. He often spent hours by himself poring over books and magazines. He tried keeping his preferences to himself because that meant being soft—or worse, being seen by others as being soft. In Yesler Terrace, that was a hard ticket to ride, Paulie's frequent intervention notwithstanding.

Now he had to ride it alone, without his brother, who would have shown him how to navigate the shoals of insults and challenges—and fear.

But two weeks short of Paulie's return date, he got nailed by a mortar. He wasn't being heroic or anything like that. He was a draftee, not someone born in red-white-and-blue swaddling clothes. In one letter he wrote that the longer he stayed, the less sense the war made. "I ain't no politician, so maybe there's a reason for this bullshit," the letter began. "But I'm sure having a hard time seeing it. I'm an accidental soldier. There's a bunch of us here." All he wanted now was to go home in one piece, take off his uniform, learn a trade, and leave the projects.

It was all too tragic, all too avoidable. Paulie could have skipped Vietnam by going to college and getting a deferment. His parents pleaded with him not to go.

His mom told him that a lot of black folks she knew had turned against this war. "Got no dog in this fight," a first cousin told her. "It's a white folks' war; let them fight it."

Later, Mom heard that that young fighter Clay—the good looking man-child who'd suddenly became a Muslim, Muhammad something-or-other—had blasted the war.

She liked her cousin, but his opinion wasn't worth much, especially since he was always unemployed, always mooching from relatives up and down the West Coast—and didn't seem the least bit inclined to change his ways. She felt the same about Clay, who had reached the top of a sport she no longer followed once her husband, Antonio, a former main-event pug, hung up his gloves. She knew Clay's loud boasts and quick hands weren't signs of wisdom.

But Martin Luther King was different. The day he turned against the war was the day before she turned against the war. What he stood for stirred the few drops of black blood in her veins.

That mix of blood had served Eula Williams well when she was young and growing up in dusty, redneck Sacramento. Her light complexion, slender figure, and doe-brown eyes often allowed her entry to a larger world denied her darker siblings, cousins, and friends. She even had reddish hair and a handful of freckles, thanks to a line of French and Spanish hustlers, buccaneers and rascals in New Orleans who thought that keeping women out of their beds because of their race or social status was an odd Northern European fetish—and the silliest thing imaginable.

"My name's Carmen," the pretty girl named Eula had often told strangers, or at least those she thought she could con. "Carmen," as in "Miranda," being code for Cuban, Creole, Hawaiian, anything exotic, anything but black.

In fact, it was one of the reasons she married Antonio, who in his prime was handsome, dapper, and athletic. "A future champ," one local beat writer wrote. "An action guy, can't miss," gushed another.

Eula considered Antonio one of the prize catches in this nation's racial underbelly. Politicians showed up at his fights, so did just-passing-through-town movie stars on their way to Los Angeles. Although Antonio was dark, he wasn't black; that was a plus in the slice of America that she knew.

But she didn't know many Filipinos then and what she didn't understand was that a lot of whites who hated blacks also hated Filipinos, sometimes even worse. It was an unforeseen drag on her dream of marriage as a vehicle to a better life.

Instead they eventually became just another colored couple trying to scrape by, especially after Antonio returned from the war, a washed-up fighter, a wounded and diminished man. Those were hard days and she'd thought of packing it in, especially after Paulie was born and she noticed her once eye-catching features beginning to stretch, wrinkle, and shift south. Sure, she still got her share of smiles and knowing glances from men she passed on the street or in the nearby IGA—just not as many as before.

But thoughts of leaving had been interrupted by the birth of Bobby, who, unlike his constantly crying brother, was a sweet-tempered, easy-to-please child. Bobby was a surprise—Eula had made sure she took precautions.

One night while dreaming of leaving she awoke and saw the infant smiling and sleeping and nestled in the arms of her husband. It was where Bobby belonged and wanted to be—a snapshot so lovely it caused her to turn away.

"I'm sorry, I'm sorry," she whispered to no one in particular.

*   *   *

For Dad, his reasons for opposing the war—or at least opposing Paulie's involvement in it—were much simpler. He didn't pay attention to politicians, protestors or even the famous Dr. King. He had a hard time paying attention to too much of anything, especially since that night at the Cow Palace in Frisco when, short on cash (he was always short on cash, especially since meeting Eula), he took a bout in December 1941 on three days notice. That night he ran into a fighter who must have been the last Neanderthal, a thick-skulled Italian buzzsaw from Chicago who hadn't read the local clips proclaiming Antonio as the next big thing.

The fight was fierce from the first seconds of the first round. Antonio, who had quicker hands, threw his best shots, blows that had stopped other guys cold. His opponent just grunted and took them, refusing to wither or even take a step back. When it was over—at thirty seconds of the seventh round— Antonio was face down on the canvas, unable to rise.

His last thought before losing consciousness was that his opponent must have been the toughest man on the planet— the type to avoid or at least stall until advancing age after the blows of other opponents had taken their toll.

The fans were so excited by the action and the bloodletting that several of them threw dollar bills and coins into the ring, a few of the quarters bouncing off Antonio's glistening back. He didn't feel them.

He woke up four days later—just in time to discover that Japan had bombed Pearl Harbor and attacked the Philippines. The newspapers predicted that a full-fledged invasion of the islands was sure to follow.

The hospital eventually released him after several months, the docs warning him to rest and not do too much. He was, they told him, lucky to be alive. Boxing, of course, was out of the question.

Antonio could have sat the war out, a course that would have pleased Eula, no doubt. But there were these memories of a younger, slower life full of family and laughter and friends. At first, Antonio thought that that was then—it was over—and that he loved Eula more than anything else. All true—but not true enough to one day keep him from hiding his condition and talking himself into the Army—not that the recruiters needed much convincing to take one more warm, gun-toting body in this brutal two-front war.

Almost three years later, Uncle Sam sent him home to his wife. They were together again—a good thing—but it wasn't the same. The money, the classy suits, the silk dresses were gone. Same with the fans waiting to talk or to shake the hand of someone on the cusp of fame.

Actually, Eula had stayed the same, but her husband hadn't. Both in his dreams and waking moments Antonio remembered too often and too well the sights and sounds of combat.

He knew that survival was mostly a matter of luck—something out of his control. So why even gamble in the first place? He figured the price he'd paid should be enough to cover the lives of his sons.

Besides, he'd just seen a photo of a captured Viet Cong on the front page of one of the local papers. The prisoner reminded him of Efren Lorenzo, one of his GI pals who was killed on the Philippine island of Leyte.

Efren was a soft, sweet soul who dutifully prayed the rosary, freely confessed his fears, and carried a picture of his mother in his wallet. He told him once that his main goal was to see her—she lived in a province up north—once the fighting on Leyte stopped. A wonderful son, Dad thought at the time, but he had no business being in the infantry.

More than two decades later, the old man couldn't imagine Efren—or anyone resembling him—posing much of a threat to anyone, much less the United States of America.

*   *   *

Paulie nodded and listened politely to the protests of his folks. But going to college was out of the question. He didn't have the grades, the inclination, the money.

"We'll pay for your schooling," they said.

"Mom, Dad, look at us," he replied. "We're livin' in the projects; we ain't rich. You need the money more than I do."

Paulie felt the same about hopping a bus and heading for Canada. He patiently explained it was too cold there, and he didn't want to learn "Canadian" or watch hockey.

"Hey, man," he later told a draft-eligible friend who was considering the move. "They speak French there, or somethin'."

There was one more reason. For Paulie, the prospect of going to war wasn't particularly frightening. He'd already been shot at at short range by an angry husband whose twenty-something wife was a willing participant in a late-summer-night backseat affair. The bullet grazed the oversized sleeve of Paulie's Hawaiian shirt as he tumbled out of the car, using the door for cover. The slug put a hole in the backside of a white flamingo, but otherwise missed its mark. Once outside, Paulie gathered himself and charged his attacker, tackling him and taking his weapon. For good measure, he started beating him with the butt of the gun until the wife, who had become hysterical, begged him to stop.

Paulie was convinced that his close brush with death was a sign from God. It added to his Yesler Terrace rep and led him to conclude that no one, short of Batman himself, could ever bring him down. That obviously included the Viet Cong.

Besides, an Army tour wasn't forever—or at least that's what Paulie said. "It's like doin' time in juvy," he told Bobby. "Did a year once, no sweat."

Two months before he died, Paulie had written and assured the family he'd almost beaten the rap, that he was down to counting the days and hours left and looking for excuses to stay out of the jungle.

"The Viet Cong," he wrote, "will have to find me to kill me."

And that's exactly what the enemy did.

Paulie got himself assigned to guarding an air base and was sleeping when the mortar with his name on it ended his life—and ruined the life of his younger brother who was depending on him.

For Bobby, losing Mom had been hard. Paulie, back home on leave, found the sorrow overwhelming and wished, for a moment, that he had never come. Dad and Bobby were lost, inconsolable. But everyone knew the cancer that was chewing

Eula's stomach would eventually eat all of it. Worrying every day about her oldest boy had made a bad situation worse. So when this vibrant, strong woman finally passed, at least a few of Bobby's tears were tears of relief.

But for Bobby, Paulie's death made daily life almost impossible. His brother would have known what to do; he'd have known what to do with Dad.

Bobby loved his father, but over the last few years, the old man began losing what little he had to start with. First came the dead-of-night screams a few years back, then the daytime lapses where Dad would stare blankly at Bobby or Paulie or Mom and squint his eyes, as if squinting would somehow repair a broken link in his chain of memory.

Mom had told her sons that the head blows from his time in the ring didn't help. Neither did the metal fragments Army docs pulled out of his neck and the base of his skull after a firefight on another Philippine island, Samar. The only thing good about it was that the injuries got him a ticket home.

At the time, he thought he was lucky. Unlike Efren or another close pal, Diony, Japanese artillery hadn't turned him into a bloody splotch and fragments of bone. Lucky, he figured, at least for a while.

"He's a good man," Mom had told Bobby and Paulie, after his luck took a hike and the screams and the memory gaps began. "We just need to understand, be patient and love him more."

On the surface and for most of the time, Dad seemed fine, no different from the Filipino fathers of the other Pinoy old-time Seattle families Bobby and Paulie knew. And other than the docs at the VA, Mom said there was no good reason to let anyone else know otherwise.

* * *

As Bobby turned east on Yesler, the shortest route home, his mind wandered to when he and Paulie were children and running unattended up and down this same street. Sometimes he and Paulie would ambush passing cars with dirt bombs and rocks lobbed from behind garbage cans and fences. They'd then duck and listen for screeching brakes—their sign to run. Once, after sunset, Paulie even nailed a police officer who had made the mistake of cruising by on a hot August evening with his window rolled down.

On Saturday nights, Dad's cronies would come visit for a night of poker and booze. One of Bobby's favorites, Manong Magno, traveled the farthest. He had a farm near Renton that the family would periodically visit. Bobby liked the array of animals, the pigs in particular.

The men—Uncle this or Manong that—would sit at the small kitchen table, hunched over and cursing in Filipino as they stared at their cards until the black-and-white Indian-head sign appeared on the screen of the small television on the counter.

No matter how late they played, Sundays were always the same. Rain or shine, Dad, Mom, and the two boys would rise early and dress in their Sunday best. But their destination was never Saint James, the Catholic cathedral just six blocks away. Instead, they would walk the other way toward Chinatown, less than a mile from their home. Dad would hand Mom a twenty and send her and the kids to eat—and he would eventually join them—but not before spending time with the other nattily dressed old Filipino men clustered near the entrances of the different restaurants, bars, and dingy bachelor hotels many of them still called home.

Bobby smiled. Great times, he thought, as he turned left on Eighth—the last short stretch before home. But that was two deaths ago.

Since then, Dad had turned inward, losing himself down a tunnel of sorrow and selective recollection. Bobby often had to remind him to cash his disability checks and a small monthly pension from some long-ago job. His father, who used to cook and clean the apartment, had stopped doing either task. Bobby now did both, and often had to serve Dad his breakfast and dinner in bed.

Bobby stopped under a street lamp and raised his watch to the light: five on the nose. Home was just a block away, and if he hustled, he could coax yesterday's bland chicken with enough crushed garlic, vinegar, grease, and soy sauce into becoming a reasonably passable meal. Bobby took his cooking seriously, at first because he had to; now, it was equal parts a matter of pride, imagination, and art. He figured he did it pretty well most of the time.

Bobby stepped back into the dark and turned toward home, distracted by the challenge of turning a lifeless chunk of overcooked poultry into something edible. That was a mistake, one Paulie never would have made.

"Be alert and suspicious," Paulie had always told him. "Especially here at night."

Bobby ignored that basic lesson of life-in-the-projects wisdom as he walked, head down, wondering about the right balance between soy and vinegar. A matter of taste, he concluded, and he would lean toward a spoonful more of the latter.

That was his last cogent thought. For Bobby, the next few minutes passed as a blur. He was suddenly on his hands and knees and wondering how he got there, what he should do next. He then felt the thud of two quick kicks to his ribs, the second one strong enough to lift him and send him sprawling face-first to the concrete.

"Sissy, high-yella punk," he heard his assailant grunt. "Too bad 'bout your brother."

The voice was familiar, but far more familiar was another voice—a man's voice cursing loudly, drawing nearer. Bobby was relieved and surprised—and couldn't decide which reaction was stronger.

"Boy, stand still so I can cut you up like, uh," the second voice commanded with a heavy accent. The speaker was stammering, struggling to finish the threat.

"Uh, like a chicken and eat you tonight, yeah, uh, like a chicken," he finally said, sounding pleased.

As painful as it was to move, Bobby glanced up to see the streetlight shimmer off a stainless steel blade thrusting forward and withdrawing, thrusting forward and withdrawing.

"Cool now, just be cool," the attacker said nervously over the sounds of a slow shuffled retreat that quickly assumed a much quicker cadence. Bobby knew he was safe now. His assailant was running, but the new sounds were odd, uneven, like he was favoring one leg over another.

"Pilay," the second voice said sadly in Filipino. "Even for a cripple, he's still too fast for me."

Bobby then felt himself being lifted to his feet and having his arm draped around a shoulder—thick, compact and familiar.

"Thanks, Dad," Bobby mumbled.

"I was dozing, and I heard this voice tell me to get up," his father said. "So I get up jus' like that and funny thing . . ."

"What's that?"

Dad paused to carefully assemble the words he wanted to say next. "Sound like your brother," he finally said.

Bobby was silent for a moment.

His father slowly shook his head. "Ah, but you know," he said dismissively. "Never mind. Mebbe just an old man's dream. . . ."

"Maybe not," Bobby finally said.

Dad smiled. "All of this, uh, reminds me."

"What's that?" Bobby asked.

"Gotta keep it together long enough to teach you, boy," he said, as they turned to walk toward the apartment.

"What?"

"How to duck, son."

Chapter Two

"You're lucky," the emergency room doc told Bobby as he patched him up. He had a couple of broken ribs—but no organ damage—and he'd eventually heal. "Just don't move around too much."

"Don' worry," Dad told the doctor. "He won'."

For the next three weeks, Dad was true to his word. He resumed cooking—or trying to—but would sometimes just stand over a steaming pot and stare at the wall or at the ceiling trying to remember what ingredients to use. When Dad got it right, the stew or the marinated pork was good to the last bite, just like when Paulie and Mom were still alive. Even when he missed something—like the liver in liver and onions—Bobby covered it with fresh steamed rice and gobbled it down without complaint.

"Oh, forgot the liver," Dad said on that occasion.

Bobby shrugged. "Still pretty good."

Bobby knew without being told that his father, who was no good with words—at least English words—was trying his best. He was showing his affection through other ways, like cooking. And Bobby showed his appreciation by eating whatever he served.

Dad also called Taft and told the principal that his boy wasn't coming to school this week or ever again, and please save the value-of-education speech because Bobby wasn't going to do like Paulie and sit through vocational ed classes crammed full of black and brown throwaway kids. Before Paulie's induction notice came, Mom and Dad begged him to grab the deferment by getting into college, any college, but he just shrugged.

"Ain't ready," he said. "It ain't like Taft ever taught me nothin'."

"One boy's enough," Dad screamed at the principal, pleased he was able to make his point without stammering. "Bobby's no grease monkey; he's more'n that."

Dad's plan was for Bobby to go to the nearby community college—like he and his wife had discussed—where he could finish high school, get ready for a four-year college and stay out of the Army. Especially stay out of the Army. Dad figured that the war would be over by the time Bobby graduated.

"He, uh, deserves better than what you gave Paulie," he said, before slamming down the receiver.

The commotion awakened Bobby, who stumbled bleary-eyed into the living room and onto an old divan. He remembered when Mom and Dad brought it home, courtesy of one of Dad's rare good days at the horse track. But that was ten years ago, when it smelled brand new and gleamed with a distinctive multi-hued luster, since reduced to must, weak springs, and a run-on reddish-brown color. Like the coffee table and the other old furniture in the living room, the divan hadn't been moved from its original spot for years.

Eyebrows arched, Bobby watched as Dad mumbled and paced, seemingly oblivious to his son's presence.

"Dad?" Bobby said softly.

"No way, uh, no way," his father mumbled.

"No way what?" Bobby asked, the tone of his voice still cautious. The old man was obviously upset, and that worried him. If it didn't hurt so much to move, he would have risen from the divan and started pacing himself.

"You ain't goin' back," he said.

"To where?"

"Taft ... told the principal, Mr., uh, well, you know, whassisname."

"But Dad, this is my last year and . . .."

"You goin' to college," his father said.

Surprised, Bobby couldn't help but laugh. The notion of him in college seemed absurd, like maybe during the next few years he should also become the King of England. "But you know, college isn't for me," Bobby managed to say. "Or for any other kid from here for that matter, and besides, it costs money and . . ."

"Me and your mom we saved some money, so you goin' to college," his father declared in a tone meant to end discussion. "Simple as that."

*   *   *

For Bobby, it wasn't just as simple as that. Over the next few days, he tried getting used to the idea, never once voicing his fears to his father.

College? One afternoon, when he was alone, he closed his eyes and tried imagining himself sitting in class, surrounded by others who knew what they wanted. A few months back, he'd heard from the friend of a cousin that the professors expected students to read books and show up for class. The memory dampened his palms. At Taft, he might do one or the other, but seldom both within the same twenty-four-hour cycle.

It wasn't because he was dumb or undisciplined. Unlike Paulie, who'd never met a teacher he could stand, Bobby liked school—at least for a while. That's why his folks paid the extra money for him to attend St. James. The nuns used to rave about Bobby's imagination, his helpfulness, his eagerness to learn; they unanimously proclaimed he had a future. But that was long ago.

His Catholic school sojourn came abruptly to an end when one of Dad's late-night dreams became the main feature of an early matinee.

At the time, the old man was working at a fish cannery on the waterfront. One afternoon, he suddenly stopped slicing off fish heads and tails. Knife still in hand, Dad approached each of his fellow workers and politely whispered be quiet, please, because the Japanese were lurking nearby. He'd seen first-hand how they could turn into snakes and slither through the night to stab or strangle young GIs in their dreams.

That bit of advice got him a red-light ride to the Harborview shrinks, who uniformly agreed that any job involving knives and moving machinery should best be done by someone else.

Dad's sudden unemployment meant Bobby's next stops would be Gatzert Elementary and Washington Junior High schools, which drew kids from the projects. As a chorus, they pronounced Washington to be the best place in the city to get high or drunk—and not get busted. Washington graduates went to Taft, but no further. Teachers had no illusions or expectations. Many were burned-out public school vets, content to serve their last days in purgatory before retirement. They freely dipped into sick days and, when in class, yawned through the motions as they listened to themselves talk.

Their students responded with vacant stares or the unbroken drone of in-class laughter and conversation. Each side knew the game—an undisguised level of indifference matched and raised—everyone killing time until time to go home.

Washington was where Bobby first learned to ignore half-hearted efforts to educate him. He came to quickly understand the school's main function—as a warehouse for kids with no future.

Now, his father was asking him to rekindle a curiosity he'd allowed to go numb. Dad said the next quarter was starting in a month or so and that when his ribs were less sore, he could catch the bus to the college and register.

"Still got time," Dad said. "Give you the money then."

Dad's willingness to put money on his education bothered Bobby. It was his father's act of faith—a faith the son didn't share. Arms folded across his chest, Bobby stared out the living room window. On the tiny kitchen table was a pile of texts, undisturbed since he put them there during the first week of his last quarter at Taft.

Can't promise anything to Dad or myself, he thought as he slowly approached the table. But lately, he'd started wondering about the subjects he'd ignored. He obviously had time, and now might be as good a time as any to find out about them.

Chapter Three

A trio of loud, rhythmic thumps—paused then repeated time and again—jarred Bobby's bed, awakening him. He bolted straight up and looked out the window, fearful that the Housing Authority was demolishing their apartment without telling his father or him.

Couldn't be, he told himself. The noise was coming from the living room. As he left his bed and started walking toward the commotion, he realized he was finally breathing and moving pain free. Surprised, and more than a little pleased, he stopped and gently touched his ribs with his right index finger—a little tender, but that was all. Relieved, he opened the door to see an old leather heavy bag—its innards kept together by rolls of black electrical tape—swinging from the beam of the walkway joining the kitchen and the living room.

"No place else to put it," his father explained between grunts of three-punch combinations. "A little crowded, sure, but this gonna hafta do."

Mouth open, Bobby saw his father as he'd never seen him before. Bathed in sweat, he seemed also to sweat off some of his sixty-plus years as he moved slowly around the bag—space permitting—then stopped and fired right jab, left cross, right hook combinations that shook the target. Dad kept this up until an alarm clock buzzed and stopped his hook in mid-flight.

"Tha's it," Dad declared, as he took off his bag gloves and rested, hands on knees, gulping down air. "Enough for today."

"Dad?"

"I told Uncle Tony to get my stuff outta storage and bring it here," his father explained, as if what he said answered any question Bobby might ask. "So, tha's what he did this morning."

Dad often stumbled into the gap between idea and expression, at least when using English. Bobby needed clarification. "Huh?" he asked.

Uncle Tony was one of Dad's long-time pals who still lived in Chinatown. Dad said that they had boxed together on West Coast cards before the war and that Tony had returned to the ring for a few paydays after leaving the Army.

Tony had tried to persuade Dad to join him—"Just like old times in Stockton, Los Angeles, places like that," Tony said excitedly—but Dad said that Mom put her foot down. Firmly.

"Except I won't be here when you get your foolish self home," she said. "I thought all you Pinoys were a little nuts, but you and Tony take the cake." His wife's opposition abruptly ended the old man's thoughts of reviving his ring career.

According to Dad, his wife didn't stop there. His wartime wounds hadn't healed, she added. *Monkey see* don't always mean *monkey gotta do*. Simple as that. Besides, he was too old. In fact, he and that fool Tony both were. And also, she had grown to hate the sport—if it could be called that. Just to be sure, she made Dad get rid of his new sparring gloves, shoes, and all of his other gear, in case he got weak and changed his mind.

That's how Dad's old equipment, now scattered about the living room, ended up in Uncle Tony's storage locker, unseen by Bobby until this morning. Now the gloves were back, freshly oiled and shining. Same, too, with his father's boxing shoes that had the sheen—if not the scent—of new black leather.

But it was one item in particular that caught Bobby's eye—an elegant black satin robe with red and white trim laid carefully across the divan. Bobby walked over and felt the smooth, cool fabric.

With his fingers, he traced the longhand name embroidered on the back—"Kid Williams"—and felt for a moment the depth of his father's twin passions.

"You took Mom's name?" Bobby asked, still staring at the robe like it had once been worn by Jesus or some top-of-the-line Catholic saint.

"Yes," Dad answered. "Wanna try it on?"

Surprised, Bobby glanced at his father, then turned away. "No," he said slowly. "It's yours; you earned it. You try it on."

Dad smiled. "Okay," he said, as he lovingly donned the robe. He smoothed out the clumps and carefully inspected the length of each sleeve before striking a pose—hands raised, right fist forward.

"Still fit," Dad declared triumphantly.

"And Mom made you give up boxing?"

"Yes," he said evenly. "Simple as that."

Bobby didn't believe him for a moment. He now knew the decision must have been a tough one; just talking about his adventures in the ring made him alive, electric, and, for a moment, Bobby was suddenly swept away in a flood of faded sepia-toned snapshots. He could see his father in his glory—athletic and young and full of himself. The image, however fleeting, surprised him. Although he was vaguely aware that Dad was an ex-fighter, neither the sport nor his father's exploits had interested him much.

For Bobby, this was a first. He'd never imagined Dad like that before—standing over a fallen opponent, arms raised, beaming and soaking in the cheers of his fans. The old man's willingness to give up the sport that made him special, that defined him, made Bobby marvel at the depth of his father's love.

Lucky man, Bobby thought, despite Dad's sadness and his long list of problems. He hoped to eventually be where his father was, feeling the same thing about someone just as special.

"Do it again?" Dad continued softly, speaking mostly to himself. "I'd do it again, by golly, no sweat."

"I know, Dad," Bobby said.

Bobby knew that from Dad's voice that he'd just boarded a train bound for a happier time. Ordinarily, he'd have let his father go. He knew that daydreams wouldn't harm him, as long as his father stayed in sight. But Bobby had a question to ask, and it couldn't wait.

Why, he wondered, had his father chosen now to show him this part of his past?

"Oh, I still got work to do," Dad explained with a shrug.

"Do what?"

"Show you the basics before I forget," Dad answered, as his eyes narrowed and his jaw tightened. "Like, uh," he stammered. "Damnit." His father violently shook his head, like he'd just taken some pug-faced brawler's best shot. The movement was necessary, a prelude to the return of composure and the classic wordless question that all boxers inevitably ask: Punk, that all you got?

Dad finally nodded, then smiled. "Like how to duck, Bobby. I tol' you that before, I think."

* * *

Dad admitted that ducking was a skill he didn't do particularly well—witness the scar tissue, flat nose, and lumps above both eyes.

"Neuro-, uh, neuro-," he began.

"Neurological?" Bobby asked, remembering Mom's reference to his father's condition.

"Yeah, yeah," he giggled. "Tha's it. The docs say I'm damaged that way, but not all cuckoo, jus' a little, uh, I think."

"Geeze, Dad, I didn't even notice," Bobby lied.

His father smiled, unsure he believed him. "You're a good boy," he finally said. "The bes'."

"No, really, I mean . . ."

"Whatever," his father said, interrupting Bobby's attempted explanation. "Now, hold up your left hand, put your left foot forward. Your right hand, hold it back by your cheek."

These instructions were barked—clear, concise, a rarity from his father—and Bobby did, or tried to do, what he was told. Dad started walking around his son—tucking an elbow here, extending or drawing back a fist there. He then took two steps back, like a sculptor examining his latest creation, and decided, nope, not there yet.

"Your chin," Dad said.

"Huh?"

"Tuck it in, your neck's too thin. Don' wanna have your head fall off," his father said, followed by a pause and further examination.

"This how I'm gonna fight?"

"Nope," Dad answered, as he continued his inspection. "Keep holdin' your hands up."

"Why?"

"Cuz most guys'r right-handed and this is how most guys gonna fight you."

"But . . ."

"To beat 'em and stay safe, you gotta think like they think, know how they gonna throw, when they throw, what they gonna bring," Dad explained.

Even to a non-fighter like Bobby, what his father said made sense. But his motionless pose was getting harder to hold by the moment. His lead left hand started dropping, same, too, with his right.

"Dad."

"Keep 'em up," the old man commanded without looking up. He was focused on figuring out the right balance, how much weight his boy should put on each foot, how deeply he should bend his knees.

"A little lower, the left knee," he said. "But keep keepin' 'em up."

Bobby sighed, but did as he was told. "Thought I was gonna learn how to duck?" he complained, trying hard not to whine.

"You are," Dad answered calmly.

Chapter Four

Dad said that Bobby shouldn't worry too much about an opponent's left hand.

"That's jus' to jab you and distract you, then nail you with the right cross when you're lookin' where you shouldn't be," he explained. "Tha's the t'under that puts you on the ground."

The right hand, he explained, was usually the knockout hand. That's why fighters held it back so that when they saw an opening, it could be launched from a longer distance, gathering greater speed and power.

According to his father, the answer was to turn around and fight southpaw—with the right hand and foot forward—and to keep circling right and away from the t'under. Dad explained that boxing was about patience and cunning, about finding the best angles for attacking and defending, not just about throwing punches. The best fighters usually find a way to hit someone, without getting hit in return—"Like that new guy, Cassius Clay," he said—and that was a skill most southpaws were pretty good at. That's how he fought, for the most part anyway. It worked pretty well, except when he'd lose his temper, abandon his strategy, march straight ahead, and brawl.

"Too hot-headed to be a good southpaw," he explained. "A southpaw's thinkin' all the time, settin' traps for the other guy. I'm thinkin' you're a smart boy, smarter than Paulie—he was more like me. So mebbe it work good for you."

Dad smiled and walked up to his son. He took Bobby's left hand and stretched it so his two big knuckles touched the bridge of his nose.

"Here, I'll show you," Dad said. "Try and hit me with your jab and right hand. One-two, fast as you can."

"But Dad," Bobby protested. "I don't got no gloves."

His father shrugged. "So, who wears gloves in a street fight?"

"But . . ."

"One-two, right here," his father said firmly, pointing to his nose and forehead. "Throw."

Bobby sighed. No choice in the matter, Dad's tone said. But just as he flicked his left, the old man—who, a moment before, had been standing in front of him—slipped under the punch, stepping outside his arm in a smooth, seamless motion. At the same time, he threw his left shoulder into a belt-level punch. Bobby felt the knuckles of his father's left hand pop his belly and stop. Another blow—delivered, he assumed, by the right hand—hooked his left kidney hard enough to let him know both punches could have been much, much harder.

Bobby grunted. Helpless, his right hand still guarding the side of his chin, he glanced over his left shoulder to see Dad standing to his side.

Hands up, his father was focused and leaning ever-so-slightly forward. He seemed to stare through Bobby, eager to attack again.

"Dad?" Bobby said nervously.

The sound of his son's voice must have turned off a dangerous switch in the old man's brain. He began to relax and started to smile, not recalling many of the details or the direction of his just completed short-circuited stroll.

"See what I mean, Bobby," he said casually. "Hard to beat you do it right."

"Yeah, yeah," he replied between deep breaths. "I see what you mean."

*   *   *

The leftover chicken fried in bacon grease and garlic had turned out pretty well—a good thing, Bobby thought, since his first workout had made him hungry. Boxing was interesting—and sure, he'd humor his father. Maybe it would even come in handy someday.

But cooking went straight to his heart. Making a good meal challenged him, the end product pleasing his senses. During his hit-and-miss culinary experiments, Bobby had concluded that enough garlic, soy sauce and salt could redeem almost any sorry piece of meat. And Dad's continuous fork-to-mouth motion further proved the principle.

Bobby finished first. He sighed and wondered for a moment about seconds as his father rose slowly from his chair, smiled at his son, and walked away, destination unknown. Bobby tensed, his mind flashing back to a day not too long ago when a deputy sheriff had called and politely asked him would he please pick up his father?

"He was just sittin' at the counter, drinkin' coffee and talkin' to himself," the deputy calmly explained. "He started cryin'. I didn't know what to do."

Dad was in North Bend, a one-gas-station town on the eastern edge of the county. Bobby eventually scrounged enough change to board the bus, fetch his father and bring him home.

"Geeze, Dad," he whispered on the return trip.

"Your mom and I useta do that," his father explained. "Back in the beginning, jus' ride the bus all day and see wha's out there. Before Paulie was born, we'd just ride the bus for fun. We saw some beautiful places, too, oh my gosh."

The old man slowly shook his head. "I don't know why, but I know that one day, I'll turn around and she'll be right next to me, and she'll be pretty and laughing jus' like old times. I don' know why I think that way. I jus' sometimes do."

Bobby said nothing, choosing instead to stare out the window at acres of lush pastureland, ringed on the horizon by snowcapped mountains and forests. Picture postcard pretty, he thought, and a surprise. He had rarely been outside Seattle and had no idea the rest of the county looked like this. Ordinarily he would have relaxed and enjoyed the vistas, but not today.

"I see her still, sometimes hear her, too," he said casually. "'Not too much longer, Honey,'" she says, and I says, 'good.'"

Crazy talk, Bobby had thought, as he sat quietly, choosing instead to bury himself in the endless snapshots of trees and cows and other pastoral scenes. But was it so crazy? Coming from Dad, sure. But he had had his own dreams and imaginings of Paulie, which he'd concluded were due to his own heartbreak and his mind working doubletime to ease his nagging pain.

"Where'd I go anyway?" his father asked.

"North Bend."

"Tha's good," he said with a smile. "Been there long time ago with your mom. I could feel her."

"Geeze, Dad," Bobby repeated.

"She was there."

Bobby didn't reply. Anything more—more words, more emotion—would have been useless. Dad had been like that since Mom's passing, just living out the days with no real plan or purpose. He'd gotten worse since Paulie's death, seeming to lose more of himself by the hour and day. On those occasions, Bobby had wanted to say, "I'm still here. I still need you." But he didn't.

*   *   *

Bobby stood up. It was time to keep an eye on his father and make sure he didn't wander out the door to yet another unplanned destination.

He grabbed his jacket, hoping to eventually coax his father to return. What he saw next, he didn't expect.

Dad, feet evenly spaced, was moving around the room, circling slowly, smoothly to his right. His lead right hand constantly pumped out and in, out and in, occasionally followed by crisp left crosses and quick right hooks.

"Dad."

"Shadow box, Bobby," his father said, as sweat began drenching his temples and forehead. He didn't look up. "Good thing to learn."

"But I thought we were done for today," Bobby complained.

"Nah," his father answered. "We were jus' warmin' up."

That's how it started. Over the next several weeks, Bobby and his father would go over the basics of the manly art—feints, slips, parries, and punches. For the most part, the training went well. Dad as teacher, Bobby as student—both relished their new roles.

Still, there were moments.

'You know, I nailed this guy with my hook," Dad said during a break. "He's champion, famous, you know, colored guy, you know. . . ."

Bobby didn't know. Eyes narrowed, he stared at his father, as if staring would help him remember.

Dad shrugged. "Ah, is jus' hard," he said, defeated.

There was another time when both were sitting on the couch after a workout, their eyes glued to the TV and the run-up to a much-ballyhooed bout between a fading champion and his brash young challenger.

"Should be good," Dad said confidently. "Maybe you pick up some tricks."

It would have been good, too, except that the fight was at the wrong place, the wrong time. "Live from the Cow Palace in the City by the Bay," the announcer said. "Fifteen rounds of championship boxing."

"Cow Palace, Cow Palace," Dad whispered, as if the name invoked and repeated began a prayer. He then tilted his head and stared vacantly at the ceiling.

"Fought there before, first time in 1940."

Bobby, surprised, turned toward his father, who had never said much about the specifics of his ring career. He was intrigued. Fighting at a topnotch venue must have meant the old man had some talent. "Did you win the fight?"

"It's where I met your ma," he said softly. According to Dad, she was sitting near the aisle as he made his way to the ring, accompanying a girlfriend whose younger brother was also on the card. "Pretty like Lena Horne, nah, prettier," he said. His father said he made sure he smiled at her during the introduction and glanced at her during the bout. He smiled again when he left the ring.

"Oh boy, after I shower and clean up good and comb my hair I hurry down and introduce myself," his father said.

"Dad, did you win?"

"Win?" he said with a chuckle. "Of course. She smile back."

*   *   *

Their training sessions—mornings, afternoons, evenings, or whenever the mood struck—revived the old man. He could put aside what he'd lost and focus on what he had left. Bobby, too, was happy with the change, even if it was just for a couple of hours each day. Then there was the other unexpected plus. The son was getting better, or so the father said after they wrapped up their latest workout in the apartment.

"You're quick," he said. "Good eyes, fast hands, quick feet, You see the punch, you move. A gift of God. You'll always be hard to hit."

Bobby smiled. This was the part of boxing that he loved— the quick and constant movement, the subtle feints and well- placed parries, the imagination needed to turn even snarling tough guys into plodding chumps. For Bobby, good defense was artistic—or at least the most artistic part of an otherwise brutal sport.

Bobby was coordinated and quick; practice made him more so. About a week earlier, he and Dad had gone to a nearby park a little after sunrise and laced up the gloves. Bobby occasionally threw a lazy jab, but mostly he danced and moved, feinted and blocked. Try as he might, the old man couldn't touch him, couldn't even come close. At the end of the session, Dad smiled slightly but said nothing as he and his son walked back to the apartment. They haven't returned to the park since.

Today, though, Dad had a point to make. Without a word, he slammed a potent double-right-hook combination into the heavy bag. The loud *thud-thud* was proof that the old man still had enough pop to bust noses, bruise ribs, and break jaws.

"Damn," Bobby whispered at the unexpected display of power.

Dad then pointed at the bag and stared at his son, who was resting on a stool. "Defense is important, but alone it ain't enough," his father began. "Fighting's also about hurtin' the other guy. Your punches look good—fast, tight—but they're pitty-pat, pitty-pat. There's no real power, no anger. The question is, can you put 'im down? Finish 'im? Even kill 'im if you got to?"

He paused and reached for a towel and began wiping the perspiration from his face and arms. "I knew the answer for your brother, but you I'm not so sure."

"Paulie and I were different," Bobby said softly.

"Yeah," Dad said sadly. "*Were.*"

Bobby didn't have the heart to continue. Although he loved Paulie, he and his brother were different, remarkably so. That much was clear. And boxing showed yet one more area with another major difference. But Bobby didn't want to ask why—at least not tonight, maybe not ever.

Bobby rose and walked slowly toward his room. He glanced at the clock—almost 8:30, usually too early to sleep. But tonight he felt different, exhausted. His muscles ached, but that was nothing new. What drained him more were the rumblings in his head and heart, both weighted down by a lengthening list of questions begetting questions.

Before opening his bedroom door, he turned to glance at his father, now seated on the divan. He knew the position, the look—back straight, hands folded, eyes staring at the wall.

Bobby sighed. "'Night Dad," he said, knowing that he wouldn't be heard.

* * *

The voice was achingly familiar. "Hey, Bobby," it said.

"Paulie?" Dream or real time, Bobby couldn't tell. Eyes still closed, he felt himself sit up. He then blinked and stared into the darkness. No Paulie, at least not yet. Sometimes, it happened this way, when he'd hear his brother's voice, nothing more.

Not tonight, though, as Paulie slowly came into view. He was sitting in a barber's chair, his legs crossed and his hands rested on the arms of the chair. Bobby knew where he was—Mama's shop on King Street in Chinatown, across the alley from the Victory Bathhouse, where a lot of Dad's pals gathered to smoke and play cards. The owner, Mama—last name unknown—was an old and kindly Japanese woman who'd taken a liking to the boys. She would slip them candies and other treats when their parents weren't looking.

It was one of the reasons Bobby looked forward to haircuts, the other being the long wall mirrors that faced each other on opposite sides of the room. From where young Bobby sat, he would stare in fascination at either mirror and see his reflected image shrink and disappear down a row that had no end.

"Know where I'm at?"

"Mama's," Bobby replied.

"This here," Paulie said, pointing at the mirrors, "is where I am on this side. Eternity, there's no time here, no end to nothin'. It's okay, though, don't get me wrong, but it's way too soon for you to come join me."

"What do you mean?"

"I got somethin' important to say," Paulie continued. "You turn eighteen, what, this summer?"

"Yeah, June."

"About five months, then. Listen close."

Paulie said that he knew Bobby had his doubts about college, but never mind that. He knew his brother was smart enough. "You like books, Bobby, and that makes you a whole lot smarter than me," he chuckled. "That by itself gives you a future, or at least a chance."

Take the money Mom and Dad had saved, Paulie advised, and enroll full-time. Maybe he could get a sole-surviving-son or hardship exemption, with Dad being how he was, but don't take no chances because the Army was now so hard up, it would take almost anyone who could walk.

Besides, their father probably wasn't long for this world, and then what? Go up tomorrow, pick up the papers, apply, get accepted. Grab the good-as-gold college deferment, Paulie continued. Rich boys did it all the time. The alternative—as one more candidate for a body-hungry draft—should be avoided at all cost.

"This world don't need one more colored boy KIA," he said.

"I know, but I don't know about this college stuff, man," Bobby replied, his voice hesitant.

"Chump, you better know," Paulie said angrily. "You better listen good or I'ma come back'n . . . Ah, damn, Bobby, I'm sorry, man, just listen close, okay? Listen to what I gotta tell you."

Bobby nodded. Despite the outburst, he knew that his brother loved him.

"I knew this dude," he explained, as he began the story of one of his closest buddies—another draftee named Marty, a *vato* from LA. Like a lot of barrio boys, Marty appeared to have the attitude—the arrogant walk, the hardcore talk, the bad-to-the-bone swagger. But that wasn't him, not really. Paulie learned over time that he adored his mom and three younger sisters, ages eight, seven and four, and worried endlessly about how they would fare without him. According to his brother, kids in the villages loved him, flocked to him like pigeons—and he loved them back. One night, he heard his friend crying over something he'd seen earlier in the day—the limbless torso of a girl about his youngest sister's age. Marty was sensitive, kind—and that's what got him killed, his brother said.

"What happened?" Bobby asked.

"He pulled a mom and her child out of a crossfire," Paulie replied. "Both of 'em made it. Marty didn't."

"Damn."

"Here's the point, little brother," Paulie continued. "Combat ain't for everyone. You gotta shut down your heart and just point and shoot—somethin' I found I could do pretty good right from the start. But it wasn't for Marty—and it sure ain't for you. You go do somethin' else with your life, otherwise . . ."

"Otherwise?"

"This," Paulie said, as multicolored lights enveloped the room, and Bobby found himself standing among a group of GIs, most just slightly older than himself. Some stared at the sky, others at the tree line of the nearby jungle. A few looked down to see another young soldier, chest and belly shattered, struggling for breath.

Paulie was cradling his head and telling him he'd make it, hold on, he'd make it—a mountain of contrary evidence notwithstanding. Paulie turned and glanced briefly at his brother.

"Or this," he whispered, as the scene suddenly shifted to a tiny living room where a mother and her three daughters sat on a couch, hugged each other and wept uncontrollably. On a nearby desk was the framed photo of a handsome young soldier, which Bobby recognized as that of the dying GI.

"Or this," Paulie repeated, as Bobby watched his brother sleeping, a moment before the mortar with Paulie's name on it tore his limbs from his body and sent fragments into his head and heart.

"Not much of me to bury," Paulie said sadly, as the lights dimmed and the room faded to black.

"Man," Bobby mumbled. As he bowed his head, his eyes welled up at the gut-wrenching sight.

"Didn't have the heart to show Dad," Paulie said, his tone matter-of-fact. "But you seein' this might actually do you some good."

Bobby, his face now streaked with tears, turned toward what he thought was the direction of his brother's voice.

"Don't cry," Paulie admonished. "It happened; it's over. Luck of the draw. Besides, you got other things to worry about."

"Like what?" Bobby sniffed, as he struggled to regain composure.

"Like the rest of your life. Eighteen's the magic number, least as far as the draft goes, and if I was you, I'd spend it here, not over there. Remember what we did when I turned eighteen?"

Bobby nodded and took a deep breath. "Yeah."

"Fishin' down on the docks, right? Caught us a mess a perch, took 'em home, fried 'em up. Just like Opie and Andy and the rest of them hillbillies. But a good time, brother, in fact, the last one I had in my too-short life. Learn from that, Bobby. You play it right, you got a lotta good times left. So don't you be doin' like I did."

Bobby knew from his brother's blunt, do-it-my-way-or-the-highway tone that he'd made his point and that further conversation wasn't needed. Whether Bobby was done talking was another matter.

"Paulie, don't leave yet, I, uh, got another question."

"What?" came back the impatient reply.

"You and me, it's been buggin' me, man, we're so different. We don't even look alike, you know that."

"So, what's your point?"

"It just bothers me, man."

Paulie chuckled. "So what? Bein' dead bothers me. Listen, in the end it don't matter. All that counts is who loves you, which means who'll bail you out when your butt's in a sling. Far as I can see, there's only one of 'em left on earth."

"Dad?"

"Bingo, bright boy," Paulie said sarcastically. "You definite college material, that's for sure."

"Paulie."

"That's it for tonight. Gotta go." As he spoke, the lights began to dim, the last image being Paulie in his chair. His brother was staring—hard—at his endless column of mirrored images.

"Man, what a trip," Paulie added.

"Paulie," Bobby repeated, as he strained to hear a whispered "later" drifting through what was now a dark, still room.

Chapter Five

Maybe Paulie was right, Bobby thought, as he left the apartment early the next day. His destination: Seattle Central Community College, maybe two miles away. He figured it was at least worth checking out and picking up the paperwork. He'd thought about telling Dad, but changed his mind when he passed him in the living room. The old man was stretched out on the divan and resting peacefully, not the tossing, turning, sorrow-filled fits of too many troubled nights past.

Bobby smiled. It was 7:00 a.m., early enough. If his luck held, he'd be back in time to wake his father with the fragrances of garlic fried rice, fried eggs, thin-sliced tomatoes, and fresh coffee.

A blast of cold winter air greeted him as he stepped outside. He pulled down his wool cap to cover his ears and buried his face in the folds of his favorite jacket, an outsized two-year-old parka from Mom. That's why he didn't immediately see rouged-up Angie, who was stumbling back after a too-long night on the town.

"Hey, Honey, long time no see," she said slowly, as she leaned against an apartment wall for support. "You never came by. Ever. Don't cha like me?"

Bobby looked up. "Hi, Angie," he said, without slowing down. "Talk later." Such a waste, he thought. She was smart enough, and pretty, too. Never mind that too much sweat and too much makeup had turned her face into a Javanese mask.

Maybe they'd even hold that conversation—sometime down the road. Right now, he was too busy to stop or to see Cortez, who was just rounding the corner. Bobby's old nemesis saw him first.

"Hey, sissy," Cortez snarled. "Don't be talkin' to my girl."

"Hey, man, I don't want any trouble. We're even; let it be," Bobby said, as he tried to make his voice sound stronger than he felt. He then stepped back. As he did, he made sure he was balanced—right foot forward, chin slightly tucked. He sighed. Without Angie, he knew they would have probably just cautiously eyed each other and kept walking—no big deal. But her presence changed the equation. Bobby didn't like it, but that was the way it was.

He knew that in Yesler, there was usually a point in every dispute, no matter how minor, when words and reason would quietly take their leave. He knew Cortez had already reached that point—he had too much at stake not to thump his chest and play this foolish drama out—and there was nothing anyone could say to change the script. Although Cortez kept his hands down and continued to talk—mostly in the form of insults and curses— Bobby knew it was a ruse, a prelude to an opening punch.

Bobby didn't reply. He was calmer now, thanks to Dad's voice inside his head, warning him to always watch the other guy's shoulders, especially the left, the side that would usually be closest to him. When it twitched, he'd move by slipping to his right, then pivot away, hands up, ready to slide in and counterpunch an exposed and out-of-position opponent. It was a classic southpaw move that Dad had taught him and that he must have practiced a thousand times.

"And your momma ain't . . . ," Cortez began, as he suddenly snapped a left jab at Bobby's head, which wasn't where it had been a split-second before. The jab was immediately followed by a hard right hand, which Cortez leaned into, shifting much of his weight onto his extended left leg. Cortez's left kneecap had once been one of the main targets of Paulie's bat-wielding revenge. It had never healed right. The extra pressure from the errant right cross caused the damaged knee to buckle and leave Cortez sprawled face-first on the pavement.

He knew that Dad or Paulie would have kicked Cortez in the head, or found some other way to inflict more pain. But that was them, not him. "He's down," he heard his father's voice whisper. "Finish 'im."

"Finish him," he heard Paulie's voice repeat.

Bobby ignored their advice. His enemy posed no threat; it was over. He slowly lowered his hands and checked his watch: only five minutes had passed. He smiled. Still plenty of time to check out the college and get back in time to greet his waking father with a pot of hot coffee and a meal of rice, garlic, tomatoes, and eggs spiced just right.

*　　*　　*

As far as buildings went, Seattle Central was hardly impressive. It was an old brick and paint-peeled wood building that had seen better days. In its decades-long existence, it had done time as a high school and then as a vocational school before this, its latest incarnation.

For Bobby, the structure's run-down condition didn't matter. He knew that what was inside counted more. But Seattle Central was *terra incognita*—a place to which he'd never traveled and couldn't have otherwise imagined. As he opened the door and walked through the main hall, some of it looked depressingly familiar—a whiff of weed and blank-eyed teens hanging out, laughing and talking loud about sex, music, the usual stuck-in-neutral stuff. Kids did that at Taft and every other public high school he knew about.

But his disappointment didn't last—and he was glad. If he'd wanted that scene, he'd have returned to Taft.

This was different, an immediate proof being the presence of a lot of students who were older and others whose nationalities he couldn't quite make out. He stopped for coffee at the school cafeteria, where a diverse collection of patrons of all ages and races formed an eye-opening slice of a larger world foreign to him. At a nearby table, two twenty-something dark-skinned men with black, wavy hair sipped tea and chatted quietly about a physics assignment. At least Bobby thought the topic was physics, judging by the imposing titles of the massive texts lying on the table.

The two were much darker than him—and a lot of the other brothers he knew. They sounded like the British actors in "The Bridge on The River Kwai"—but not quite.

He looked at his watch and gulped down his coffee. He'd better get going if he was to make it back home before his father awakened.

As he reentered the hallway, he heard voices start arguing loudly and turned to see two young white men standing nose to nose, their faces tight, their voices rising. Both were dressed in fatigues, with their units' insignias still on their shoulders. "Guys 're dyin' for nothin'," the taller one said. "And folks like you, who still think otherwise, are worse 'n fools. You're helpin' to keep this useless war goin'."

The argument was quickly drawing a crowd, some of whom immediately weighed in on one side or the other. Bobby didn't hear the other veteran's response—or even if there was one. His attention was focused on a sign that said the admissions office was at the end of the hall. Close enough.

He was nearing his destination when he passed a small group of students quietly discussing Plato and Aristotle, names even he had heard of. Then a long-haired young woman in a high-pitched voice said something about someone named "Manuel Can't," who, in her opinion was the most important of them all. "Can't" moved her, she told her friends earnestly, and spoke to her "essence."

Bobby slowed down, pretending to look a little lost as he carefully read the signs on nearby office doors. Cute, Bobby thought, as he caught a glimpse of her dark, angular face framed by long, black hair. Or at least, not ordinary. For a second, he thought she had also glanced his way, but it happened so quickly he wasn't sure.

As he began walking away, he remembered a girl named "Essence," but she moved away when her parents split up. He'd thought "Essence" was just a first name, nothing more. Maybe he'd grab a dictionary and look it up.

He knew a lot of Manuels, all of whom were either Filipinos or Mexicans. But he thought it odd that anyone, no matter how famous, would take as a name two short words joined together by an apostrophe. He shrugged and slowly resumed walking. Personal choice, he figured, like stars who change their names, that sort of attention-grabbing thing.

Whatever.

A contraction, Bobby suddenly recalled, as he stood before the admissions office door. That's what it's called. He'd learned about contractions at St. James. He beamed, confident he'd do pretty well here. The nuns, he figured, would have been pleased.

                    *   *   *

Dad wasn't there when Bobby got home. Panicked, he rushed into his father's bedroom, then the bathroom—no Dad. He took a deep breath and sat on a chair, compiling a mental list of where he should look next. He then stood up and walked to the closet, picking out a scarf for what could be an all-day search. He'd start with Chinatown, where he could talk to Dad's cronies and check out the coffee shops and dirt-cheap noodle joints. Besides, he was starting to get hungry—and he could do worse than begin his search with a bowl of hot noodles on a cold Seattle day.

Bobby left the apartment and hurried down to Yesler Street, a major east-west arterial that cut through the housing project, sloping downward toward town and stopping at the waterfront. Chinatown was on the other side, south of where he and Dad lived. The still-green traffic light meant that if he hurried, he wouldn't have to break stride. Standing still and giving the wind a clear shot to bite him—even for a moment—wasn't what he had in mind.

Yet, that's just what he did. He blinked hard and saw—or thought he saw—Dad running toward him. In his almost eighteen years, he'd never seen his father—or any older Filipino man he knew—run. Or even walk briskly. He knew them to drink, smoke, gamble, wear Borsalino hats and Florsheim shoes, watch boxing matches and tell him and Paulie outrageous stories about the old days that made them laugh—but he never knew them to run.

Maybe they ran as kids in the islands, but as grown men? Never. Bobby had come to conclude that running just wasn't an adult Filipino trait, at least not in their adopted land. Yet there Dad was, dressed in baggy sweats and high-top black tennis shoes, huffing and puffing up the steep Yesler incline. In truth, he was moving rather slowly—slower than many younger folks walked—and Bobby, not believing, furrowed his brow and stared harder. But his father's pumping arms, grimacing face, and other telltale signs removed all remaining doubt. Dad grunted at Bobby as he passed and stopped only after he had finished what for him was a brisk, down-the-stretch sprint.

As Bobby walked toward the old man, he could see steam billowing from his head, shoulders, and back as he bent over, resting his hands on his knees and sucking air. He eventually composed himself, straightened up and greeted his son.

"Hi," his father said simply.

"Dad, why?" Bobby began.

"Do this?"

"Yeah, this."

"Oh, I dunno, didn't do nothin' like this for a long time, jus' after the war I think," Dad explained. "But I felt fine this morning, strong, you know? So I thought I'd test myself. Seemed like a good idea at the time." He paused and chuckled. "Mebbe not so good," he said as he coughed, cleared his throat and spat.

Bobby gently put his arm around his father and nudged him toward home. "Come on," he said. "Let's get you outta the cold."

The old man smiled but didn't budge. "Oh yeah, there's one other reason I did that."

"What?" Bobby asked, trying not to sound impatient. Try as he might, he couldn't stop his teeth from starting to chatter.

"I was first thinkin' that you should do that. Tha's what got me started," he explained.

"Huh?"

"I mean the runnin' part," Dad said. "All boxers gotta run. And then I remember how I useta be when I was a boxer and how I love the sport and even useta love runnin', trainin', all of it, and so I go outside and . . ." He shrugged. "Oh, what the heck."

Bobby nudged his father again. This time he didn't resist.

"Even if I can't do it no more, I still love it," Dad said, as they neared their apartment.

"What?"

"Boxing."

"Why?"

"It brought me your ma," Dad said quietly.

*   *   *

Over a breakfast of eggs, garlic fried rice, and sliced tomatoes, Dad explained that he started boxing because it was a way to make good money. In those days, he said, a lot of whites didn't like Filipinos—same as now, just worse. The only work he could get when he first arrived in the States was washing dishes in Oakland or cutting asparagus near Vallejo and other Bay Area towns. Then one day, Uncle Tony says they should go see then-welterweight contender Ceferino Garcia. The great Garcia, he said, was headlining a local card and was training every day in a gym in downtown San Francisco. So he and Tony and three other Pinoys hopped into a borrowed Packard for a day-long trip to the city.

Bobby listened carefully. This was a story he hadn't heard before. "So, what happened?" he asked.

Dad said that when they arrived at the gym, Garcia was in the middle of four bruising, fast-paced rounds. He was sparring a black fighter bigger than him—maybe a middleweight or even a small light-heavy. Despite what was at least a ten- to fifteen-pound size difference, Garcia was able to give as well as he got, often rocking the bigger man with his trademark—an exaggerated right uppercut nicknamed the "bolo punch."

Even though it was only a sparring session, Dad said that Garcia's name "was magic in those days," enough to draw hundreds of fans from all over. That included a lot of Pinoys, some of whom his father knew from work in the fields. They "oohed" and "aahed" at every heavy punch the great man landed—and even at a few that missed.

When the sparring was over, Dad struck up a conversation with Sam, a Pinoy he'd once worked with on a San Jose farm. Sam, who claimed to be a friend of the cousin of Garcia's assistant trainer, said that Ceferino would make $5,000 for his upcoming fight. His father said that when he heard that amount, his jaw dropped.

"Big, big money those days," he told Bobby wistfully.

But that wasn't all. Dad also liked the adulation heaped on Garcia—not just by other Filipinos, but by other savvy fight fans. At the time, he couldn't imagine a Pinoy in any other line of work earning such across-the-board respect.

On the drive home, Dad casually announced he was changing careers. He'd been a pretty good scrapper both in the Philippines and here, so fighting for money seemed to him like a natural and lucrative step up. Good-natured laughter, boxing poses, and encouragement filled the car until Manoling, the driver, spoke:

"You're nuts," he said quietly, adding that his favorite cousin was a boxer in the Philippines—and a pretty good one at that.

"Did he come over here?" Tony asked.

"No," Manoling answered. "He died, brain injury after a fight in the province. Never regain consciousness. A good sport to watch, jus' don' never do."

The cousin's fate triggered a small wave of "Ohs" and "I'm sorrys," followed by an uneasy silence lasting from the outskirts of Oakland to Vallejo. Dad and Uncle Tony got off at their destination, a Japanese-owned farm just outside town.

As both men made their way to the bunkhouse, Dad said he told Tony that he'd had it—he was tired of it all. Tired of the pre-dawn start time, the heat, the lousy wages, the outhouse stench, the back-breaking work. He said that over the past year, he'd managed to save a little—enough for two months' worth of groceries and rent at any fair-to-middling flophouse in Central California. It was enough time to see if he'd be any good at what he planned to do next. He had decided to head to Sacramento the next morning, where he knew some other Filipinos were training for the ring. Would Tony like to come along?

"That's how me and your uncle got started," he told Bobby. "We were fightin' for money three weeks later. Four rounds for fifty bucks."

Bobby was shocked by the lack of preparation for such a brutal sport. "Phew, Dad, that was pretty quick."

"Yeah," he said, nodding his head. "Hard way to start. Took my lumps, too, but I learned." He then touched his right eyebrow and traced a line. "Got cut here, first round, first fight, but no matter, I win in the end."

"Still . . ."

"Yeah," Dad said. "I know, hard way to start. But then times were tougher, too, so you jus' adjus'."

"Guess so."

"But some things don' change," his father continued.

"Like?"

"Ringwork," Dad replied. "Gotta getcha to a gym, put you in a real ring."

"Sure, sure," Bobby said, his tone distracted. Dad's story had been fascinating, but that had run its course. He soon found himself thinking about the girl with the "essence" and everything else he'd seen at the college. It certainly was different, maybe even exciting. He wanted to go over the application forms and figure out what had to be done next.

"Today," his father said.

"Huh?"

"I said we go to the gym today."

* * *

Especially for newcomers, a boxing gym can be intimidating, a second home for skilled, angry men capable of inflicting great bodily harm. Bobby was intimidated. He stood quietly by the door and watched fighters of all shapes, sizes and ages go through their paces. Nearby, an Italian-looking guy with a pug nose and slightly puffed eyebrows blasted multiple hooks and other heavy punches into a taped-over heavy bag as an old white man stood to the side, leaning on a silver cane and barking orders.

"Five punch combo," he yelled. "Again," he screamed just seconds later. "Stay on him, your only chance. Jeeze, you call that punchin'? Louie, you're costin' me money."

Bobby's attention shifted to the other boxers, some of whom were shadow boxing in front of body-length mirrors, while others were skipping rope. But the real action that day was in the middle of the gym, where two young fighters were sparring in the ring as their trainers shouted instructions. For most of the round the taller of the two, a young white kid, seemed to be boxing smartly. He was keeping his stocky opponent away with good footwork, well-timed jabs, and occasional rights.

Bobby smiled. That's just how he would have boxed him.

Then the other boy—a stocky Mexican named Alfonso— suddenly turned it around with a flash of his hand. In this case, Alfonso threw a hard right over a lazy left jab, its impact on his taller opponent's jaw buckled his knees and sent him reeling into the ropes. Bobby flinched; he knew what would happen next. But the bell saved him from further harm. "That's it," his trainer said, and motioned for his still-groggy fighter to leave the ring.

Bobby then spotted Dad seated on a ringside chair and chatting amiably with another old-timer, a Filipino man dressed nattily in a sport coat and tie.

"Bobby," he said, as he motioned his son to join them. "Come here."

He did as he was told, but not before a brief flutter told him he might soon be in waters way over his head.

"This is your Uncle Mariano," Dad began. "We boxed together on the same card, when? Thirty years ago? Stockton?"

Bobby vaguely recalled seeing him before, possibly in Chinatown at the pool hall that Dad and the other Filipino old-timers favored. The old man looked like a character out of an old gangster flick—slacks, sports jacket, black Florsheim shoes, dress shirt and tie. Even monogrammed cufflinks.

To Bobby, he looked more ready for a post-dinner nightcap at Rosellini's than a few hours in a boxing gym. But Mariano was like so many of his father's other Pinoy friends. They'd come to this land thirty or forty years earlier when the Philippines was an American colony and had worked for pennies an hour at backbreaking jobs most white men wouldn't take. But when the work day was over, they'd shower and dress up and strut into the night. Dressing well, Dad once explained, was their way of saying they belonged in this new and hostile land.

Mariano smiled as he straightened his tie. "Nah, closer to thirty-five, and it was Sacramento."

Dad nodded. "Time flies. Anyway, Mariano runs this place and manages a lot of the boys here. I been tellin' 'im about you and he wanna see how you look."

"I'm just startin', Uncle," Bobby said humbly, worried about where this conversation was going.

"Tha's okay," Mariano replied. "Today, I jus' have you warm up, hit the bag, move aroun', see how you look." He then reached into a nearby sack and handed Bobby a pair of old bag gloves and new hand wraps.

Bobby relaxed, treasuring the reprieve, however temporary. "How much, Uncle?" he asked.

"Never mind, gift to this guy," Mariano said, pointing at his father. "Then after warm-up, you work two rounds."

"Huh?"

"I put you in with one of the beginners."

Bobby gulped.

"Yeah," Mariano said evenly. "Alfonso, he needs more work cuz he's got another fight comin' up."

*   *   *

As Bobby stood in his corner, he was comforted little by his Everlast headgear—the biggest leather hat he could find—and the oversized fourteen-ounce sparring gloves. Big deal, Bobby thought. Alfonso had nailed the last guy with a fourteen-ouncer.

Across the ring, Bobby's opponent was mumbling in Spanish and pacing, eyes down; he kept slamming his gloves together. Earlier, as Bobby was warming up, Uncle Mariano had told him that Alfonso would take it easy on him, seeing as how he was new.

He wondered if Mariano had told Alfonso that—or even if he had, whether his fighter had been listening. Judging by what he saw, Alfonso looked a little too eager to fire both fists—hard.

During Bobby's warm-up, Dad had stepped aside and turned him over to his old friend, who mumbled a word here and raised an eyebrow there. The only advice his father gave him was just before he stepped into the ring.

"The other guy's short, leads with his left," Dad whispered. "Stay to your right, counter fast, keep movin', don' let 'im trap you against the ropes, don' stop."

When the bell rang, Alfonso came out quickly to mid-ring, where he slowed and began methodically stalking his prey. He shuffled forward, gloves against his cheeks, his head and shoulders bobbing and weaving. He wasn't in punching range yet, and his pencil-necked opponent—moved by skills, quick reflexes and no small amount of fear—was equally determined to not let him get there.

Bobby began dancing, first to his right, then quickly to his left, then back again. His effortless zig-zags made it tough for the slower Alfonso to get close enough to land punches. Not that he didn't try. But his left jabs, right crosses and left hooks occasionally landed on a glove or a well-placed elbow, but most caught nothing but air. Bobby would occasionally counter with quick and accurate right jabs and hooks—pop-pop pitty-pats—just hard enough to let him know he could hit him whenever he wanted to.

Bobby, his fear suddenly gone, began to enjoy what he was doing. He was now late into the round, and he felt like he was flying—his feet never touching ground—like he'd seen Fred Astaire do in a late-night movie. For a second, he imagined he was the elegant Astaire doing star-turn after star-turn as the cameras lovingly caught close-ups of his winning smile and unmussed hair. He knew that if he'd been a more attentive boxing fan, he might have picked a more appropriate model, like the silky Ali, or before him, the elusive Willie Pep.

Nah, he thought, as the bell rang ending the first round, Astaire, top hat and black tux, would do.

As he turned toward his corner, he noticed all other activities in the gym had stopped. His father, still seated in his chair, smiled and clapped. The other boxers and their managers were staring at him, a couple of them turning to each other and nodding knowingly.

Mariano, who was working his corner, quickly wiped him down and told him to breathe deeply. "You doin' good, but he's gettin' closer," he warned. "Keep movin', sure, but sometimes you gotta jus' set your feet and throw those hard punches. And I mean hard enough and often enough to keep 'im off."

As Bobby left his corner to start the final round, he nodded at Mariano, more out of politeness than anything else. He quickly resumed his game of quick flicks and constant movement. Alfonso, he figured, was strong, but also slow and unimaginative.

So, off he went, zigging and zagging and frustrating Alfonso's efforts to clobber him. At about the two-minute mark, Bobby tired of the game and decided to make it interesting. He stood in mid-ring, flat-footed, chin out, hands down. He dared Alfonso to hit him.

Was it arrogance? Boredom? Stupidity? Bobby wasn't sure himself. It just seemed like a good idea at the time.

"Bobby," he heard his father scream.

But no matter, he stayed where he was and easily avoided the first two jabs by deftly moving his head to his right.

However, the third jab was different. That's because it started out straight like a jab then arced into something he didn't expect. Alfonso's jab-turned-left-hook exploded in a sweet spot above Bobby's right ear, sending bolts of numbness to his knees.

Alfonso, seeing his advantage, got ready to launch his right. But Bobby—whether by instinct or luck—made the perfect move. He fell into his opponent, grabbing his arms and shaking his head. Someone from the audience yelled "break," but Bobby, still wobbly, refused to let go, knowing well enough that if he did, his next destination would be the ring floor. Finally, Alfonso used his greater strength to wrestle himself free.

By then, Bobby had recovered somewhat, but not enough to resume dancing. He was suddenly exhausted, his legs felt dead. The most he could do was move back against the ropes, the worst place in the world for a groggy fighter. Though his mind was half-fogged, he was still able to see Alfonso move toward him behind a pawing left jab.

His only advantage was that Alfonso was slow and predictable. It gave him enough time to remember Dad telling him that a left cross to the belly followed by a right hook to the head were a southpaw's best friends. Using the ropes like a slingshot, that's exactly what he threw as he launched the combination with every ounce of power and desperation he could muster.

Alfonso grunted as the left dug deep just above his belt line. Bobby then felt his opponent's head turn violently as his right hook landed. The combination had done its dirty work, momentarily stopping Alfonso, his brain now as foggy as Bobby's had been just a few seconds earlier.

"Finish 'im," he thought he heard his father say.

"Finish him," he thought he heard Paulie repeat.

"Thirty seconds," someone else shouted.

Not much longer, he thought. He knew he'd survive the round. Bobby then resumed dancing, a little wobbly at first, but soon his balance returned. Just before the bell rang, he was gliding across the ring in a style worthy of the incomparable Astaire.

*   *   *

A good meal just wouldn't be good enough for Bobby that evening. He wanted a spectacular dinner to mark something significant. His survival in the ring? His visit to the college? He wasn't sure. Mostly, he wanted to make his father smile. So, as Dad napped, he lifted a couple of bucks from his wallet and went to the market to buy fresh garlic, bay leaves, onions, and soy—some of the staples for pork adobo, the old man's favorite dish.

He then labored over that meal, taking hours to sample the sauce and adjust accordingly—too much soy, add some vinegar, too much vinegar, add brown sugar and maybe a little water. On and on he went—stirring, sniffing and sampling—until he was convinced he had come up with something special, maybe the best Dad had ever eaten, or so he fervently hoped.

Bobby wouldn't be disappointed. His father suddenly appeared in the tiny kitchen, explaining that he'd awakened earlier than planned and tried unsuccessfully to go back to sleep. The reason? The scents were so fragrant, so good, that sleep was impossible.

"Hmm," Dad said, as he stood over the oven and dished out two scoops of fresh rice and a generous helping of adobo.

"Hmm," he repeated, as he savored his first bite. "Very good, Bobby."

"The best?" his son asked casually.

Dad didn't immediately reply, preferring instead to sit at the table and nibble the last remnants of a soft bone. "Let's put it this way," he finally said. "For me, once your mother learned how to do it, she did it bes', no question—not until now anyway."

Bobby smiled at his father's attempt at diplomacy.

Dad then folded his arms, leaned back in his chair, and began staring at the wall. Bobby was a little worried, thinking that maybe the reference to Mom had prompted Dad to board the bus in his brain that allowed him to escape a flood of sad, unbearable memories. He knew what to do. Just let him be, he thought, just like always. He then gathered the plates and utensils and put them in the sink. The sound of running water almost drowned out what his father said next.

"You did good today," Dad said quietly.

"Huh?" Bobby said, as he turned off the faucet.

"I said you did good today," he said, this time a little louder. His gaze was still focused on the wall.

"You mean cooking?"

"Yeah, for sure."

"Boxing?"

"That, too."

"But I didn't finish him," Bobby said. "You told me to. Paulie would've knocked that guy into tomorrow."

Dad laughed and turned to face his son. "Yeah, he would've, but tha's jus' how he was," his father said. "You're a different boy—and for my money, jus' as good."

Bobby blinked, not believing he'd heard what had just been said. "Jus' as good, jus' as good," he thought, replaying the words like the hocus-pocus, eyes-closed chants he'd loved as a kid—"salim salabim," or something equally exotic and nonsensical. But no matter, it was always fun to say and he'd wanted to believe the incantations had the power to save him, his family, and maybe even the entire civilized world from destruction.

The challenges he currently faced certainly weren't as dramatic as those of his childhood imaginings. In fact, he'd been mostly happy then, thanks in no small part to his folks and to his always vigilant older brother. He knew that other kids in Yesler had to make do with less. But over the years, one thing had lodged in his craw. For as long as he could remember, Paulie was Dad's favored son. His father never seemed to play favorites, at least not overtly, but he knew in the way second sons do. He once thought that if he and his brother had been on baseball cards, Dad wouldn't have traded one Paulie for ten of him, maybe not even twenty.

But who could blame the old man? Dad and Paulie looked alike, acted alike. They were blood of blood, no doubt. But strangers couldn't tell he and his brother were related—a contrast picked up on by some of the neighborhood kids.

"Least I know who's my daddy," one of them sneered a few years back during a pick-up game at the Yesler gym. Play had gotten rough—equal parts jump shots, hard fouls and mean-spirited put-downs. All afternoon, the speaker, a new kid named Andre, had had a hard time taking Bobby off the dribble.

But he was quick with his lip—a skill useless against Paulie, who was standing nearby and heard the curare-tipped words. He ran over and grabbed Andre by the throat and pushed him hard against the wall.

"Don't never say that again, new boy," Paulie had snarled. "It ain't polite, and one warning's all you get." And Andre never did, nor did anyone else in the gym.

The sound of a chair moving jarred Bobby, bringing him back to the present. "Good adobo, son," Dad said quietly as he rose and shuffled slowly toward his bedroom. "Sleepy now."

"'Night, Dad," Bobby said, as he folded his arms, looked out the window and smiled. "Salim salabim," he whispered, as something once stuck in his craw began working itself free.

*　*　*

Bobby smiled as he lay in bed, choosing to linger on the slim ledge between consciousness and sleep, the perfect place to begin sorting things out. The day had gone bing-bing-bang, starting with the drama with Cortez and picking up speed from there. He'd had no time to reflect on what seemed like a half-year's worth of important events played out in a day. Now was his chance.

Tomorrow, he planned to go back to the college and sign up for the GED exam. Bobby wasn't particularly worried about passing it. No sweat, one of his many drop-out pals assured him.

"Dummy basics," an acquaintance named Chico declared. "Easy, unless you're a junkie or an idiot." Chico should know. For years, he'd managed to sample every drug on the market and although he'd been clean for several months, the mind-robbing ghosts of the old bad days stuck around. Sometimes he'd forget in mid-sentence what he wanted to say or utter sentence fragments that made no sense to anyone, maybe not even to him. But somehow, despite occasional bursts of gibberish, Chico passed the exam and was admitted to college. It was the rest of his life he resumed flunking. School bored him; night life never did. About mid-term, he stopped going to class, and the last thing Bobby had heard, the Army had punched his ticket for Vietnam.

That night Bobby promised himself that what had happened to poor Chico wouldn't happen to him. He'd study to pass the GED—the sooner the better—and stick around long enough to get to the heart of a sure-to-lengthen list of matters.

Such a change. At first, college had been just the easiest way to get out of the draft—a down-to-the-bone practical point hammered home by the always protective Paulie and his parents. But that was before today. Actually setting foot on campus—for him, the first time—started him thinking that there may be more to education than just keeping him out of a war zone.

At Seattle Central, young people actually talked about ideas, intriguing and serious ones, not like the high school knuckleheads who got drunk or loaded before first period and zombied their way through English and math. He wanted to be part of what he saw, felt, and heard at the college.

It might also be nice if he bumped into the interesting young woman who said her essence had been spoken to. He could see her face—a mix of some sort just like him. If he saw her again, it might be a common point in a future conversation. Or maybe he could ask her about the famous fellow whose name was a contraction.

Just then he realized it had been awhile since he thought of a girl that way. Amazing, he thought, as he yawned and knew he was moments away from sleep. He fluffed his pillow and pulled the blankets snug, feeling for the first time in months that maybe, just maybe, something decent might finally work out.

Chapter Six

Monkey see, monkey do, Bobby remembered Dad always saying. It was one of his ways of getting by in the Army, when he didn't always understand what the white officers were saying—or Filipino GIs chatting away in different dialects, for that matter.

So that's what Bobby did as he sat in the college cafeteria, surrounded by students, their noses buried in books, their pens scribbling furiously. He took the cue and stared at a pile of pamphlets, practice questions and papers explaining the mysteries of the GED, all picked up earlier that morning from the admissions office. For good measure, he'd also brought his high school English and math texts, figuring there was no time like now to begin getting up to speed. The next exam was sometime the following week—plenty of time to get a grip on dummy basics.

He sipped his coffee, relieved that the sample questions didn't look too hard. Not quite who's-buried-in-Grant's-Tomb simple, but close.

"Man, this chemistry midterm's gonna kill me," he heard someone at the same table two chairs down say. Bobby briefly glanced up to see the speaker, a young, scruffy-looking white guy with bloodshot eyes. Private stuff, he figured, and returned to the task at hand. Still, he was too close to the principals not to hear their conversation.

"Nah, James, in this class you're already dead," his bearded, overweight companion said evenly. Bobby thought he sounded like a straight man in a not-ready-for-the-big-time comedy team. While he spoke, he remained focused on a thick, expensive-looking book—reading slowly, carefully, mumbling and nodding before turning a page.

"Unfortunately," he added, "chemistry is one of those things you actually have to study, even memorize, and, uh, knucklehead, I told you I'd help, but did I ever get that knock on the door? That telephone call? Uh-uh."

"Albert, that ain't funny," came James' answer. By tone and inflection he was telling his friend that lame attempts at sarcasm weren't particularly appreciated.

"You know I been workin' full time, just barely scratchin' by in school. . . . Man, chemistry was a mistake especially with this old fart Anderson, but I had to take it 'cuz it was the only one open and I had to do a full load. If this goes south and I lose credits, I got an eager-beaver draft board waitin' to snatch me for an extended, rifle-packin', expenses-paid visit to Southeast Asia."

Albert ignored the hint. "Heard it's nice there, nice beaches, nice exotic women, no winters," he said blandly. "Too bad you're a picture of health, a former athlete, grade-A beef. Not like me—flat feet, weak eyes, irregular heart beat, asthma—a poor candidate for anything remotely rigorous, like blowing up those I don't even know. Fortunately, I will be spared that moral decision. My doctor says I've got every physical flaw imaginable. According to him, with proper care and enough meds I should be able to live a full but boring life and die a natural death."

Albert paused and looked up. "It just goes to show that sometimes fate has a way of evening things out."

"You don't think he'll give me a break?"

"Not likely. I heard Anderson's an old Marine. Shot up on Tarawa, that's what I heard. *Semper fi, semper die*, that sort of thing."

"Yeah, yeah, right. Remember Danny Wilson?"

"Sure, Mr. once-upon-a-time hot football star, college scouts interested, all the young ladies, too," Albert answered without looking up from his book. "Good hair, good teeth, a prince of the city—or so he thought. But dumb as a doorknob. You played with him, right? Whatever happened to Danny after graduation? Did he miss the Saturday night lights, the adulation?"

Albert paused, possibly to catch his breath or wait for an answer. Bobby was amazed such scorn could be so blandly delivered, like he was ordering a burger, hold the onions, please. Where he came from, words of scorn ran the scale from *basso profundo* to the purest *falsetto*, all accompanied by a full range of hostile stares and chest-puffed swaggers. Understatement, Bobby figured, must be a white guy thing.

"Did it cause him to have an epiphany," Albert continued. "A piercing existential moment of despair during which he'd realized that he'd peaked at seventeen and that life would be all downhill from then on? Did he then choose to end it so that those who saw him in his glory would remember him as he used to be, as opposed to what he was fated to become—nothing, zero, a former fast-for-a-white-guy figure in the history of the city's high school sports?"

Bobby tried not to laugh. He didn't know what "epiphany" or "existential" meant, but most of the rest of it sounded like a lot of guys he knew.

"I wouldn't put it past him," Albert snorted, as he turned another page. "Just too full of himself, if you ask me. I didn't like him much, to be honest."

"Heard from his sis," James said quietly. "We used to date and we're still pretty close. She'll call maybe near the holidays just to touch base. Danny couldn't cut it in college, so last year he dropped out—Utah, Utah State, somethin' like that—and signed up. You know how it goes."

James paused and slowly shook his head. "The last time she called she said her brother just got out of the VA, rehab, minus an arm and a leg . . . and most of his mind."

Albert suddenly looked up and stared at James, searching for a tiny smile or some other sign that he hadn't just heard what his friend had so clearly said. No sign.

"Good God," Albert finally whispered, any hint of sarcasm suddenly gone. "I'm so sorry."

"It's okay, man. You didn't know."

It was obvious to Bobby that Albert didn't like Danny Wilson and, after this moment passed, he'd probably resume not liking Danny Wilson. But for a moment at least they shared the same DNA passed on by a pair of common ancestors from a primordial European past. Just knowing Danny had made him more than a statistic on the dreary list of unfamiliar names from far-flung places on the daily roll call of America's dead, wounded, and maimed. Finding out what happened to him was a jolt, an uncomfortable reminder that life can do cruddy things, even to the young, maybe even to safe, secure, plump-as-baby-pig boys like him.

For Albert, disliking Danny had suddenly become not that important. He had no further reply, other than the chunky fingers on his right hand drumming rat-a-tat-tat on the table.

Turnaround. For some it happens quickly. It happened, the sisters claimed, to Saul on his way to Damascus. It was apparently happening to Albert now.

He began writing on an index card. "Formulas," he explained, as he handed James the card.

"Copy them on your hand or forearm. I don't know, but maybe they'll come in handy. I've had Anderson before, an intro class, and sometimes he just leaves the room during an exam—he goes outside to grab a Pall Mall moment—especially near the end of the hour and most of the students have left."

Albert paused. "So, you stay right to the end. I'll be there next to you. Understand what I'm saying?"

James nodded.

Nodding also was an unkempt, dark young man who stood quietly and slightly behind Albert. Like a lot of other young men in the bustling cafeteria, he was dressed in a hodgepodge of civilian and military garb—in this case, light blue ski jacket, black Converse high-tops like Bob Cousy used to wear, and khaki pants.

He nudged Albert softly on the shoulder. "You did good, my man," he said. "Righteous, real good."

Startled, Albert looked up. "Uh, yeah, man, thanks," he stammered. He was not a little alarmed that someone else, maybe another chemistry student, had snuck up and heard this conversation.

"Uh, have I seen you before?" he asked, hoping dearly that the answer would be no. He wiped and rewiped his palms on his new blue corduroy pants. A sharp looking pair, a great deal—and absorbent, too.

"Maybe, but I doubt it," he said, as he began to walk away. "Don't worry, bro, you never said what you did and I ain't sayin' nothin'. No big deal."

"Uh, what's your name, just in case I see you again."

The young man stopped in mid-step and turned but didn't immediately respond. He was staring intently at another young man—more a boy, really—sitting at the same table but slightly apart from Albert and James. He remembered any number of girls saying he reminded them of Harry Belafonte, only younger and prettier. He nodded. They were right, he concluded. He is prettier. In particular, his brown, wavy hair made the ladies wish he'd drop by for a visit and stay long enough to get in trouble.

As he shifted his gaze toward Albert, the corners of his mouth turned slightly upward.

"Ain't highly likely, my man," he said, laughing. "Don't plan on seein' you again; college ain't my thing. But just in case, the name's Paulo. The fellas call me Paulie."

"Okay, Paulie," Albert said, extending his right hand. "I'll remember that."

Bobby looked up, curious why someone he didn't know would say his brother's name. What he saw was Albert who'd turned away from the table and was apparently talking—his nodding head was a giveaway—to no one but himself. Then there was that hand—connected to the wrist then an arm slightly bent—his fingers curled as if grasping something, moving up and down, down and up, up and down.

Bobby flashed. Maybe it was a Jimmy Stewart/Harvey the invisible rabbit type of thing that he'd once seen on late-night television. Or maybe it was chemistry that had made Albert so crazy?

He shuddered and decided then to avoid that class and old Professor Anderson at all costs. He swore to himself he would never be a chemist, even if a thousand angels, his mother,

Paulie, and the Blessed Virgin Mary herself came flying out of the skies to tell him that's what he should be because mankind's future depended on it.

What did that leave for him to study? He smiled. Everything else, he figured.

* * *

The gnawing in the pit of Bobby's stomach told him that he was hungry. Small wonder, he thought, as he glanced at the clock on the wall. It was 2:00 PM, or almost five hours since he'd had his first cup of weak cafeteria coffee. Sure, there were distractions, like eavesdropping on the nearby conversation about chemistry, war, and one sad young man's despair.

Interesting? Sure. Educational? That, too.

But that wasn't why he was here. Mostly, he spent his time going over the sample questions and rereading long-forgotten chapters in the texts. He was surprised by how much he'd forgotten, surprised, too, by his ability to focus on the materials—and pleased that he still could.

When Bobby was younger, focusing wasn't a problem. He would often lose himself in a book—or several books simultaneously if he liked what he was reading. But coming home on Saturday afternoons with an armful of library books made him stand out even more—and he was already standing out too much.

As he got older, he stopped going to the library and began shedding other habits.

Blend in, he thought. School, Cortez and the other delinquents said, cut into time better spent getting over—getting what you can, whenever you can, however you can.

Going to St. James, with its uniforms and starched white shirts—hard-to-miss emblems of better than the rest—was tough enough. Bobby endured the stares and occasional insults of public school kids who wondered what made *him* so special? What gave *him* the right to dream? Although he loved the nuns and their devotion to teaching, they didn't have to walk home, or at least not to his home.

When his parents could no longer pay for his tuition, Bobby, at least on one level, was secretly relieved. He recalled the afternoon his mother broke the news that he'd have to transfer to public school. Mom was solemn and, Bobby thought, ready in a heartbeat to take it all back and declare that with the Good Lord's help and a second job they would somehow find a way to make it work.

He didn't give her a chance. "Okay," he said, as he forced what he hoped would be a convincing smile.

Big mistake, Bobby now knew, as he stood up slowly and walked toward the counter where he scanned the offerings before settling on a slice of cherry pie and a small carton of milk.

"Ninety-five cents, hon," the middle-aged woman behind the cash register said. "Are you a new student?"

"Hopin' to be," he answered, as he fished in his pocket for what he hoped would be enough change. He pulled out what he had and totaled up the small mix of coins in the palm of his hand. He did it again just to be sure. But each time it was the same result—two dimes short.

"Ah, that's all right, forget the milk," he said, as he nudged the carton toward her. As he did, he felt his face warm.

"How much do you have?" the cashier asked.

"Seventy-five cents."

"You can pay me tomorrow," she said. She winked at Bobby and pushed the carton toward him.

"I, um," he stammered. Bobby was embarrassed by her kindness, more so by his all-too-naked need.

"Oh, Hon," she said airily. "Don't worry. The college won't go belly up overnight."

"I'm not usually like this," he mumbled.

"I know," she replied. "I've got kids your age."

"Well . . . um," Bobby began, his tone undecided.

"Put it on mine," a voice behind him said. Startled, he turned toward the speaker, the young woman who'd gushed over a Mexican with the contraction for a last name.

"There, it's settled, Honey," the cashier said. "That'll be two-fifty, young lady."

"You didn't have to do that," Bobby said softly.

"I know," she said. "But it's government money, financial aid."

He wasn't sure what to say.

Unlike his peers in the projects, Bobby was new at liking a girl, or at least being interested in one. Sister Victor and the other nuns had made sure of that, especially when students hit fourth grade. Couldn't start too soon, the good sisters figured.

They would constantly warn about the dangers of lust and that those who gave in committed mortal sins—never mind the ongoing mysteries of Jesus' resurrection, the virgin birth, meatless Fridays, or the new-look church of Vatican II.

"And you know what dying in a state of mortal sin means," Sister Victor warned.

The earthly penalty, the nuns said, was doubly bad for girls, who would end up shaming their families, losing their friends, and living in the diocesan home for unwed mothers. Like Lori,

Sister Victor said, referring to a recent Saint James grad. Beautiful, a Filipino *mestiza*, smart, too. But two years ago, during her first year of high school, she hooked up with a rascally fellow and, rather than go through the messy list of pre- and post-coital specifics that might provide hints on how such things were done, Sister ended the lecture on a general but somber note.

"Her life is ruined," she told a hushed class of nine-year-olds.

Boys, Sister added almost as an afterthought, had options, like leaving town, joining the Navy, or staying put and daring the mothers to come after them to prove paternity.

The only way lust was okay, Sister Victor and the other nuns explained, was for it to occur within marriage—and that was years in the future. Catholic marriage made lust sacramental, a divine green light for husbands and wives to shed their clothes and rub on each other to their hearts' content, all for the greater honor of God.

"But even then," she sniffed. "A life of chastity is still preferred."

Like most things the nuns said, Bobby took the message on outside-of-marriage lust to heart. Sister Victor was not to be messed with, not with her cold blue eyes and hint of a blonde mustache. She was an odd-looking woman with a Karl Malden-like nose. But she'd found her calling as God's enforcer. Besides, he liked how Mom and Dad treated each other, so maybe there was something to this sacramental stuff, which also coincided with where he was—wherever *that* was.

Girls, he'd concluded, were just too much trouble. He'd seen young guys in the neighborhood strut and preen—not a hair out of place—then start senseless *mano a mano* battles over them. One fight was especially memorable; the combatants were two husky fifteen-year-olds that nine-year-old Bobby had seen around, each on different occasions, in the company of Luisa, a striking and slender fourteen-year-old brown-skinned sister who drew winks and nods even from old men.

They fought after school on the infield of a nearby park—wrestling, punching, and gouging each other for about half an hour until hoots from assembled spectators caught a passing cop's attention. They resumed the carnage the next day—same spot, same fight fans, same time. From Bobby's perch on the edge of a small knoll, he saw the two resume their brutal, artless combat, neither one noticing that Luisa was slowly drifting to the back of the crowd and leaving the scene at about the same time as Eddie, the street-savvy eighteen-year-old Mexican half-brother of a Black-Mexican friend of his.

Bobby yawned and leaned back. Too obvious, he thought. Predictable, too.

Eddie and Luisa walked slowly in opposite directions until each had left the park. Once outside, Eddie, cigarette in hand, sat casually on the hood of his tricked-out, talk-of-the-neighborhood '57 Chevy. About five minutes passed before Eddie slid off the hood, walked to the passenger's side and opened the door for Luisa. They kissed, then slowly drove off just as a siren's wail signaled the end of the latest round of bloodletting.

This tacky rendezvous simply confirmed what Bobby was beginning to suspect—that Luisa and the other pretty girls were a source of unending confusion and trouble. Case closed, at least for a while.

But what if he was thinking of changing his mind? What then? His main problem was that years of avoidance had dulled his instincts and thickened his tongue.

Here, in the cafeteria, this intriguing young woman had given him a gift. She was expecting him to say something.

"Uh, thanks," he finally managed to mumble.

As Bobby listened to himself speak, he felt a little like Opie telling Sheriff Andy that under the current circumstances, maybe he'd just as soon go fishing. Perch and crappie don't require conversation, just a decent worm, properly hooked and suitably uncomfortable. Fishing was less complicated with fewer opportunities for public humiliation.

But there was no easy out here. Reflexively, Bobby lowered his head as his eyes began bouncing side to side—one result of a nervous effort to pretend that the only thing interesting wasn't standing right in front of him. He was blushing again and imagined the other patrons staring at him; he hoped she didn't notice.

She smiled. "You can look at me, you know. I don't bite, at least not hard. That crazy eye thing, though, you gotta lose it."

"Huh?"

"It's making me dizzy."

Bobby was amazed that someone who didn't know him could be so bold. He blinked, shrugged his shoulders and, despite his embarrassment, started to chuckle—a quiet, self effacing laugh. He knew he was ridiculous, pathetic—insert the right adjective—and that the only good thing was that no one from Yesler was watching.

"I guess I just have to practice," he said.

"What?"

"Oh, I don't know, I guess talking to girls," he answered.

"Women."

"Okay, yeah, okay, talking to women."

"That's better," she said with a smile. "And besides, I can help you."

"Do what?"

"Talk to women," she said with a smile. "Starting with me."

Chapter Seven

Her name was Deena. "That's double 'e' in case you decide to write me a love letter, and your name, please, especially since we're sitting down and about to share a meal."

"Bobby Vincente."

"I noticed you the other day and you looked interesting," she continued. "I was just curious, that's all."

She said she was named after her wild-as-a-shewolf aunt who ran a bordello in San Francisco, her hometown. The cops, she explained, knew all about it, but so too did the police chief and several important city officials—all patrons at one time or another. She'd moved here two years ago when she was eighteen because she was tired of the scene and had heard Seattle was slower.

"It was too hard and way too fast," she explained. "I was bored and got sucked in, but I wanted to slow down, go to school and at least make it to twenty-one."

She then stared at Bobby, focusing her gaze upon his eyes. He smiled and looked briefly away. "So, Mr. Bobby, what are you?"

"What do you mean?"

"I mean, what wonderful mix of races produced you?"

"Well," he began slowly, unsure how to answer. "My mom's part black and my dad's Filipino."

Deena, arms across her chest, looked skeptical. "You know, the Bay Area's full of Filipinos and you don't look . . ."

"I know," he said quietly.

Bobby was trying hard to stay calm—not the easiest thing to do. Her round, dark eyes and full lips made her pretty— maybe even beautiful—sans makeup and any recent effort to tame her long black hair. Dangerous, confident, older, Bobby thought, what more could he possibly say to someone like this? He felt like he was trying to swim underwater and wondered just how far in over his head was he getting.

Deena added casually that her flirtation with hardcore street life wasn't a raised-on-the-wrong-side-of-the-tracks-thing, please don't get her wrong. She came from a respectable family and money, a lot of it, and had gone to the type of private schools that fed the Stanfords and the Vassers. She never lacked for anything courtesy of her mother—a Spanish, not Mexican, beauty, she stressed—who married her father, a Persian oil executive and adviser to the Shah who died in a plane crash when she was a child. The insurance paid out handsomely, same with the will, and her mother used the money to play the market. She kept marrying well and kept playing the market until she'd built up a nice upper seven-figure sum, complete with Swiss accounts and a fat trust fund her daughter couldn't touch until she turned twenty-five.

"Pretty funky," she grumbled, referring to the out-of-reach cash. "Guess she doesn't trust me, probably for good reason," she added, before taking the first bite of her sandwich.

Rich, too, Bobby thought, as he felt himself sink deeper.

The ensuing silence as Deena munched on her meal showed how one-sided the conversation had been. She intended to change that.

"So," Deena finally said. "What about you? Are you from around here?"

"Yeah," Bobby answered.

"And?"

"Well, it's just up the hill, a, um, housing project," he said, spitting out the last two words and hoping she didn't notice. It was the first time he'd ever been embarrassed by being poor. He didn't like the feeling.

"Ooh, a tough guy," she squealed. "I can't help it, but I just love tough guys."

"Nah, I wouldn't say that."

"Well, then, how would you describe yourself?"

"Just an average guy, you know, get an education, stay out of the Army, get a better life."

"Just average?"

"That'll do for now."

Bobby was about halfway through his pie when he put down his fork. His expanded role in their conversation had given him a rare burst of confidence, enough to ask a question.

"Who's this Mexican guy you were talkin' about the other day, Manuel Can't?" he asked, and suddenly regretted it.

"Immanuel Kant. You're kidding, right? The great German philosopher Immanuel Kant." Her eyes stretched wide like she'd just seen Jesus or maybe Kant himself walk into the cafeteria.

"Of course," Bobby lied. He poked at the pie crust with his fork, then pushed the saucer to mid-table. "Gotta go," he said suddenly, and just as suddenly rose from his chair and began gathering his books and other belongings.

"Why?" Although Deena sounded surprised, Bobby couldn't be sure because he was glancing there and here and everywhere just to avoid eye contact. Not that what she was feeling at this moment mattered much to him anyway.

Mistake, way out of your league, ignoramus, forget it—
chump thoughts roared through his mind. Sophisticated,
worldly Deena, he knew, was just being herself. Same with
him. But how could he expect her to accept him, which meant
understanding this gurgling mess of emotions and insecurities
in his head. He concluded that she couldn't—she was a woman,
not a saint—no one could, and that there was no point in
pretending otherwise.

The priests, he thought, had it all figured out—just pray
and read and think and pray again, a serene, simple life with
three squares, a warm bed and skip everything else. It wasn't
too bad considering the alternatives. Maybe he should check
it out?

"Was it anything I said?" he thought he heard her say as he
walked away from the table.

"No," he mumbled, an answer spoken more to himself
than to anyone else.

*   *   *

A few blocks from the college, Bobby's head began to clear.
Simpler things—getting dinner ready, touching base with Dad,
catching a nap so he could go at the books again—started to
replace the play-rewind-play movie in his mind starring Deena.
He'd concluded that starting anything with her would be
complicated, too messy; it would pry open a trunk of subjects
he didn't want to think about, at least not now. She was pretty,
sure, maybe even beautiful. Toss in smart and worldly—what's
not to love?

But he knew from observation that women such as that
had certain expectations—loud-talking, chest-thumping, pack-

leading standards he wasn't interested in meeting. For Dad in his prime and for Paulie, no sweat, they'd have taken the bait. And if his brother were still alive, he would have suggested—politely, of course—that maybe Deena should meet him. His unshakable ego matched hers; maybe they'd have more in common.

He sighed. It wasn't enough to be kind. Shyness, awkwardness, insecurity—each one of them, deal-busting traits as far as young women went. But that was who he was, and it was too bad, he thought, as he turned onto the short walkway leading to the apartment.

As Bobby reached for the door handle, lingering memories of Deena abruptly gave way to multicolor images, as vivid and inviting as a *Look Magazine* holiday spread. He envisioned whole gingers, green peppers, green onions, garlic cloves, bottles of soy and vinegar and what he hoped was by now a thoroughly defrosted chicken.

Like any good cook, Bobby paused for a moment, savoring an array of possible tastes, products of continuous experimentation, meaning that he never cooked the same dishes exactly the same way. He loved the surprises, with shifting aromas and intuition dictating a pinch more of this, a lot less of that.

Garlic, he knew, was always safe, a can't-miss favorite. In fact, he and Dad had had garlic fried rice yesterday and garlic-flavored pork chops the day before that. Delicious. But twice in the same week was reason enough not to feature it again.

Bobby slowly opened the door. By the time he closed it behind him, he had made up his mind. He smiled; soy sauce and ginger would co-star tonight.

*   *   *

"Tha's good, by golly," Dad declared, as he savored the taste of a tender slice of chicken smothered in sauce. "Smells good, too."

"Thanks, Dad," Bobby replied, knowing that his father loved everything he cooked. It felt good to know he was appreciated. But he was withholding his own judgment on the meal until he could nibble on a wing.

A quick bite delivered the verdict. Bubby was disappointed. Sure, it was good, good enough—tasty and nutritious, but workmanlike, a standard he'd already mastered. As he sat staring at the piece of chicken on his plate, he wondered what he could have done to make it more interesting, make it really come alive?

It was something about the sauce. It seemed too bland, pedestrian, like the sauces smothering a five-and-dime store Salisbury steak. Less soy? Less or more ginger? Perhaps some wine would have helped? If so, red or white? Or maybe a little brown sugar to sweeten the taste?

Then there was the presentation, a notion he'd picked up from a cooking show on television. Top-shelf chefs would have also made the meal a pleasure for the eyes. He briefly imagined the same chicken, its head magically reattached, nesting in a valley surrounded by snow-capped peaks. It was almost too pretty to eat.

He chuckled. Nah, too Heidi, too much.

Still, a great chef would have somehow made the chicken look different from what it was now—a dead brown bird lying on its back in a silver baking pan.

That was a challenge for Bobby. Most of the Filipinos he knew weren't big on aesthetics, at least when it came to food, where function always trumped form. His father's buddies were hardscrabble, working-class men who'd survived the Depression, migrant labor camps, white racism, and, later, Japanese bullets. For them, a good meal was one that warmed them and eased the gnawing in their bellies, fueling them enough to push through another dreary day. He had often sat with these men at dinner, when they'd mix meat or fish with their rice and vegetables and gobble it down with a table spoon.

Five-minute meals, functional but artless, form be damned. They would then move on to drink, tell stories, play cards or watch Sugar Ray Robinson smoke some artless pug on TV.

Art *should* matter, Bobby thought, as he continued carving up the chicken. He wasn't sure why he thought that way, but he was glad he did. Other guys might be smoother with the girls. They might also be smarter, bigger, and faster; but in this kitchen he was king—or at least a leading pretender to the throne. He knew he was good, but he believed that cooking was one of the few skills he had the talent to perfect. Besides, a great meal—or even one that was passably decent—brought pleasure to those he loved.

All he had to do was look at Dad, who, Bobby's self-criticisms aside, was quickly lining his plate with breast and thigh bones and was now focused on gathering the last grains of rice. For his father, the lack of presentation obviously wasn't a problem.

Bobby couldn't help but smile, a moment of contentment soon clouded by something he remembered. He suddenly wasn't sure how many more dinners he and his father had left. Sure, over the last few weeks, he'd seemed sharper, more focused, the Dad of old, especially when it came to teaching Bobby how to box.

But there were times, like late last Sunday, after Bobby had gone to bed. He was awakened by the sound of a voice coming from the kitchen. He opened the door and tiptoed outside to see his father, sitting at the table in the dark. He was talking to his mother, his tone solemn as a prayer, telling her how much he missed her—Lord, how he missed her. They weren't meant to be apart.

Then his father did something he didn't expect. He giggled like a schoolboy and said, "Sweetheart, you jus' stop worryin' now. I swear I'll be with you soon."

How soon? Bobby had wondered, as he slid along the darkened walls and slipped quietly into his room.

That told him that each meal of a finite and dwindling supply had to count. Although he didn't see her, he had no doubt that his mom had been in the kitchen and that Dad knew that his end was near. He'd come to believe that sometimes the dead, for whatever reason, didn't immediately go away. Just look at Paulie.

But that was no guarantee that Paulie and his mom would stick around forever. If they did, it wouldn't be so bad. But that probably wasn't the way things worked in the afterlife. That meant to be with his family, he'd have to wait, decades maybe if he stayed out of the Army—a mixed blessing at best.

Bobby sighed. Dad's passing would make him an orphan—like the big-eyed poster kids in India, the Philippines, and other Third World corners. But those young photogenic phenoms had him beat. They could guilt-trip Americans into opening their wallets. They were objects of cooing—passengers on a jet flying to this land of immigrant dreams. Instead, he was about to become just a native-born orphan—just an average poor American—who still wasn't sure how he'd make it on his own, or even if he could.

Bobby breathed deeply. That helped.

Besides, he told himself, maybe he'd sort it out later. All he could do for now was promise himself that whatever the number of breakfasts, lunches and dinners he and Dad had left, all of them would be great. It was the least he could do for someone he was already starting to miss.

His father's voice ended his reverie.

"Eat, Bobby, you should eat," Dad urged.

"Not that hungry, Dad. I had something at the college," he said softly, and pushed his barely touched meal toward him. "You can finish mine, or I can turn it into chicken salad for tomorrow."

"Hmm, a chicken salad sandwich for lunch? You'll make one for yourself, too, huh? I worry about you sometimes, like you worry too much and study too hard and you don' eat enough. . . ."

Bobby looked at his father, lingering a bit as if to memorize his features. But he was careful not to stare too long so as not to give away suspicions he couldn't shake. He forced a slight smile, then shrugged and turned away as his eyes began to mist.

Deep in his heart, Bobby understood that Dad longed to be with Mom and Paulie. He belonged with them, especially with Mom. She was the strong one, the wise and patient *bruja* who could dig into her Creole past and find the right *hoo-doo* words to talk Dad down whenever his wounded mind spun out of control.

Years ago, when Bobby was ten, he was snooping around his parents' bedroom and came across some faded black-and-white photos of his mom sitting, legs crossed, in a high-back chair. She was wearing a dark dress, narrow at the waist, that showed her figure well. He was stunned by the images—how lovely she was, how elegant, the type of young woman for whom doors opened. He wondered then would some of the doors still be open.

At the time, Dad was going through an especially rough zombie-like stretch, and she had to pick up a second job just to make ends meet. Bobby was also getting tired of other kids saying he didn't look like his dad.

One day he asked his mother on one of her rare days off wouldn't they all be better off somewhere else? Then the unasked part: With someone else?

"Don't you ever ask that again," she hissed, in a tone so full of venom and threat that it chilled his blood. "Your father is too good a man for you to even think that. You got no idea what he's done for you."

Even now, the memory of his behavior shamed him and he could feel his cheeks redden. A very good man, Bobby concluded.

He now realized that Dad was sticking around to make sure he could take care of himself—what a good man would do. Of course. It was also what his mom would have wanted.

"It'll be the best chicken salad you ever tasted," Bobby managed to say, hoping that his voice didn't crack in the telling. He had wanted to talk about his day at the college, about meeting Deena, but that would have to wait.

"Oh, I never worry 'bout that, son. I got no doubt a' tall."

*   *   *

The dishes were washed, the chicken was put away. Dad was sitting in front of the tube glued to Dr. Richard Kimble's long-running ordeal. Bobby smiled. Everything was in order, he thought, as he walked to his room.

On another night, he might have stayed up and commiserated with his father about the horrid fate that had befallen an innocent, likeable man.

"He's a good guy; why do they chase 'im?" his father asked after a recent episode.

"Dad, it's just a television show," Bobby explained. "Make believe."

"But he didn't kill his wife and that guy, that Detective Gerard, I get so mad at 'im. He should be fired, or at least spend more time finding that one-armed guy. Tha's how I see it anyways."

"Oh."

Dad then folded his arms across his chest, his gaze focused on the show's credits. His stern demeanor spoke volumes about how unhappy he was that the obsessed and humorless Gerard had gotten so close to his prey.

Usually, his father was able to tell the difference between reality and fantasy, at least when it came to Pa and Hop Sing and the boys or the characters on other popular television shows. But Richard Kimble was somehow in a class by himself. Bobby guessed later that maybe it was because the old man identified with the good doctor's unspeakable burden—how tragedy begat sorrow and, later, injustice, and a life that all of a sudden stopped making sense. Kimble's response was to run and play for time; he figured that in a way Dad's was, too.

So Bobby adapted. On "Fugitive" evenings with his father, he would cheer Kimble, sometimes even giving him advice on what to do next, whom to trust—useful suggestions for a fellow on the run. It was fun, but he was too tired to play the game tonight. He guessed that he could last another fifteen minutes, if that—time enough to re-read a short section on the correct use of semi-colons and colons.

*   *   *

"Semi-colons can be used to separate items in a sequence," Bobby mumbled, as his eyelids grew heavier, and he began drifting into what he hoped would be a deep, long sleep.

He would have made it, too, except for a pesky, unanswered question that nagged him. "Dang, so what makes them different from commas?" he added.

"Man, who cares?"

He recognized the voice and quickly pulled the covers over his head. "Come on, Paulie," he groaned. "I'm so tired, go away and come back in the morning."

"Boy, I gotta tell you, for such a smart kid, you can be such a major chump sometimes."

Bobby sighed, aware that his brother's I'm-gonna-tell-you-somethin'- and-you're-gonna-listen tone of voice meant that he was going to speak now, not a minute or an hour later. No way out. Checkmate.

He slowly sat up, rubbed his eyes, and turned toward the sound of Paulie's voice.

His brother looked different. Paulie, his hair meticulously pompadoured, was leaning against a wall, casually smoking a cigarette—a better-than-most version of Frank Sinatra cool. Instead of Army fatigues and tennis shoes, this evening he was wearing a gray, narrow-lapel shark-skin suit and black Italian boots.

"Nice threads," Bobby said.

"Thanks, little brother."

Bobby paused, as his eyes grew accustomed to the dark. "That suit, man, it looks . . ."

"Yeah, I know, familiar," Paulie replied. "I wore it to Mary Sandoval's junior prom. Remember her?"

"Oh yeah. Real pretty, smart, too," Bobby replied. He remembered seeing the prom photos and thought at the time what a handsome couple they were—how stunning she was, how happy Paulie was. His brother had had his share of street corner conquests, but Mary was different.

"How'd it go, anyway?" Bobby asked. "You never said much."

"Not much to say."

"Huh?"

"It went good, too, maybe too good, but back then, the Army had me by the balls. I figured I'd survive, but couldn't promise her nothin', just 'if I'm still livin' next year, we'll see,'" Paulie said, followed by a mirthless chuckle. "Ain't much of a promise, you ask me. Every day I was over there, I thought about you and Dad and Mom. I also thought 'bout Mary, 'bout what could be, 'bout seein' ya'll again. Nothin' else mattered."

For a moment, Bobby wasn't sure what to say.

"She was there, you know," he began softly.

"Where?"

"At the funeral, crying."

"I know; me, too," Paulie said softly.

Bobby didn't expect that comment; he cleared his throat, wondering what he should say next. "So, uh, why'd you dress up today?"

"I dunno, maybe I was thinkin' 'bout Mary, what could'a been, ain't never gonna be, that sorta sentimental thing."

"I saw her at Safeway a few weeks back," Bobby said slowly. "She's taking accounting classes, asked about Dad, found a nice guy."

"I know, I was next to you, man," Paulie said, his tone curt.

"Oh. So what're you going to do next?"

Paulie stared at Bobby as if his book-smart brother had suddenly turned stupid and was starting to drool. "Nothin'," he finally replied. "I'm dead, our story's over, but yours ain't, startin' with that girl."

"Huh?"

"Geeze, dumbass, the fox you met in the cafeteria and been dreamin' 'bout ever since."

Bobby, who started to blush, was glad it was dark. "Deena?" he managed to say.

"Yeah, yeah, that's her name. Good lookin', real sharp, too."

"You were in the cafeteria?"

"Sittin' at your table."

"So, how come I couldn't see you?"

"Hey, it's my business if I wanna be seen or not."

"So, why didn't you?"

"What?"

"Want to be seen."

"Didn't wanna cut into your play."

"Shoot, there wasn't any play."

Paulie threw his head back and laughed. "Ain't what she told me, Romeo."

"Thought you couldn't be seen."

"I couldn't, but I read her mind and believe me, for her, there was plenty of play," Paulie said. "She saw you walkin' her home, coppin' a feel and kissin' her, God's truth. You just too dense to know it. But even so, I guess it's a start, with all that talk back then when we was kids, with you bein' so soft and pretty and never with a girl—different, you know, almost . . ."

"Homo, fruit," Bobby said evenly.

They'd had this talk before. "Man, you gotta stop actin' that way," Paulie would warn. "People be thinkin' you a sissy."

He frowned and nodded. "Faggot and yeah, sissy, before I forget," he continued.

Bobby then sighed. He'd heard the whispers and innuendos and had grown tired of them, tired of explaining to his brother and to anyone else that he was just the way he was, whatever that was. He didn't dislike girls and wasn't attracted to boys, but beyond that he couldn't say.

"Somethin' like that, yeah," Paulie said. "I use'ta bust dudes upside their heads I hear 'em talk like that 'bout 'cha. It disrespected you, it disrespected us."

"So," Bobby began calmly. "What if I was?"

Paulie folded his arms across his chest, his dark brown eyes focused on his brother. The look said, without a word uttered, "You gotta' be kiddin'."

This time instead of looking away—what he usually did—Bobby stared back, a stalemate broken by the hint of a smile on Paulie's dark, otherwise somber face. "You ain't," he finally said.

"But humor me, Paulie. Just say I was?"

"And I was still here?"

"Yeah."

"You my brother so I catch someone sayin' that, I'd do just like I done before," Paulie answered. "But I know I won't have to cuz you may be soft, but I also seen you make Cortez

look like a chump. You took his balls sure as you'd cut 'im
down there with a knife; he'll be goin' outta his way to avoid
you now. And then you top that by goin' and handlin' yourself
in the ring. Me and Dad was proud. And I'm thinkin' ain't no
fairy can do that."

"Fairy," Bobby thought. A new one to be added to the
homo-fruit-faggot-sissy list of hate-filled labels sometimes
directed at him, but also at an old Puerto Rican bachelor named
Orlando, a rouged-up queen who lived in a bachelor hotel near
the projects. Orlando mostly kept to himself. Although folks
in the neighborhood snickered about his long eyelashes and
whispered about his boom-da-boom Marilyn Monroe walk,
they learned to leave him alone, the lesson driven home one
night when the old man found himself cornered by a group of
young thugs shouting faggot this and sissy that.

As the story went, Orlando casually pulled out a switch-
blade and, in a move too deft to counter, casually sliced off
the lower corner of a young man's ear. He then handed the
ear lobe to its original owner, said good night in Spanish and
walked home.

The incident drove home a painful message throughout
the neighborhood: not all sissies are punks. Sexual preference
objections aside, everyone in the projects soon learned the old
man was no one to be messed with.

Bobby admired what Orlando had done—so smooth, so
calm, so bold. But at the time, he hadn't earned that type of
respect. He knew he was still fair game, especially with Paulie
gone. Maybe humiliating Cortez would finally change things.
Maybe. He could only hope that it would.

Bobby was sure there were other insults even more vile
that he hadn't heard of yet. But that would be for later. For

now, he was pleased by Paulie's response because he understood that, given who his brother was, he was confirming their bond the best way he knew how.

"Thanks, Paulie," Bobby said.

"No sweat, younger brother."

"You know, I was scared out of my mind when I faced those guys."

"So?"

"I've never seen you scared."

Paulie shrugged. "We jus' different, that's all? Myself, I liked fightin', liked takin' some dude's rep and wearin' it like a badge, you know?

"Even if someone was bigger, supposedly badder. I'd do stuff to provoke 'im, talk smack, talk 'bout his mom, that sorta thing. It was a game, really, gettin' inside his head, makin' 'im think I was crazy, that maybe takin' me on wasn't a good idea. And that's when I knew I had 'im. When I seen that moment of doubt. Can't never remember bein' scared."

"Not even in Vietnam?"

"Nah," Paulie said softly. "Least not at first."

"What happened?"

"I started thinkin' of home," Paulie said softly, as he started to look away. "How this war stopped makin' sense and that if I didn't make it back, my dyin' would be a waste. And I started thinkin' about the kinda impact it would have on you, on Dad—you know, he ain't got much left. So, I started bein' more careful, cut the gung-ho stuff way back." He laughed. "Guess it didn't work."

"Wasn't your fault."

"Just water, brother, water under . . ."

"The bridge," Bobby said.

"You see?" Paulie said, pointing and wiggling his right index finger for emphasis. "You finish my sentence. How close is that?"

"Close."

Pailie beamed. He then lifted his left arm and stared at his wrist as if he were wearing a watch. "Better get up."

"Why?"

No answer, other than a mumbled "ten, nine, eight," the drone broken by a barked, "get out of bed," followed by a "three, two."

Bobby's feet touched the floor as the hallway phone rang at "one."

"It's Deena," Paulie announced calmly.

"Dang. How'd she find . . ."

Paulie laughed and winked, like Sinatra would have done. "We're listed, man. As I remember, you told her your last name and you also said you lived just up the hill. She checked out a map and let her fingers do the walkin' and so on." He paused. "Hmm, obviously a smart girl. Nice fingers, too, I might add."

Chapter Eight

It wasn't just the brisk night air that made Bobby shiver as he walked down the path leading to the sidewalk connecting him to the world beyond Yesler. He was on his way to a late-night rendezvous suggested by Deena, who seemed determined to be his friend—or something.

"See you at ten," she said in a tone oozing confidence, as if his meeting her was a foregone conclusion. Poor boy, he just needed a destination.

"There's a coffee shop a block south of the college," she added.

Bobby had never had a rendezvous before, at least not with a woman—late night, daylight, dawn, or dusk. Just the word itself and the way she said it—slowly, in a low whispered growl—excited him, releasing black-and-white stills of Bogart and Bergman meeting again in Casablanca.

He picked up the pace, forgetting for a moment Paulie's warning about always being aware in the projects, especially at night. Had he been, he might have seen a man dragging his left leg and walking slowly toward him on his right. He also might have seen the man—who must have heard the footsteps—suddenly stop, then slide silently toward the shadows created by a nearby porch light. There he stood, still as a statue, waiting for Bobby to pass before resuming his journey. Had Bobby been paying attention, he may even have recognized the silhouette, the uneven gait, and his role in making this pitiful man's painful condition even worse.

*   *   *

It took a moment for Bobby's eyes to adjust to the dim lighting of the coffee shop. Despite the late hour, the room was almost packed with patrons talking, reading books and newspapers. A few were even taking notes. He glanced quickly at his watch: ten on the nose. He scanned the room as his gut churned and he danced a subtle jig, twitching and shifting his weight from one foot to the other.

He was relieved. No Deena, at least not yet. Not too late, he thought, to turn around, go home, forget about it, avoid the confusion.

That option ended when he caught a glimpse of a slender young woman in a far corner rising, mouthing his name, and motioning for him to join her.

Bobby shrugged and whispered a prayer, a reflex from his St. James days, that whatever else happened that he should not be embarrassed—or embarrass himself. Was there, he wondered, a patron saint of fools? Sadly, he couldn't remember.

Bobby then took a deep breath. Right foot, left foot, he told himself, repeat. Simple as pie.

As he drew closer, he was struck even more so than earlier in the day by how stunning Deena was. Her long black hair—glistening and straighter than before—framed her pale, angular face, putting just the right accents on her large eyes, high cheekbones and full red lips. On this evening, her tight blouse was open a button short of proper, giving Bobby an intimate view that he hoped was for his eyes only.

"Hi," Bobby said shyly, as he paused in front of Deena's table and looked around. Not an empty chair in sight.

She smiled. "Then you can sit next to me," she said coyly, as she patted a spot on a long padded bench affixed to the wall.

Of course, Bobby thought, as he slipped onto the bench. Side by side, no separate chairs—this, too, had been planned. He sighed. No going back now, he thought.

The two of them looked like a long-time couple, a case of contrasts like so many couples are. Deena was lively—chatting, laughing, then casually wrapping her arms around his and pressing it to her breasts, their shape and feel causing Bobby to blink repeatedly. Otherwise, he looked straight ahead, impassive—sitting erect with his hands folded on the table. But his lips, which moved slightly and only on occasion, were proof the two were holding a conversation, no matter how one-sided.

After ten or so minutes, Bobby finally turned to look at Deena, an occasion he knew was laden with risk. They might lock eyes—she would love that, further proof of her power. He might just stare or maybe stammer like a just-off-the-gangplank immigrant new to the language. Still, he forged ahead because he had a question needing an answer.

To the point, Bobby told himself. Keep it short.

"Why?" he asked.

Deena smiled. "Why what?"

"Why me?" Bobby was pleased with his question. Two words, he thought, not quite eloquent, but better.

"Cuz I like you, silly," she answered, still smiling.

"Not good enough," he said evenly.

"Okay," Deena replied slowly, sensing that their conversation had suddenly taken a serious turn. She then gently unlocked both of her arms from his, creating for the first time that night a sliver of space. This time, it was Deena staring straight ahead, sorting through feelings, gathering and arranging words.

"You're handsome, almost pretty," she began, as she whisked back a stray strand of hair. "But more than that, you're different. Gentle, thoughtful, just plain different from any man I've known or will ever know. I knew that from the first time I saw you."

"In the cafeteria?"

"No, earlier, when I saw you in the hall," she answered. "I've had my share of men, you know—smart, driven, obsessed, controlling, the usual suspects. Good catches for most women, I suppose, just not for me. After the last one. I figured I needed a change—celibacy, sure; maybe a woman, tried that, too. Just something, anything, to break the cycle."

"What did he do?"

She sighed and closed her eyes. "What didn't he do?" she whispered. "Beat me? Yeah. Threatened to kill me if I left him? That, too. I left anyway. It's one of the reasons I'm here instead of San Francisco."

"I'm glad," Bobby blurted out, his spontaneity surprising him.

"You are?" she asked, as she turned toward Bobby and quickly closed the just-opened space separating them. Her smile had returned.

He glanced down, nodding reflexively, wondering if he should have said what he said, so clearly and without qualifiers.

"Say it then," she said.

A mumbled "yes" the reply.

Right answer, wrong style. "Then look at me and say it," she demanded.

Her tone told him, come on, recognize the obvious. You swallowed the hook when you left your apartment, or even earlier when you agreed to this rendezvous. Relax, her tone said, the rest of tonight will unfold as it should. We'll both be fine in the morning.

He turned and focused his eyes on hers. "Yes," he said, this time clearly, without a qualifier, without regret.

Chapter Nine

Outside of the coffee shop, snippets of the tail end of a recent conversation played, rewound, and replayed in Bobby's mind. Deena had asked if he wanted to kiss her. Yes, he'd answered, just not here.

"Not here" led to her tiny, book-strewn apartment less than a block from the college. Inside, they snuggled on a couch, a picture of easy familiarity—his arm across her shoulders, her head on his chest.

With Ella Fitzgerald crooning softly in the background, they chatted and told stories; she laughed. He smiled, then sipped a glass of mid-price merlot, its flavor prompting an approving "hmm." It wasn't the first time he'd tasted wine, just the first time it didn't come in one of the screw-top brands favored by Paulie and his pals.

Bobby was feeling more at ease than he could have ever imagined. He gently rested the side of his face atop her head, making sure to slowly inhale her scent and commit it to memory—fresh, he thought, like a pine bough. He loved the way she felt—firm and trim, her waist in particular.

More than that, he liked her; that much was clear. But as a girlfriend? he asked himself, the two of them as a couple? Would she change? How would it change him? Would he become—would she expect him to become—jealous and possessive, suspecting strangers, doubting friends? He didn't think he would, but he was less than eager to put it to the test.

First things first, he decided, take it easy. He could care about her, maybe deeply over time, and that, for him, was good enough for now.

Or so he thought. A soft caress of her hair, then a peck on her cheek—innocent gestures of affection most of the time, just not tonight.

"That's it?" Deena asked, her tone oozing disappointment.

"What?"

"A kiss on the cheek for the kiss you promised?"

He shrugged. "I guess not."

"You can, you know," she began.

"What?"

"Kiss me, but shsss, where we want to go tonight, words won't take us," she whispered. She then shifted her body and raised herself slightly to where their lips touched and their mouths opened, gently at first, a delicate introduction to a looming intimacy delayed not much longer than a moment.

Soon, two pairs of hands were holding, massaging, exploring, and removing articles of clothing. Deena's blouse went first, then Bobby's shoes, socks, and pants.

"Undress me, Bobby," she murmured, as Bobby lay on top of her. "Finish the job." Deena still had on her bra, an ankle-length skirt and a pair of cowboy boots.

Bobby paused and sat up, his legs straddling her body. "This is my first time," he said quietly.

The admission embarrassed him, unleashing an army of doubts marching through his mind, triggering fears of unfavorable comparisons to unknown lovers. But that mattered less at this moment of truth. He felt strongly that she should know.

"If you don't want to," he stammered.

"Then I'll just make sure I give real clear instructions," she answered evenly, as she raised her right leg toward him.

She then began to giggle. "You can start with this boot."

* * *

Three hours weren't enough sleep, but Bobby awakened anyway. The reason, not the rays of a bright mid-morning sun flooding his room, but a grating cackle so loud, so near, it caused his head to lift and his back to arch. The sudden movement, more a spasm, crashed into the limits of gravity and human flexibility which, just as suddenly, forced him back down where he lay, eyes still closed, wondering when a rooster had become his roommate.

At the moment, he was still a little foggy on how he got home or when he climbed into his bed. But at least he was alone. It would have been tougher to explain otherwise.

"Ooh, man," said an unknown voice. "That's just gotta hurt."

Strange, Bobby thought, chickens can't speak, although an old friend of his father's would have claimed otherwise. Manong Carlo used to raise fighting cocks on a farm in Auburn. One day, when the boys were visiting, Carlo claimed that his prized rooster, Big Bill, would chat with him in Ilocano every morning at chow time.

As Carlo spoke, he was holding Big Bill and gently stroking his feathers. Paulie, ever the bold one, demanded proof.

"Manong," Paulie said. "Get 'im to talk now."

Carlo looked at the boys, first at Paulie then at him. His dark brown face, creased and expressive, was solemn as he continued petting the bird.

"Is not morning," he said simply.

But is not English, Bobby thought, his mind still muddled by exhaustion, as he forced his eyes open to see the room filled with his brother and a host of long-ago friends and acquaintances. Some of the street boys were there—gangsters-in-progress whose lives ended early. Carlo and Big Bill were there, too, same with Danny, a childhood chum who was squashed by a bus running a stop sign when Bobby was six. Transit officials, aghast, offered his parents $25,000 to go away.

They took the cash and disappeared, using it—rumor said—to put a healthy down payment on a three-bedroom, ranch-style house more than a bus ride and a transfer from the projects and pay for private school education for the younger brother and two sisters. One less mouth to feed, not a bad deal under the circumstances, Bobby heard an unsympathetic neighbor say.

"I bumped into Danny and them here and they asked how you was doin'," Paulie explained. "So . . ."

"I see," Bobby mumbled, still not fully awake.

"Hey," his brother continued. "Think of it as a neighbor-hood party, 'ceptin' you the only one still alive."

The comment drew a smile from Manong Carlo and a chuckle from Danny and a couple of others. Bobby, who was now sitting up, didn't share the humor.

"Paulie, how long have you guys been watching me?"

"Oh, since last night," he answered casually before turning toward his companions who nodded in agreement.

Bobby froze and took a deep breath as his palms began to dampen, his throat began to dry. "So, ah, what time?" he managed to ask.

"Ten or so," Paulie answered casually.

"And you were all in the apartment?"

"Sure, but I left after you took off her boot," Paulie said, smiling. "Figured you needed some privacy. Can't say for these other fellas, though."

Bobby closed his eyes and felt his chest tighten. Over time, he had grown accustomed to his solitude, wearing it like a favorite hooded sweatshirt—warm and comfortable, better still, no messy surprises. Then last night happened and far worse than what he'd ever feared had come to pass, turning what should have been sacred into the public and profane.

Would he now be expected to hang out on the corner, chain smoke Camels, stick out his chest and brag loudly—between puffs—about his prowess like the other bedroom buccaneers?

He shuddered at the image.

Yet, he knew how they thought: there was something strange about Paulie's younger brother—indifferent, soft, shy, maybe even, well, who knows? For them, the possibility never arose that maybe, given the choices, being alone was the way he wanted to be.

Last night erased their doubts. Ooh, a score and with such an outstanding fox, the thinking went—the first, if belated, notch on his belt with more to come. Love was just a game, after all, a contest of wit and guile—nothing more. They were players and, thanks to last night, he'd just joined their ranks.

Welcome to the club, young man, their smiles and nods of approval said. It's about time, Bobby imagined a few of them adding.

"I tried tellin' 'em you wasn't no sissy," Paulie continued, his voice smug and proud, like what his brother was—or wasn't—reflected on him. "And obviously you ain't."

Bobby, eyes still shut, imagined their grimaces and smiles, hearing in his head their different voices as they chatted and laughed, hooted and howled at every murmur or groan, each word of affection.

At that moment, he thought that he hated them, all of them, including Paulie. No, he decided, even now hate was too strong a word. But whatever he was feeling made him angry enough to sit up and do something he'd never done or ever dreamed of doing.

Bobby pointed his finger at Paulie, who was smiling and still unaware of the emotional storm he'd unleashed.

"Get out of my room," Bobby said icily, using the kind of bring-it-on tone that on the street would have signaled the end of discussion and the impending launch of fists and elbows, feet and knees.

He stared first at Paulie, then slowly shifted his eye-to-eye gaze to each of the others. No one was laughing now; a few looked away.

"You have no right, no respect, none," Bobby continued as, one by one, they began to disappear.

"We didn't mean to," Paulie began. "I didn't mean to . . ."

Bobby cut him off. "Turn me into some sick joke? So you and your buddies could have a laugh just so you could say, 'You see, he ain't no faggot. Even with 'im speakin' good English like a rich white boy, readin' books and his other sissy ways—but goddamn, even I gotta admit, the boy don't sound like he's from here, do he? Okay, he ain't a good fit. But that's different from him bein' a queer and he ain't one of those, oh no, no, no, uh-uh-uh, cuz he got the same blood as baaad-as-I-wanna-be me, the one and only Paulie Vincente and, by the way, don't you never be doubtin' me again.'"

Bobby, his face now fully flushed, paused to catch his breath. He felt sad, empty. For him, it was a moment of firsts—

the first time he had ever been furious with Paulie, the first time he'd ever seen him back down.

But as tired as he was, Bobby still wasn't through. He had a question to ask.

"Paulie," Bobby whispered, as his eyes locked even more fiercely onto his brother. "Who I am, what I do, who I'm with, all of that is secondary. It's really all about you, isn't it?"

Paulie didn't respond. Instead he just stood quietly, striking the classic pose of a penitent—head down, hands folded, like a St. James schoolboy nailed in the act by the vigilant Sister Victor.

"Well, isn't it?" Bobby repeated, as he watched his brother slowly disappear, his hands still folded, his head still down.

* * *

It was well past noon, Bobby guessed. His clue: the sunlight flooding through the apartment's tiny westside windows. He had just left his room and was shuffling down the hall toward the kitchen where he hoped to find enough coffee—Folgers or instant, it didn't matter—to finally jolt him awake.

Inside his head, a projector was quick-clicking images of him and Deena, of Paulie and his friends. By then, the rage he'd just felt had mostly disappeared. He was confident his brother would get over it; he had no choice. Paulie had often said that a blood tie resembled a cockroach—virtually indestructible, the only thing living at the end.

Inelegantly put, Bobby thought, as he rubbed his eyes. He would have used a different metaphor. But the meaning was clear—one he shared and swore by. Paulie, he knew, would return.

Deena, though, was another matter. When they were together, skin to skin, he was engulfed by the swirl of scents, beguiled by her contours and the sound of her voice sprinting through octaves—from growls to screams to whispers.

As lovers new to each other often do, he remembered they had said a lot—and nothing at all. They shared flat jokes and laughed. Deena also told him she sometimes thought her beauty was a mixed blessing. Sure, she got attention and the right compliments. But sometimes, she felt her beauty trapped her, made her a prize. She had a feeling deep in her gut that he wasn't that way.

Bobby said he didn't believe in trapping her or anyone else. "You're not a gopher," he said.

He added that like a puzzle she'd intrigued him and, this night aside, her essence—he'd looked up the word—had burned an impression in his memory. She seemed so full of imagination and life, so open to the new. Her talking about that fellow Kant was proof enough of that. Despite his doubt, he just had to follow up. Years after tonight, he declared, he was sure he'd remember that the most, long after the seductive moment-by-moment details of this evening had blurred or vanished altogether.

Many young women he'd known had been preformed by expectations, spiritually bent and disfigured by what everyone had told them they had to be. They had been trained to bore themselves and their men—old, tired women with young women's faces just going through the motions by age twenty, tops. He had a feeling that, okay, her past mistakes aside, she really wasn't that way.

That's what had pushed him out of her bed and later, out the door. Although here—he thumped the mattress for emphasis—wasn't where it had to go.

"Odd boy," Deena said.

Bobby smiled. "I guess."

They continued talking, buckets of words filling in the gaps, each word a brick in a foundation supporting reasons why—why what they did was good, why it was destined. But it was Deena's whispered "I love you" that made Bobby blink and that had slowed for a moment the surging sensuous wave that had been sweeping him along.

Bobby to Earth, he remembered thinking. How could she possibly say that? Love—at least as he understood it—was the quiet and unglamorous product of time and patience, of unswerving loyalty, openness, generosity and complete acceptance.

A priest at St. James had once told Bobby and his fellow classmates that "God loved us all without trade-offs or preconditions—we're loved just because we are, completely, I might add." The definition was fierce and uncompromising, frightening and powerful. To love someone that way meant surrendering self and abandoning expectations. It also meant keeping the door to the heart open all day, all night, weekends and holidays.

But as uncompromising as it was, in Bobby's mind the standard made sense: black and white, no negotiation and no "I will love you if" to stumble over. He'd seen it in his family— in his parents and even Paulie, although his brother would have to work on the complete acceptance bit.

Bobby recalled thinking that maybe Deena was rattled, intending to say that she *could* love him over time, or misusing "love" like his friends who always said that they just loved James Brown's latest cut. Or perhaps she really meant to say "like"—"I like you a lot tonight" or "Please keep doing what you're doing because I really do like it"—but decided not to because it lacked sufficient heft.

He didn't think love this soon could happen between strangers—and that's what he and Deena still were. But he was willing to be convinced otherwise, possibly starting later that afternoon when he and Deena were going to meet.

But first things first and that meant coffee. He resumed his kitchen-bound shuffle before pausing again. He smiled, amazed at the power of positive thought. From where he stood, he could hear the tin pot percolating and smell a welcome and familiar aroma.

Odd, he thought, Dad rarely drank coffee this late in the day. As he drew nearer to the kitchen, he could hear his father and a nattily dressed older Filipino chatting in a mix of English and their dialect. As Bobby turned the corner, he saw the two of them seated at the table. Dad's friend, his head buried in his hands, laughed uncontrollably while his father, also laughing, jabbed him with his finger.

"Boy oh boy, that blondie in Stockton, she was . . . ," Dad began, before glancing up and noticing his son.

"Hi," Bobby mumbled, as he grabbed a cup before turning toward the stove.

". . . a very nice girl," his father added.

"I'm sure she was," Bobby said over his shoulder. It amused him that his father thought that his son's ears still needed protection. He wasn't so young and, after last night, not nearly as innocent.

Filled-to-the-brim cup in hand, Bobby turned to join Dad and his friend, Uncle—Mariano, the name finally came to him—at the table. The last time he'd seen Mariano was at the boxing gym, where he was doing his best to stay in one piece.

He'd succeeded, but at some point between the left hook that rocked him and the end of the spar, he'd decided that boxing could survive nicely without his participation. To please Dad, he'd checked the sport out and even liked some of it, especially the feints and quick steps, the dancing—but the hurting part, himself or others, he decided he could do without.

Although his adventure in the ring was just the other day, he'd pushed most of it out of his mind. That included Mariano, whose slight smile couldn't hide the fact that he was giving him a head-to-toe inspection complete with occasional head bobs, furrowed brows, and unintelligible mutterings

Bobby felt uneasy. Dad acted the same way when he would check out roast ducks dangling by their necks in the windows of Chinatown restaurants.

He squashed a sudden urge to quack. Too impolite, he thought.

"Hi, Sonny," Mariano finally said.

"Hi, Uncle Mariano."

Mariano then turned toward Dad. "What's he weigh?"

"My guess? One-fifty, tops. He cooks—oh, I tell you, my boy can cook—but is funny that he don' eat much. I don' know why."

"How tall?"

"Five-ten, mebbe more," Dad replied with a shrug. "Still growin', though, hard to tell."

"Tall for his weight, mebbe gonna grow, tha's good," Mariano said. The old man then sat back in his chair and clapped his hands. He was beaming now. "Southpaw, too, and real quick, hard to hit. Also good, real good."

Dad—still an old fighter at heart—smiled at the string of chip-off-the-old-block compliments. He couldn't help it.

"Uh, Dad, Uncle Mariano . . ."

The two old men glanced at each other. Mariano nodded first, Dad answered in kind.

"Well, Bobby," Dad said. "Your uncle says he wanna manage and train you. A few amateur fights first, then turn pro and make some quick money, save, you know, then get out when you wanna. You could go to school, then afterwards, go to the gym. No problem. Make sense to me, but mebbe not to you. I tol' your uncle is your call."

For Bobby, Mariano's proposal was hard to digest. Five minutes ago, he would have scrunched up his face and said, "No, no way, uh-uh, end of story." Especially the pro part.

At least as an amateur, he could wear big gloves and headgear—not enough to protect against a really heavy punch, but a level of safety nonetheless. The same wasn't true of the pros who fought hatless and slugged each other with eight-ounce mitts—not much bigger than a big man's fist.

Bobby knew the differences were huge. He remembered one night as a kid when he and Dad sat in front of their black-and-white and watched in horror as Emile Griffith hurled punch after punch at a trapped and helpless Benny Paret. Paret later died of his injuries. Bobby wondered in the days that followed how Griffith could have unleashed such cold-blooded fury on another human being.

He found out just last year, when he was standing behind two older men at the IGA checkout line. They were chatting about an upcoming Griffith fight on television. One of them claimed that his cousin back East had a pal who'd actually heard Paret insult Griffith, calling him a faggot—or so the story went.

"That so," his companion answered casually. "I don't care if he is a fruit, the man can box. And besides, I already heard the story."

For Bobby, the answer, for whatever it was worth, didn't make what happened to poor Benny justifiable. But he could at least understand Griffith's rage—and he wondered as he left the grocery store if he had a little of that rage himself.

In the months since, he hadn't thought much about Emile Griffith or Benny Paret. But Mariano's proposal jogged his memory, conjuring images of violence best forgotten.

To his surprise, though, he felt honored and at least slightly intrigued, uncomfortably so, that the old man thought enough of his skills to come to his home and pitch the deal. It meant he had at least a smidgen of talent in a tough, brutal sport where men challenged each other every day in the gym. At least Mariano thought he was a man—some kind of man, anyway.

Sure, he still hated the idea of nailing someone or, worse, getting nailed—just not as much as he did five minutes earlier. But as he pondered how to reply, he glanced from one old man to the other.

The scar tissue around Dad's eyes and his father's slightly flattened nose made him shiver. The same for the missing incisor on the left side of Mariano's mouth.

"But Uncle," Bobby said. As he spoke, he tried hard not to look at the gap in Mariano's smile. "I'm not tough, not like Paulie, and besides, I don't hit very hard."

"Hard enough," Mariano said, balling up his right fist for emphasis. "Game's change. Look at that guy Clay, he don' punch hard. He stay outside, dance aroun', make the other boy look slow and stupid. Sometimes he don' never even punch at all. And look at 'im: he wins, no one hits 'im, he's champion."

"He change the rules," Dad added.

Mariano nodded. "Yes, tha's it. Not like before with Joe Louis, now that was a fighter, a tough guy, a real champion. Sure, he get hit, sometimes even knock down, but he always get up. Got punch like a mule, knock you out either hand, no question."

He paused and smiled, as if remembering one of the grand old champ's Kodak KO moments—Schmelling, Baer, Sharkey, and Carnera—falling and fallen. Name the year, the site, the unfortunate and unconscious victim.

"Don' really like how it is now, but they don' ask what I think," the old man added, as his lips curled into a frown. "Clay wouldn' las' back then, not with Louis. He'd have to go forward, not backing up and dancing-dancing all the time. But now is different and is prob'ly good for me to change, whether I wanna or not. Clever and quick. Nowadays, tha's good enough."

Mariano was relaxed and smiling now. By its nature, beating the snot out of an opponent (or the reverse) makes boxing a hard sport to sell.

But it was his job, his livelihood, the only way to stay tied to the game that took him out of the asparagus fields near Stockton. Boxing gave him a break, when other Pinoys got no break at all.

During his 1930s heyday, he was a main eventer, a big money draw in West Coast arenas. Other Filipinos knew his name; white fans did, too. Sure, he knew too well that prize fighting had its flaws, but without it he'd be living in Chinatown in a hotplate room, his afternoons spent on street corners with other old Filipinos, all dressed up to kill time and just wait for the end—whenever that would be.

The sport kept Mariano busy, alive. He'd been a trainer since after the war, scouring the bushes for good prospects, sometimes settling for much less—boys whose courage, desperation, or lack of common sense outweighed their talent.

"Flesh peddler," a pregnant young woman once screamed at him after her not-too-skilled fiancé was knocked cold in the first round. "You're nothin' but a pimp."

Mariano shrugged. Maybe so, although he'd never thought of himself that way. No matter. He once dreamed that he would die exactly one day after he turned in his gym keys. He wasn't superstitious, but he also wasn't eager to test the dream. That meant to keep doing what he'd been doing, perhaps finally finding a youngster with enough raw talent that he could shape and call his own.

Bobby, the old man knew, had talent. Perhaps enough to one day steal a title—which he'd never done as fighter or trainer. It was the only missing item on his resume. A title, now that could lead an old-timer who'd lived a full life to do strange things, like turning in his keys and testing the dream.

Mariano was hopeful. Despite his reservations, Bobby hadn't said no, get out of here, you've lost your mind, Uncle, and I've lost mine if I sign on. That meant he was at least nibbling the bait.

He had made his point and was confident he was close to signing, sealing, and delivering his first quick and clever protégé. All it would take would be for the kid to imagine the hand-raised "thrill of victory" and to ignore the face-down, lips-kissing-the-canvas "agony of defeat."

Just to be safe, Mariano whispered a prayer asking Jesus, Mary, and Joseph—individually or in concert—to lend a hand, making sure not to whisper too loud. He hoped they hadn't forgotten him. It had been awhile since he'd invoked their names—more than five years, in fact, when he'd learned that his sister had died in the Philippines. He then glanced at Bobby, who smiled politely and looked away without saying a word.

"He's not sure."

The sound of the voice startled Mariano. Sure, it was a message, just not the one he wanted to hear. He turned slowly toward the messenger and shrugged.

"Guess you're right, Antonio," he said.

"You know, it was differen' back then," Dad began. "You and me fight cuz we have to. Not so much for young guys nowadays. Times change, is easier. Bobby's gonna go to college and if he fights, is cuz he wanna real bad."

Mariano nodded and slowly started to rise. He walked over to Bobby's father, who was still seated. "Good to see you," he said, before putting his hand on his old friend's shoulder.

He then turned to Bobby. "You know where to find me, Sonny. Every day, even Sunday."

"Yes, Uncle," Bobby answered.

Mariano smiled. "Your dad's proud of you; he says you're a good boy. I think he's right."

Bobby blushed and turned away. Before he could respond, Mariano was already out of the kitchen and down the hall, the last sounds being those of a door quickly opened and closed.

Bobby fidgeted slightly, wondering how Dad really felt. Like Mariano, boxing had made him more than he otherwise would have been. It had also brought him Mom. Like father like son—like countless other fathers and sons? Were those his expectations? God, he hoped not.

"So, what do you think?" Bobby finally said.

His father shrugged. "Nothin', really."

"What do you mean?"

Antonio turned slightly toward his son. He sighed and silently wished he had spent more time with him as he was growing up, but the boy preferred being with Eula. "Bobby's just different," his wife would say. So he had focused his attention on Paulie, who was handful enough and so much more like him.

The old man studied Bobby's smooth, unmarked features, and recalled a moment almost eighteen years ago when he first held him in Columbus Hospital. He was struck by the boy's delicate beauty—by his long eyelashes and large brown eyes— and realized immediately that it was both blessing and curse. Over the years, the equation hadn't changed.

He had thought then and was thinking now that such a handsome face—so like his wife's and so unlike his own—should never be cut or even bruised. At least not in the ring, where hard men regularly dished out cuts and bruises, sometimes even death or permanent injury. For fighters, the risks were just part of the game.

"I mean, you're almost a man and you're gonna have to choose on this and everything else," his father began. "For me, I like boxing."

He then chuckled and pointed at his nose, broken more times than he could recall. "Besides, I got the face for it. But tha's jus' me, mebbe not you. Mariano's right. You're a good boy and I'm already proud of you and what you decide to do won' change a thing."

His father's words touched him and for a moment, he thought of going over to hug him. But no, Dad had never been the hugging type, at least not with Paulie and him. Hugging was Mom's job.

In that sense, the old man was like a lot of the other Filipino dads he knew—all dedicated non-huggers, something he promised himself he would never become. He figured that the small and large defeats endured decades ago and over time had taught Antonio and his friends to go easy on affection, even with their kids.

But love? Sure, Bobby knew it was there in the bottle, just with the cork screwed down tight. He suddenly decided it was time to loosen it a little.

"Thanks, Dad," he whispered, then paused before adding, "I love you."

Three simple words, the simplest of sentences, a not-so-simple response. Antonio, blinking hard, looked away, leaving Bobby to wonder if the strength of their bond was best left unspoken. But he felt it and knew in his bones his father did, too.

Bobby couldn't have known that Antonio was suddenly remembering a time before he was born, when he and Eula had bitterly argued and he'd asked her to give up this child. For him, the pictures and sounds were still painfully clear.

Then as the boy grew, he recalled hearing the whispers and titters from neighbors, leaving him embarrassed, a shrunken man, and wondering whether he should have been firmer, more adamant with his wife. He wondered then if he'd made a mistake, if he should have drawn a him-or-me line when he could have and dared her to cross it?

That was all such a long time ago, but not long enough to block rivulets of shame from seeping out of the folds and corners of memory, soon forming a wave that swept over him. And over that time, he'd also come to love this boy as he loved Paulie. But no matter, in his mind it didn't make right what he'd once felt.

Face flushed, the old man couldn't stop blinking as he composed another simple sentence in his mind, deciding to add two words to Bobby's three-word declaration.

Antonio, eyes still blinking, cleared his throat. "I love you, too, Son."

* * *

As Bobby walked briskly down the path leading to the street, a tune kept playing in his head, eventually burrowing into his throat to become a melody hummed in perfect pitch. He didn't hear himself humming, focused as he was on what had just happened between his father and him.

No, he and Dad hadn't hugged. Some endings were too much to hope for. The moment happened and then it was over—like turning off the television—allowing father and son to catch their breaths and focus on other things.

Bobby recalled saying he was going out and would Dad be okay? How about picking up something on the way home?

Yes, he'd be fine, Dad had assured him, and no, no need to worry or stop by the store; just go have some fun. And by the way, his father added slyly, he noticed that Bobby didn't come home until late last night, or was it early morning?

"A girl, huh?" Dad had asked.

"Yes," he'd answered.

Dad smiled.

A girl, Bobby thought. Who would have imagined it?

But there he was on his way to meet Deena on a sunlit afternoon for a day after the rendezvous at the coffee shop. He smiled, suddenly hearing "Somewhere Over the Rainbow," the tune he'd been humming. He just loved *The Wizard of Oz* even more than the dance extravaganzas of the great Astaire. In fact, he'd stayed up to see it again a few days ago on late-night TV.

But more than anything, he loved the song and would sing along with little Dorothy as she poured out her heart. Over the years, Bobby had often tried to imagine what was over his rainbow.

He chuckled. The black and Filipino boys he knew in the projects were hard into James or Sam and Dave, with maybe a little Wilson Pickett and Junior Walker on the side. All rhythm and blues royalty, all manly men growling manly messages over throbbing bass licks and blaring horns. Bobby liked them, too, and if the mood moved him, he could skate across the floor on one leg, do the splits, and pop back up without a single hair out of place.

But there was something about Dorothy hoping for a better world that touched his heart in a way that James and the other brothers couldn't. A sissy thing? Sure, and tough to explain. So what?

Bobby chuckled again as he wondered if Mariano would still be interested if he knew his taste in music? As he neared the street, he also thought about Emile Griffith and wondered if late some night he had ever sung along?

* * *

Same table, same lovers, different day. Last night, Deena whispered, was special and could they please, pretty please, be together again soon? She giggled and added that she didn't say "please" very often, didn't have to, but for him she would make an exception.

Bobby eyed his oversized coffee mug and didn't immediately reply. He glanced down at Deena, whose head was resting on his shoulder, her hand holding his. He sighed. What a beauty, he thought, and he liked her, maybe even a lot. But she was pedal-to-the-metal on this and he was still riding the brake.

"Deena," Bobby finally said. "Last night, did you say you love me?"

"Yes."

"Why?"

"Because I do."

Bobby sighed again. "It's not that simple," he said, hoping his brother wasn't nearby, leering and cracking jokes with his friends. He looked around the room—the coast was clear—and relaxed.

"It is for me," she said, smiling. "I'm just telling you what I felt and what I'm feeling right now. I know, I know, it's early. Maybe it's because you're different, I dunno. But if anything, I feel stronger about it now than I did then. I've had my share of men, but I've never had this feeling before, Bobby. That's all."

A beautiful woman's offer of love, there on the table, there for the taking. A first for Bobby, maybe an only. How should he respond?

As he carefully assembled the words, he imagined tiny black question marks suddenly appearing and covering his eyes—the current objects of Deena's gaze—and her standing up, hands on her hips, demanding to know how the hell did that happen? A mood-breaker, for sure.

"Deena," he said quietly. "I'm open to you and to this relationship, whichever way it goes. We'll know over time."

For Deena, Bobby's measured response was a first—it was code for patience, please, one step at a time. Men had usually professed their undying love to her during and immediately after their first night together, and once even before. With that history, she was a bit disappointed, at least until she remembered that their loves had all died, often because hers had rarely gotten started.

"There's more than one way?" she asked, and immediately regretted it.

"Yes."

An honest answer, sure, just not the one she preferred. She wanted to draw him out and figured it was time to roll the dice.

"Do you love me?" Just the sound of the question, unneeded in the past, made her wince. She'd never had to ask it before and, just by asking it, she felt exposed, like a cat on her back. How would he answer? Yes, but I already have a girlfriend. Yes, but I'm not ready for this. Yes, but I love my dog more. Yes, but I'm joining the service to get away from you. Yes, but . . .

A girlfriend had once told her it's what follows the "but" that will kill your heart. She took a deep breath just in case.

Bobby, sensing her vulnerability, took a deep breath, too. He then gazed at her softly and lifted her hand to his lips.

"I could love, you, Deena," he said softly. "Deeply."

Still not quite what she wanted, but not too bad given who she thought he was. Deena knew that Bobby was a man without artifice, rare in the men she'd been with. She also knew he meant every word—a realization that prompted a smile. In her mind, she did some minor editing, joining "deeply" with "love" and changing "could" to "will."

"But love requires knowing, complete openness, patience," he droned on. "And that requires time."

For Bobby's sake, Deena nodded and tossed in an occasional "yes" and other signs of agreement. But God, she thought, he sounded like a nun or that new-age Jesuit she'd seduced in Frisco. The church, she had assured him, was changing quickly and chastity would soon be buried in history's dust bin. Lead or be led, she said as she lit up some bud and began unbuttoning her blouse. He removed his collar.

"So, um, how do we get there?" Deena asked, hoping that sometime soon she could figure out a shortcut.

"This is a pretty good start," Bobby said. "Being together, talking, getting to know each other, that sort of thing."

"Talk about what?"

"Whatever we want."

"Anything?"

Bobby nodded. "Yes."

Although Deena thought it was silly, she played along. She loved him, they were good in bed, she felt safe with him—end of story as far as she was concerned. For her, all talking did was fill minutes better spent on other activities.

But she was uncharacteristically patient because she didn't want to tango alone—or with anyone other than the young man sitting next to her. Besides, she figured that if she talked enough, maybe by tomorrow Bobby might say, "Shut up, take off your clothes. We're goin' to bed."

"Okay," she said. "Movies, what's your favorite?"

Sure, it was a dopey question, one asked by every thirteen-year-old American girl. But she had to start somewhere to begin filling Bobby's word jar. She was laying odds in her mind, betting on a James Bond flick. They were all the rage and why not? Hot girls, hot guns, hot cars—what wasn't to love?

To her surprise, Bobby smiled and moved closer. "It's a secret," he whispered. "But I'll tell you."

Chapter Ten

A couple of pages more and Bobby figured he'd roll over, pull up the sheets and call it a night. He'd been reviewing steadily since after dinner with Dad—almost four hours now— and was surprised by how easily the rules of grammar, the math equations and the lessons of history were coming back to him. That afternoon, he'd received a letter from the college telling him his GED exam was next Tuesday, more than enough time to cram and get the basics down. When, not if he passed, he would sign up for classes and become Bobby Vincente, college student.

He sighed and put the history text down and stretched out. Such a day, starting with Mariano's surprise visit and the father-and-son chat to the last lovely moments with Deena.

Of course, she had asked him to spend the night. Of course, he declined. Dad, he explained. He didn't want to leave him alone.

She said she wanted to meet him. Today? No. Tomorrow? Maybe. Please? Maybe. They then giggled like children and kissed like lovers.

The part about being with Dad, with his mind blitzes and prone-to-wandering ways, was true. But also true was that Bobby wasn't ready yet. At least that's what he thought before leaving the apartment. But an afternoon filled with laughter, conversation, and genuine affection might persuade him to stop riding the brake sooner, not later.

Plus, "The Wizard of Oz" wasn't a deal killer, although Deena confessed that when she first saw it in a film criticism class, she wanted to march onto the screen and slap the little bitch silly.

"Why?" he asked, trying hard not to scowl.

"It would've been fun."

"Huh?"

"No one's that innocent and pure," she said, as they left the coffee shop and walked down Broadway hand in hand. "And that Hollywood happy ending crap, I tell you, mindless candy for a nation stuck in the Depression and on the edge of war. I didn't buy it, not for a moment. College can be dangerous, Hon; sometimes you learn about things you really don't like."

Deena tightened her grip on his hand. "And besides, if she was real, she'd be my rival and I'd have to kill her."

An absurd thought, almost funny, in fact. But the words of jealousy and possession made him a little nervous. A warning sign? Maybe, he told himself, but he would sort it out later; he was enjoying the moment too much. Besides, she was kidding, right? A quick, sideways glance, but he couldn't tell.

Bobby cleared his throat. "Well, I know what I won't be getting you for Christmas."

"You thinking that far ahead?"

"Why not?"

Deena smiled and kissed him on the cheek. "What won't I be getting, Lover?"

"Little red shoes."

"Not unless they're high heeled and strapless, Baby," she said, chuckling.

*　　*　　*

Deena was a woman of her word. She walked up to Dorothy, called out her name, and right there, in front of the Tin Man, Cowardly Lion, and Scarecrow, began slapping her silly. Bobby, who was standing stage right, jumped in to separate the two.

He had just completed his task when he heard a familiar voice say, "Paulie, that ain't funny."

"Mom?"

"It's me, Honey," Eula said, as she came into view, and Dorothy, Deena, and the others disappeared. Mom was young and lovely once again and seated in a high-back chair, just like she was when she posed for those pictures decades ago. "You know your brother; he was just messin' with your dream and havin' fun. He didn't mean no harm."

Bobby, heart still pounding, failed to see the humor. "Where is he?"

"He wanted me to tell you he was sorry."

"Why didn't he come?"

"You know how hard-headed your brother is," Eula began. "Besides, you'd never tell me no if I asked you to forgive him. So, do you?"

"Okay," he grunted.

"He's your only brother."

"Yes, okay, yes, Mom, I forgive him."

"That's better," she said soothingly. "Aren't you glad to see me?"

The question changed his mood. "Of course, Mom," he said softly. "You know I am."

"Good boy," she said, then paused. "There's another reason I'm here."

She waved her hand from left to right and before the motion was finished, Bobby could hear the driving beats of conga drums, then the trumpets, then the deep, rich voice of a man singing in what he guessed was Spanish.

With each passing moment, the sounds became louder and images slowly came into view. The singer was a handsome, light-skinned man with wavy brown hair, slicked back for the gig with not a strand out of place. He gripped the microphone as he worked the room, dancing and twirling, crooning and making eye contact with the patrons, especially the high-fashion ladies who made up most of the first two rows.

"The next song's for Carmen," Bobby heard him say in slightly accented English, before Eula waved her hand again and the singer and his band disappeared.

"Who's that?"

"Your biological father."

Bobby slowly shook his head. He felt numb, like he'd just seen Jesus walking on water or Ray Charles driving Stevie Wonder and the Blind Boys of Alabama, all of them, down King Street. He wondered why was she telling him this now?

"Honey," Eula said softly, "Dad and me were havin' a hard time then, but we worked it out and had a good life together. I guess I'm apologizing to you, too. I should've told you; it might've made your life a little easier, or at least answered some of the questions that bothered you. I wouldn't ask Dad to do this because it's too hard for him to relive that past. You should know I'm sorry for the affair, but I don't regret having you—and neither does Dad."

"I know," Bobby mumbled.

"Do you forgive me?"

Bobby stared at his mother. "Of course, Mom. I love you."

Eula smiled. "There's one other thing. He's playing here tomorrow night at the Black Cat Club. Dad and I thought you should know that."

Information overload—Bobby's head began to throb. "Huh?" was the best he could muster.

"What am I supposed to do?" he eventually added.

"See him, don't see him. Whatever you want, Honey," Eula said, before disappearing.

In his dream, Bobby saw himself sleeping and remembering what a friend once told him about dreams. Michael was a half-Indian boy whose Colville mother firmly believed that dreams were real. It was so obvious, she said. Michael, always skeptical, asked why non-Indians didn't see things that way. She answered that Whites and others prefer a toned-down slice of reality, something they can control. Dreams, she added, can be disturbing and overwhelming, totally out of control. It's the way of the world, she said.

Bobby then saw himself turning over and pulling up the covers. He heard himself mutter, "Boy, she got that right."

* * *

It was easy enough for Bobby and Deena to get into the Black Cat. Paulie had been pals with Jimmy, the bouncer, whose parents owned the club. Before Paulie shipped overseas, he and his brother had caught a smokin' R-and-B review here, confident the club was police free. According to Jimmy, that was because of the under-the-table courtesies paid by his folks to the beat cops.

He had thought about going alone, but Deena had insisted otherwise. Earlier that day, they'd met at the college library, where Bobby continued preparing for the GED. During a break—and somewhere between Lincoln's debate with Douglas and the end of the Civil War—she'd asked him what were his plans for the evening.

He'd casually mentioned he was going to see the Caribbean All-Stars.

With Leonard Gomez?

You've heard of him?

Hasn't everyone?

No, I'm just a Pinoy from the projects. My thing's rhythm and blues, not Ricky Ricardo and Lucy.

And you're going without me?

Hadn't thought about it.

Deena's pout prompted an "Oh, Baby, of course, you're coming with me" reply, full of contrition and a belated realization he hadn't thought through the consequences of his invitation.

He sighed. When did he start acting married?

That night, though, potential consequences were the last things on his mind. Deena was hot, with her short black dress and a tight v-necked blouse that showcased her dark, dramatic features and her model-perfect figure. Although he wasn't much into style, he'd managed to scrounge up a pair of dress slacks, a blazer, and a blue shirt.

Thanks to Jimmy, they were seated at the front in a room that was quickly starting to fill. Bobby was surprised. Other than the old queen Orlando, he didn't know a lot of people in Seattle who spoke Spanish, much less grooved to the music. But here they were, dressed to kill and ranging in hues from black to white, all talking and laughing in a language he didn't understand.

It wasn't uncomfortable, just odd. When he was young, Dad had once told him that when he worked the fields, he learned that Mexicans and Filipinos were like cousins, sharing similar histories and values despite different languages. Bobby was intrigued with what he had heard about these distant relatives and wanted to know more about them.

Ever since birth his world had been filled with blacks and Filipinos, some Whites, a few Asians and Mexicans and mixes of all kinds. But he had no idea there were so many Mexicans in Seattle, and what he guessed were Puerto Ricans or maybe even Cubans.

Most of them weren't White so, Bobby figured, they had to be poor. In Bobby's experience, this rule of thumb had never failed.

But Mexicans and the others were a mystery. He rarely ran into them in the projects or in the nearby neighborhoods. Not a lot of rich folk in any of those places.

So, where did they live? Where did they go during the day? Maybe he could find them in college?

He began tapping his foot. Finding so many Mexicans, Puerto Ricans, and Cubans—for Bobby, one more reason to get this night over with, go home, cram some more for the GED, and pass it.

It wouldn't be long. One by one the musicians made their way to the darkened stage—a sign that the show was about to go on. Bobby glanced at Deena and smiled. She was into it, enjoying the buildup and anticipating the live performance of a musical style she professed to love.

Suddenly, the two conga players started up, slowly and softly at first, then building, building to a point where they were joined by the blare of trumpets and a spotlight that shone on the man Bobby had seen in his dream.

The light caught him in mid-stride as he, almost running, began singing and churning his arms, moving to a beat that Bobby found frenetic—not effortless and smooth like the steps of great R & B singers, hardworking James Brown being an exception. Whatever, it seemed to work, as the cheers and whistles of the audience drowned out the announcer's introduction of "the one, the only, the Puerto Rican legend . . .

". . . Leonard Gomez!" It was his face that Bobby was carefully studying, searching for similarities and hoping to find none. He then slowly shook his head. The results were coming. He recognized the older man's hair, complexion and every other feature he could see. It was so obvious; a blood test would not be needed.

Damn, he thought after a few more minutes. No doubt. Sonny, this is your new daddy. Oh, and incidentally, now you're Puerto Rican—no longer any need to go looking for them.

In his mind, a series of black-and-white photos flashed—first of Mom, elegantly dressed and seated in her high-back chair. Then of Mom, still seated and holding a baby who stared blankly into the camera—himself, Bobby guessed. Leonard, nattily dressed, was standing to her right—a perfect, photogenic family. Finally, a third photo, with Dad standing where Leonard had been. Bobby winced. Antonio wasn't as handsome as Leonard—the prize ring had seen to that. In this shot, though, the toddler was smiling.

Bobby, suddenly exhausted, slumped in his chair. He couldn't wait for this night to be over. Not so for Leonard and everyone else, as the singer danced and preened, flashing a pearly, perfect smile and eyeing the ladies who smiled back as they followed him across the floor. That included Deena, who moved sensuously to the music.

Or was it to Leonard? He couldn't tell as he loosened his collar. Bobby was sure he noticed Deena—she was the best-looking woman in the house—and thought Leonard had noticed him as well. What he did know was that he suddenly felt irritated and wasn't sure how to handle it. Jealousy? He didn't know. This reaction was uncomfortable new territory for him.

Bobby then touched Deena's hand. "Bathroom break," he explained, before rising from his chair as a troubling scene kept playing in his head. He then walked to the back and stood next to Jimmy as the band changed songs and slowed down the tempo, leaving only a soft conga beat and the mournful, minor-key riffs of a Spanish guitar.

Leonard then strolled confidently over to Deena. He flashed a smile and whispered in her ear. She whispered back.

"The next song is for Deena," Leonard declared, as he extended his hand toward her. "I would be honored if this lovely señorita would grace me with this dance."

Bobby watched Deena rise to the sound of applause. He then turned abruptly toward the door.

"Hey, Bobby, the show's just startin'," Jimmy said.

"I'm not feeling well, Jimmy," he said, and then nodded toward Deena. "Make sure she gets home okay."

Jimmy wasn't born yesterday. He snuck a glance at Leonard and Deena—now cheek to cheek and moving slowly, rhythmically across the dance floor—before turning to look at his friend.

"That's just Leonard, man, ain't no big deal. He's just playin' with your girl, you know, Latin Romeo, show-biz stuff."

Bobby sighed and shook his head. "Leonard's not playing, Jimmy. Deena's not either."

* * *

Bobby flipped his collar up to provide a little more protection against the chilly night breeze. He could have walked home, but that required more energy than he had and more time than he wanted to spend. He decided instead to catch the bus, the next one due in ten minutes. All he wanted now was to go home, climb into bed, and forget this night.

He wished he smoked, and not because all the street-smart boys did. Years ago, one of Dad's old Pinoy pals said that he smoked two cigarettes each day—one at night to relax him, one in the morning to clear his head. It was, he claimed, his secret to health, long life, good hair, and teeth that wouldn't fall out of his mouth. Never mind that he died two months later.

Even as a kid, Bobby didn't buy it, at least not all of it. But he wasn't too picky now, not with his heart racing and his brain turning into mush.

"Hey man," a voice said, as Bobby tensed and turned toward the sound. He put his right foot forward just in case it was a strong-arm or worse. That way he could at least stick the dude with two quick rights and finish him with a left cross. But no one was there, and Bobby wondered for a moment if this Deena/Puerto Rican-daddy thing was causing him to lose his mind.

Suddenly, Bobby heard laughter. "Thought I'd change my voice and watch you jump."

"Paulie," Bobby said, as his brother came into view wearing shorts, an orange-and-blue Hawaiian shirt, and sandals.

"Hey, weather don't bother me no more," Paulie explained, as he lit a Camel unfiltered and handed it to Bobby. "Thought you might need one."

"Thanks," Bobby said, as he took it and inhaled for the very first time. Several hacking coughs later, he tossed the still-lit cigarette into the street.

'Why'd you come?" Bobby eventually managed to ask.

"I saw the scene," Paulie answered.

"In there?"

Paulie nodded. "Wasn't doin' too much else. Besides, figured I should be here."

"Why'd she do that?"

Paulie shrugged. "Ladies be that way sometimes."

"Come on, man," he said, trying hard not to whine.

In the distance, Bobby could see the bus drawing nearer.

"Listen, Bobby, you got this notion of love and such," Paulie began. "Love's not selfish; love's not jealous; God loves this way; blah, blah, blah. You on your way to bein' Jesus, his own damn self. Myself, I'm a little simpler. I see the girl; I get the girl; she's mine; she stays mine until I say otherwise. Just like that."

Paulie paused and put his hand on Bobby's shoulder. "But you got different standards," he said softly. "Musta been all them Catholic school lessons and, yeah, it looks so good on paper. But lemme tell you, it's a helluva lot easier to think like that when you ain't all tied up in it."

"What are you getting at?"

"Youngster, you gotta find out who you are, whatcha really believe in."

"But why did this happen?"

"Hey, this is cool," Paulie said. "Watch this."

Bobby cringed as Paulie casually jumped off the curb in front of the approaching bus, which passed harmlessly through him. "Damn, I always wanted to do that," he said, as he yawned and fished in his pocket for another Camel.

"Paulie, why?" he asked, as the bus door opened.

"It's probably a test a' some sort," Bobby heard his brother say.

* * *

A test of some sort, Bobby thought glumly, as the bus pulled away. If so, he wondered if he was flunking it. He sighed and leaned back in the seat. It could have been worse.

Even before it happened, he had visualized the scene— Leonard smirking, striding over to their table, Deena rising to the bait. In it, Leonard had stared at him, his look saying, "Punk, I've done this before. What's yours is now mine."

He then saw himself stand up, walk over to the singer and drop him with a wicked hook. Leonard then fell to the dance floor, eyes still open, hands at his sides. He was out cold before he hit the floor, maybe even dead; Bobby didn't know.

The surge of adrenalin made him feel pretty good at first. But then Bobby heard the screams of patrons; he saw the look of horror on Deena's face and Jimmy rushing over. He was standing in the spotlight, with traces of blood on his now-swollen knuckles. He was as still as a statue, mumbling, "I'm not like this, no, really, this isn't me, I'm not like this."

Then some of the dead street boys appeared. They were laughing and passing around a bottle of cheap wine in a brown paper bag. They surrounded Bobby and mocked him with their reply: "You are now, son. You wanna go do this and that, but give it up, sucka; you ain't no better than us."

That's why he had to leave—and he was glad he did. But God, it wasn't easy.

*   *   *

It wasn't easy. It was the last thing on Bobby's mind as he pulled up the covers and began drifting into sleep. In the hallway, the telephone was ringing. Deena, he thought. He knew that Dad, a heavy sleeper, would snore right through it. The ringing stopped for a couple of minutes, then started again. He was lying on his back, eyes half open. Although Bobby was tempted to pick up the phone and ask her why, he decided not to.

That wasn't easy either.

Chapter Eleven

It came to Bobby the moment he awoke. He'd figured out a plan, not long term, but probably good enough to get him through the next few days. Less than perfect? Sure, but under the circumstances, he would gladly take it.

The key was to avoid Deena at all costs—no phone calls, no coffee dates, no random sightings at the college. His focus now was to study hard, pass the GED, and get into college. It was at least something—one of the few things—he could actually control.

Deena—and sorting out the mess—would have to wait. He was disappointed in how he had reacted, but that would have to wait, too.

The only possible problem of this best-laid plan was that Deena wasn't the waiting kind. If this was going to work, his father would have to be part of it.

"*Dad,*" he imagined himself saying, "*if a woman calls, tell her I'm not home, and if she asks where I've gone, tell her you don't know. Or better yet, tell her I've joined the Foreign Legion because I'd once seen Buster Crabbe on a Saturday matinee and, boy, he sure looked sharp in his legionnaire uniform, his kepis in particular. Or tell her whatever other smoke you feel like blowing.*"

Bobby giggled and was glad he could still laugh. Such a difference a night of sleep makes. Control what you can, let the rest of it go, he thought, as he walked slowly into the kitchen. Dawn had long since come and gone and his father would be waking soon. He'd be greeted by fried rice and eggs and the aroma of a fresh pot of coffee—a good meal for a good man. Bobby smiled as he greased the pan and began heating it slowly. Taking care of Dad for whatever time he had left—that was something he could control.

*   *   *

This is my father, Bobby thought, as he sat at the table across from his dad and watched him gulp down the last spoonful of rice. That's the main story; Leonard was just a sperm-donor footnote. He had no more curiosity, no need to inquire further.

As Bobby watched, he marveled at their almost eighteen years together—at Antonio's love for him, at Antonio's love for Eula and Paulie.

Sure, there had been rough spots. It could have easily gone south. But that didn't happen. In fact, he couldn't recall any violence between his mother and father, rarely even a harsh word.

What magical reservoir had the old man tapped to heal the damage from Eula's betrayal? What more did he have to do to accept, support, and love a boy who popped out of nowhere and wasn't his own?

He couldn't have asked for a better father. For Bobby, an important question had suddenly been answered. Before last night, he'd talked a good game—love was this and, puny humans, it certainly wasn't that. But his brother was right; it was easier when he wasn't into it up to or maybe even above his neck. Now he wondered whether love in its best sense was really possible, or was it something real only in the realm of angels and the better saints?

He smiled. His father, who was neither angel nor saint, had done it—quietly, and for a very long time. He had managed to do what the priests and nuns extolled as an ideal—a gift of selfless and pure love, a divine act, or very close to it.

"Very good, Son," Dad said, as he pushed the plate away and patted his stomach.

"I'm pleased, Dad," Bobby replied, as he began cleaning the table.

"Whatcha gonna do today?"

"Nothing much," Bobby said casually. "Just study for the GED." He turned on the faucet and began washing the dishes. The warm water on his hands comforted him.

Dad nodded. "Tha's good," he said. "And, uh, how's your girlfriend?"

Bobby, his back to his father, winced. "Deena?" he finally said. It hurt just to say her name. He wanted to add, *Dad, she's not my girlfriend. I don't know what she is*—but didn't.

"Yeah, she call late last night."

"You answered the phone?"

"Yeah, I always sleep good, but after the third time . . ."

Bobby turned toward his father. "So, what did you say?"

"Well, she was crying," he said slowly and began tapping his fingertips on the table. "I tol' her, Honey, is gonna be okay. He's a good boy, kind, you know?"

Bobby took a deep breath before speaking. "Dad, please, if she calls again, tell her I'm not home," Bobby said slowly. As he spoke, he could feel his body start to tense. Last night was too soon, too raw. His father meant well, but dealing with Deena—if that's what he chose to do—would be later, not sooner.

"Forever?"

"For a while."

"She seem like a nice girl, mebbe make you happy," his father began. "Mebbe you give her a second chance?"

Bobby was amazed. When did Antonio Vincente turn into Ann Landers? What the heck, the old man loved him and was only trying to help. He shrugged and managed a faint smile.

"We'll see," he said in a sing-song tone.

Antonio recognized the brush-off. Eula did it the same way. Sure, it was polite—Bobby was always polite—but it was still a brush-off. Antonio nodded and blinked and found a new topic. "You gonna study at the college?" he finally said.

"No, I'm going to the library downtown," he answered, as he held up a plate for inspection. He then declared it clean and put it in the cupboard.

Bobby then walked over and kissed his father on the top of his head. "Gotta go," he said. "But I'll be back, maybe five, but no later. It'll give me to time to cook. Pork adobo, right? One of your favorites."

Dad smiled. "Sure," he said.

But to Bobby, Dad seemed a little tired, withdrawn. "Are you going to be okay?"

"Oh yeah, no problem," Dad replied, making sure to amp up his smile. "Don' worry 'bout me."

Bobby put his hand on his father's forehead—temperature normal. "Good, Dad," he said, as he walked out of the kitchen.

Antonio remained seated, eyes closed, hands folded on the table. He was, for the moment, buried in memory.

"A second chance, Honey," he mumbled. "I give you that. Mebbe Bobby could do the same thing? It was the bes' choice I ever make."

He paused, his eyes starting to water. "Ever."

*   *   *

Less than a week now, Bobby thought, as he yawned and stretched, then pushed a tattered grammar book away. He had found a small table in a quiet corner of the library and, for the last four hours, had been steadily reading, memorizing, and taking notes. Bobby was satisfied as he slowly turned his neck to the right until it cracked, then to the left until it cracked again.

Better still, his Deena-be-gone plan seemed to be working. He hadn't thought about her; she didn't distract him from what he needed to do.

Bobby was satisfied because he didn't know any better. Had he been older, he would have known that love can be merciless, a confusing force that pokes and prods its target, each jab a reminder of heartache and absence. Had he been older, he would have filled his day with an impossible list of tasks—an endless array of mind tricks to numb the pain, to distract and exhaust, to fill every waking moment so that sleep could more easily follow.

Bobby gathered his books and put them in his book bag. He then leaned back in his chair, eyes closed, and locked his hands behind his head. To other library patrons, he was a picture of contentment—like a cold-weather tourist on a sun-drenched Hawaiian beach.

Bobby smiled; he thought so, too. Productive, he thought smugly—an instant before he was to learn about the folly of smugness.

Deena, with no textbooks to compete against, was about to make a grand entry. In his mind, he could see her as she strode confidently to center stage. He could hear her voice. "Bobby, why?" she said. He could smell her scent and feel himself missing her.

He quickly opened his eyes, but that didn't help. Not even the library's bright overhead lights could chase Deena away. Then he tried to deaden his heart, telling himself that his pre-Deena life was so much better. That didn't help either.

He sat up and slowly shook his head. *Aloneness*: that's what he was feeling. Bobby wondered was there even such a word?

He didn't know what to do, how to make it better. Whatever the answer, he knew he wouldn't find it here.

*   *   *

After wandering through Seattle's downtown streets, Bobby found himself sipping coffee while sitting on a waterfront bench, close to the pier where he and Paulie used to fish for sea perch and shiners. He had come to this spot when Mom died and, again, after his brother's funeral.

Then, as now, he gazed at the roiling blue-green waters of Puget Sound and beyond, at the snow-capped peaks of the majestic Olympic Range. Then, as now, he marveled at the stunning beauty that gave him solace and a chance to heal.

For Bobby, this was a place of staggering power—enough to persuade even those with the most broken of hearts that their sadness would pass. Just look at this beauty and say life isn't good, that you won't survive—if you can.

Bobby thought that perhaps the natives had blessed it, or maybe it had always been this way. Whatever the reason, he felt safe here, serene. Sure, Deena was still on his mind, but he was pain- and confusion-free, at least for now.

He then closed his eyes and began to pray to the native spirits, to Jesus, to a handful of martyred saints, and to whoever else was around who could be helpful. Although Bobby was raised a Catholic, he was no longer a purist. He figured the recipients of his prayers were all dead, all invisible, all nosey, and all heavy-hitters.

His was a fervent prayer of thanks, first of all for loving parents and a good, if somewhat judgmental and hard-headed, difficult-to-deal-with brother.

He then whispered a thank you for Deena's having entered his life. Whether they were together or apart, he told whoever was listening that she would continue to matter. He vowed that however this turned out, he would keep her in his heart forever.

Bobby believed that once he said it, someone somewhere was hearing it. Spoken words had power, a prayer in particular. It wasn't just a stump speech on a campaign trail. He had come to learn that the dead aren't really dead; they can hear what you say. Hence, the need for caution, not to say more than you can do.

No matter. Here in this place, Bobby felt strong. His prayer was a promise he intended to keep, whatever the costs.

When Bobby finished his prayer, he crossed himself, rose, and began walking east toward downtown, which would lead him eventually toward home. He wasn't aware of others who had gathered as he passed through them.

Paulie was present, as was his mother. But so, too, were others like several native medicine men and St. Polycarp, a revered early Catholic bishop and martyr, burned at the stake for refusing to renounce Jesus.

By any measure, Polycarp and Paulie were an odd pair. But they had become friends because the old bishop's name had intrigued the younger man. He thought that the first part was cool—obviously—so why mess it up by joining it to a fish? Paulie never got the answer to that, but it didn't matter because their friendship quickly deepened after Polycarp told Paulie the grim details of his death.

Paulie winced throughout the telling. "And after them Romans was yellin' and burnin' you and stuff, you still didn't give 'im up?" Paulie asked.

"No," Polycarp replied calmly. "Of course not."

"I would'a," Paulie said. "In a heartbeat."

The bishop smiled benignly. "I am sure you would have done just fine, my son."

"You one baaad mutha'," Paulie said admiringly.

"Pardon me?"

"It's an honorary title sorta thang," Paulie explained. "We useta say that in the neighborhood. It's all good."

The bishop nodded as if he fully understood. "So, now I'm Polycarp, the Bishop of Smyrna, and a baaad mutha'?"

"No shit, my man," Paulie replied.

This afternoon, the bishop and Paulie, as was their habit, were engaged in casual chit-chat. They watched Bobby cross the street and head toward downtown.

"Your brother is such a good, pure-hearted boy, he'd make a wonderful priest," Polycarp said. "But his theology, I must say, is a little confused. His style of prayer goes far beyond what was intended by Vatican II."

Paulie shrugged. "Hey, Poly, cut 'im some slack. He's just a kid. Right now, consistent theology's the least of his worries. Besides, he's a little rusty on the Catholic stuff cuz he had to quit St. James when our folks sent him to public school."

"Do you think he'll ever solve his dilemma?"

"Give me some odds, man," Paulie replied.

"Two to one he doesn't."

"You're on, Bishop," Paulied said firmly, as he shook his hand. "My brother may be soft, but I say he'll surprise the hell outta you. I say he figures it out. When I win, you can get me a cigar. Myself, I'm now into Bolivars."

It would have helped Bobby if he had heard his brother's vote of confidence. He may have reacted differently to what he thought was a Deena sighting. A young woman with dark hair was standing by a bus stop on First Avenue. She turned her head briefly and Bobby thought he recognized a familiar silhouette.

Never mind that Bobby had sworn her off, at least for now. Never mind his fervent prayer earlier that day. His resolve suddenly evaporated. He quickened his pace and was almost sprinting as he neared her.

"Deena," he said breathlessly.

The young woman turned slowly and stared at him. Bobby's heart sank. Her resemblance to Deena was remarkable, save for her fuller lips and for her eyes—green not brown. But close wasn't good enough.

"I'm sorry," she said sweetly. "I think you've mistaken me for someone else."

"Oh," Bobby told the lookalike. "I'm so sorry, you just, uh . . ."

"Look like someone you know?" she said, smiling.

Bobby blushed. "Yeah."

"I'm sorry I'm not her," she said, still smiling. Her bus was approaching and she started looking in her purse for change.

"Me, too," Bobby said, as he turned to slowly walk away, fully aware that he was floundering, his guts churning. After a respite, Deena had returned with a vengeance. What other reminders was he doomed to see today?

With eyes downcast and hands buried deep in his pockets, Bobby was a forlorn sight. To other pedestrians, he must have looked like someone born to lose, a bum in progress. Younger and a little neater, yes, but drenched by the sense that nothing would ever get better; it would only get worse. On this afternoon, his despair was thick enough to touch. Those he passed gave him a wide berth, careful not to stare or do anything that might set this strange, possibly dangerous young man off.

Bobby would look up, but only to get his bearings. Cherry Street, where he would take a left, was less than a block away. He was so oblivious to everything else, he didn't hear his name being called—twice, and from nearby.

"Hoy, Bobby," the voice screamed loudly above the traffic din. "Bobby!"

No reaction. It took a tap on the shoulder to get that. Bobby turned around.

"Hi, Sonny," a beaming Mariano said.

"Oh, hi, Uncle," Bobby replied.

"So, you comin' by to see me?" the old man said, and pointed to the door of the Cherry Street Gym. "Come on, then," he added, before Bobby could answer.

What the heck, Bobby thought, as he followed Mariano. He was wearing tennis shoes and loose khaki pants—not the ideal outfit for a workout, but it would do. Besides, a couple of rounds on the heavy bag, some shadow boxing and sit-ups—a chance for Deena-free time. Maybe he'd even become tired enough to sleep soundly tonight—eight more hours of Deena-free time. An hour or so in the gym, it couldn't hurt and might even be worth it.

* * *

"Hi, Dad," Bobby said, as he entered their apartment, which was quickly filling with the aroma of boiling rice. He then walked over to his father, who was seated in the living room, and kissed him on the forehead. "Sorry I'm late."

"Half an hour, not bad. I figure you was studyin' hard," Dad said, smiling at his son. "So I jus' put the rice on."

"Yeah," Bobby said, as he walked into the kitchen and shifted quickly into high gear. He grabbed the sharpest knife and was soon slicing and dicing onions and peppers and everything else that would make up tonight's meal.

Bobby smiled. He was enjoying the movement—the process and end product, the comfort of cooking, the hope for perfection. For him, this tiny kitchen was a sanctuary, a Deena-free zone.

"That girl call," his father said.

"I'm sure she did," Bobby answered casually, as he carefully mixed a cup of soy with what he thought would be just enough vinegar. Just to be sure, he dipped his pinky finger in the sauce and then placed it on the tip of his tongue.

Satisfied, he then poured the sauce into a pot, soon to be followed by crushed garlic, sliced onions and peppers and thick chunks of pork.

"You're not with her no more?"

Bobby shrugged. "I don't know, Dad," he said, as he turned the burner to low and began stirring the ingredients. He had come to learn that most meat dishes were best cooked slowly. It made a cheap piece of meat more tender. It also gave him a chance to sample the sauce and add, when needed, a pinch of garlic here, a splash of vinegar there.

Bobby, a wan smile on his face, turned toward his father, now seated at the kitchen table. "We'll find out in a few days, I guess," he said, as he pulled up a chair and joined him.

Antonio leaned forward, his gaze focused on his son's face.

"Your right eye," the old man said. "It swell up."

Bobby gingerly touched the area described. Sure enough, it was swollen. He was surprised. It didn't look that bad an hour ago, when he'd checked himself out in the mirror before leaving the gym.

"Dang," he whispered.

"What happen?" Dad asked.

Bobby sighed and sat down. He explained that he'd gone to see Uncle Mariano just to, well, you know, check it out.

"You do that?"

"Sure," Bobby said, adding that he really hadn't planned to. It was just the way things had worked out, he said, without getting into the details. He said he was warming up and breaking sweat, hitting the bag and minding his own business, when one of the trainers announced that his boy was fighting a southpaw next week and would some lefty please give him some rounds.

"So, I said I would," Bobby said.

Antonio listened intently, a look of concern on his face. He knew gym culture well enough to know that beginners were often used as ego-building punching bags for more experienced pugs. It had happened to him those many years ago, until he got good enough to dish out more than he took. Antonio suddenly winced. Even now, he could still feel the pain—the neck-snapping upper cuts, the broken ribs, the first two broken noses.

"You say that?" he finally asked.

"Yes."

"So, what did Mariano say?" He didn't think Mariano would be so careless, especially with Bobby, but if he had been, Antonio was planning to have a few not-so-friendly words with him.

"He told me not to do it. The guy was experienced, a young pro with a couple of four-round fights," Bobby said.

Antonio was relieved; the old trainer said what he should have said. He liked Mariano and it had pained him to think he might have to end a decades-old friendship.

"And then?" he finally asked.

"I told him I'd be fine, I wanted the rounds," Bobby replied. "And Mariano said he would stop the spar if I got hit hard. I smiled and said, 'What if he's the one that gets hurt?'"

"And then?"

"Uncle Mariano just shook his head and said, 'You too much like your daddy. More heart than common sense sometimes.'"

Bobby was looking at his father when he spoke. He heard him giggle and saw him smile—a reaction that gladdened his heart. Then the old man blushed, something he'd never seen before. It amazed Bobby. He couldn't imagine his dad ever doing that—oh, maybe in the old days when he was young and dreamed championship dreams, or when he was courting Mom and tomorrow seemed to promise more than it would ever deliver.

Bobby had thought that old Filipino men—Dad and his pals—weren't good candidates for blushing. For these old-timers, there were few, if any, surprises left. They had seen and endured too much, whether it was life in the fields, the war, both, or more. In Dad's case, it was more, so much more. But with Dad sitting not two feet from him and turning a different shade of brown, he might have to reconsider his assumption.

"Dad," Bobby said. "You're blushing."

"No," his father replied, still smiling as he patted his temple. "I don' do that. Jus' got hot is all. Mus' be the boiling rice."

"Okay, if you say so."

"Is jus' the rice, Son, tha's all."

* * *

Bobby knew it hadn't been just the rice—and knew Dad knew it, too—and that made Bobby happy. As he lay relaxed in his bed, he inventoried his day, starting with the later, more pleasant things first. He was tired and, for the first time, could feel the pervasive ache in his muscles. His condition was due, no doubt, to his determined effort to relieve another young man of his senses. He hadn't told Dad that, saying only that he did "okay" in his two-round spar.

Antonio didn't press it, satisfied that his boy had come home in one piece. When he was fighting, he never bragged much about what he had done. It was old school, the right way to do things. Bobby must have picked up some of that—somehow, some way, blood ties be damned.

Actually, Bobby had done better than okay, so much so that Mariano nodded and smiled and other fighters stopped what they were doing to watch him work. They looked at each other and nodded when he left the ring, satisfied that this thin, soft-looking stranger was one of them.

He touched the mouse and remembered how and when he got it. It was near the end of the first round when his opponent—a thick white kid named Mike—had him pinned in a corner.

He remembered Mariano screaming, "Tie 'im up, or get out, get out."

It was good advice, but heeded too late.

Up until then, it had gone really well, with Bobby staying in center ring and using his long right jab and superior foot speed to pile up style points and keep himself safe. Despite his experience, the shorter Mike had no chance of hitting him unless Bobby stopped moving—and that's what he did. Once again: boredom or stupidity? Once again: possibly both. Whatever the reason, he came down off his toes and stood flat footed, signaling for his opponent to come forward. And that's what Mike did.

He bulled Bobby into the corner and hit him first with a hard right to the gut, the prelude to a wicked left hook to the head. The glove missed as Bobby leaned back, but not the raised elbow which caught him just under his right eye.

The elbow, in particular, hurt. Bobby was furious; he knew the elbow was no accident. As the bell rang and he walked slowly toward his corner, all he could think about was payback. In his mind, he could hear him laughing, telling his trainer that he'd really fixed this punk.

In the corner, Mariano, a look of concern on his face, toweled Bobby down and asked if he wanted to continue. He grunted, of course he did.

Less than a minute later, Bobby shuffled to center ring where he greeted Mike, his confidence restored, with a stiff right jab to his nose and a hard overhand left to his forehead that stopped him cold. He probably could have followed it up and taken him out then, but a round lasts three minutes and he intended to use the two minutes and fifty seconds remaining to pay him back in full.

Bobby then began dancing, right to left, left to right, all the while beckoning Mike to come play with him. This time, though, would be different. To hell with Fred Astaire—no more dancing for the sake of art, no more pitty-pat jabs.

For the next two plus minutes, Bobby danced and a dogged Mike came forward behind a strong but slow left jab that usually fell an inch or two short of its mark. On those occasions, Bobby would punish him. He would pivot to his right, then set his feet and fire swift and hard combinations— his right hook over Mike's left, a straight left to the face and another right hook.

"Thirty seconds," one of the trainers yelled. "Thirty seconds."

Bobby, still dancing, looked at Mike, who was bleeding from his nose and breathing heavily through his mouth. He was finished, but Bobby certainly wasn't as he fired a stiff right jab to the face followed by a left to the body that made his opponent grunt. He followed with a flurry of punches that drove Mike into the ropes, where he desperately tried to grab and hold on.

"Ten seconds."

Bobby was disappointed. Not enough time, he thought.

"Let go," Bobby growled.

Mike tightened his grip.

To break the hold, Bobby leaned forward then quickly stepped back, freeing his right hand. He then stepped in and threw an uppercut that landed fist first then elbow on the poor man's chin. Mike was upright, but just barely, as the bell rang and Bobby finally backed off.

Bobby felt giddy, almost light-headed. He glanced around the gym and caught the knowing nods of other fighters, silent confirmation that he'd done well. For the first time ever, he felt invincible and was tempted to thump his chest, thrust his fists skyward and declare, "I'm a bad man, a baaad man. Who's next?"

He was, of course, savoring an adrenalin rush that comes with survival. It was more than that, though. It was also the first time vengeance had driven him to stalk another man and pick him apart, piece by piece. For Bobby, malice and efficiency were potentially addictive.

Most of his young life had been so bland and uneventful, he didn't understand why he was feeling that way. What he did from the opening moments of the second round was so unlike him—or who he thought he was.

But Paulie could have told him about adrenalin and malevolence; it was an addictive combination and one of the reasons he loved to fight. The bigger the other guy's rep, the bigger the charge after the dust had settled and the winner, usually Paulie, was clear. His brother's exploits on the street had fed his legend. For Paulie, the danger and pain of fighting were worth it, even if meant taking some bone-shaking shots to get close enough to land his punches and put his opponent down.

Bobby didn't strut or gloat. Although tempted, he didn't—at least not outwardly—because he began thinking about what Dad would have done. Bobby nodded, then walked over to Mike, now slumped and seated on a stool. He patted him on the shoulder.

"Good spar," he mumbled, unsure if Mike could even hear him.

"Good spar," he repeated to Mike's trainer, an old Mexican with a pock-marked face and flattened ears. He also didn't respond. The trainer was kneeling in front of his fighter, gently cupping his head in both hands and staring into a still vacant pair of blue eyes.

As Bobby walked away, he heard the old Mexican tell his young charge, "It's over, Son, you're not meant for this game."

Life's tough, Bobby thought at the time. Oh well.

Bobby also remembered his long walk home, especially the climb up Yesler. At the foot of the hill, he passed a group of four young men, none of whom he recognized. They were leaning against the wall of a convenience store and sharing a bag-covered bottle of rotgut wine.

Normally, he would have averted his eyes and walked close to the curb—I recognize your territory, the street-smart gesture said, I'm just passing through, please. He might have even crossed the street. But not today. They were looking for trouble and so was he.

He slowed his pace, looked at each of them like they were apples on display and shook his head disapprovingly. Good bait, he thought, as he continued walking. He was smiling, knowing what would happen next.

"Hey, pretty boy," one of them said. "Punk, you better stop. I'm talkin' to you."

As Bobby turned around, he was careful to put his right foot forward and to check his balance. His opponent, an Indian, tall and rawboned, taller than Bobby, was walking toward him, scowling and balling his fists.

"Kick his ass, Virgil," one of his friends yelled, as he reached for the bottle.

A newcomer, Bobby thought, not from around here, maybe from Montana. He was built like Sammy Arsenault, the oldest of three Blackfeet brothers from the neighborhood who'd spent their early years causing trouble in Browning near the Canadian border. Their parents, nice enough folks, couldn't control them. They were rambunctious. They were tough, even Paulie admitted they were.

"Sure, I'd fight Sammy and then I'd haveta go nail the other two," his brother told him once. "I ain't never backed down from no one, individual or family."

He paused, possibly imagining the opening scene, then feeling the pain of what would have been the fight of his life. "It'd be one helluva brawl," he'd finally said.

Bobby recalled that in the run-up to fights, Paulie would always take several minutes to insult and threaten his opponents, telling one soon-to-be victim that he hoped he wasn't his mother's only child. "Can't be, though," Paulie added, his brow furrowed, his voice oozing sincerity, "cuz yo mama's such a ho'."

After the fight, which was shorter than the prelude, an unmarked Paulie explained that words were also weapons. "Get inside the motherfucker's head," he said.

But Bobby wasn't especially good with words. Virgil had stopped and was standing in front of him, not two feet away, cursing and breathing hard. He looked focused, confident. Maybe he was expecting a round of pre-fight insults or maybe even an apology. What he didn't expect was the straight left to his solar plexus that sucked out his wind and drove him to the ground.

Bobby stood over his victim. "You know Sammy Arsenault?"

"No," Virgil grunted.

"Good," Bobby answered, as he launched a kick to the Indian's ribs. He felt the impact—solid—heard the crack and saw the grimace. He heard the groan.

"Welcome to Seattle, motherfucker," Bobby growled, as he turned to walk away. Although it was the first time he'd ever used *that* word, it sounded right—with the accent on the "fuck"—like he'd been saying, "Motherfucker, would you please pass the motherfucking toast" since he'd left his high chair to sit at the breakfast table.

The truth was that Bobby had hated the word when he first heard it at age eight—from Paulie, of course, who patiently explained in general terms that it was among the most potent of insults. Hence, Paulie's fondness for it.

But Bobby was suspicious. "Mother" was fine, but the second half, well, it sounded out of place, nasty. It took an afternoon conversation with Angie—even at ten, an older woman of the world—to find out what it really meant.

"It means a boy sticks his weenie in his mother between her legs," Angie explained in a matter-of-fact tone between slurps of an extra-large soda. "My boyfriend told me."

"You have a boyfriend?"

"Sure, he even kisses me," she replied, before pointing to the appropriate anatomical spot—the perfect way, she figured, to conclude her lecture. "It's right here," she added casually.

"Oooh," Bobby said, scrunching his face. He blushed and turned away, promising himself he would never use such a vile word, not even in anger.

But use it he did almost a decade later and under conditions he never before could have imagined.

As Bobby lay in his bed, he remembered what he felt after putting poor Virgil down. Before the fight, he had thought it would give him just what he needed—another adrenalin jolt to blanket the pain.

He recalled getting the jolt, all right. But it had worn off by the time he neared home, replaced by a sudden down-to-the-bone weariness and what seemed like an enormous anchor that had affixed itself to his soul.

He had taken out Mike, messed him up and probably ended his career. He could justify that.

But going out of his way to bait Virgil and hurt him, especially the second time when he was defenseless—how could that square with common decency? He used to think he had that and more, his very own well-defined code of "thou shalt nots" and "thou shalts," courtesy of the nuns at Saint James with Bobby adding a few more rules on his own.

Sure, his long list of how-he-should-be rules limited his choices, sometimes keeping him from having "fun"—at least as the word was defined by his peers in the projects. But he figured it was worth it. For starters, he liked who he was. It was also what made him different from the street boys, even from his brother. After today, however, he was no longer sure.

Was he becoming—or had he already become—someone he wouldn't like, perhaps even fear? He didn't know but the possibility bothered him. The time spent cooking dinner and later, chatting with Dad, were lovely distractions, now hours past. Alone in his room, he repeatedly whispered the question, thankful that exhaustion would postpone the answer.

* * *

Dream or real time, at first Bobby couldn't tell until Paulie told him. "Keep sleepin', man, you been a busy boy," his brother said. "But I got somethin' to say."

"What?" Bobby said.

In the dream, Paulie furrowed his brow and folded his arms across his chest. It was an ominous image, one that said pay attention—or else.

"I ain't sure if I like where you goin'," Paulie began.

Bobby sighed. He knew what his brother meant. He asked anyway. "What do you mean."

"Me and Polycarp, we wuz with you," Paulie said. "Right from the docks to the gym, then over to Yesler and . . ."

"Polycarp?"

"Yeah, he was a bishop or somethin' way back when, but that's another story," Paulie replied, a tinge of irritation in his voice.

"Anyways, the reason we wuz tailin' you was cuz him and me had a bet goin'. I was braggin' on you and said no doubt Bobby'd figure out this Deena thing in his sweet, kind way. And Poly says let's go check it out, or somethin' like that. So that's what we did."

In his dream, he and Paulie were standing by the east goalpost on Broadway Playfield. As kids, they'd spent countless hours between the chalked lines, playing pick-up games of baseball or touch football or whatever sport was in season. It was also one of Paulie's favorite places to pick fights, usually with kids on the other team, but sometimes with teammates.

Bobby watched himself frown as he also folded his arms across his chest. "So?"

Paulie shook his head, surprised by the slight tone of defiance in his brother's voice. "You already know what I'm gonna say, so I'll just say it," he said. "Fightin's one thing, but whatcha did to Virgil was bad, cold-blooded, flat-out wrong." He paused, waiting to see if his message had any impact.

Bobby was expressionless. "Like you've never beaten someone up before?" he asked calmly.

Paulie was surprised and a little flustered at the suddenly turned table. "Yeah, sure, I done it, but what you did was, it was . . . ," he sputtered, unable at first to complete his sentence.

Paulie, red faced, collected himself. "It was *immoral,*" he blurted out, using that word for the first time.

"Immoral?" Bobby repeated. For him, the word touched on God and the angels, black robes and incense, the clearest sense of right and wrong. Moral people didn't lie, steal, or murder; they also didn't set up suckers just to beat them for fun. His brother was right; what he'd done was immoral.

In his mind, he relived the moments—the feel of the punch and kick, the animal sounds of his badly hurt victim. Somewhere, he thought, a loved one—maybe Virgil's mother—would have screamed or cried if she had seen her boy crumpled on the sidewalk. He then thought of his own mother; Eula would have done no less. It was then that he understood the enormity of his deed—his utter lack of decency—and felt the onset of guilt and remorse.

But even then, Bobby still couldn't help smiling just a little. The word "immoral" sounded so strange coming from his foul-mouthed brother. Must be the bishop's civilizing influence, he guessed.

Paulie grunted. "Hell, you know what I mean."

Bobby nodded. He did.

"And besides, I've had a chance to think about things, sort stuff out," Paulie began. "Like my life, you know, with me runnin' the streets, jackin' dudes up—a lot of 'em right here—earnin' all kinda rep. I was livin' hard, high, and fast. Ooh, yeah, and I loved the feelin' of winnin' a fight. Damn, good times, or I thought they was anyway. I wasn't scared'a nothin' cuz nothin' could kill me. Man, ain't no one gonna kill Superman, right? Join the Army? No problem. Fight the Vietcong? Charlie, come get me."

Paulie paused and looked down, then shook his head slowly as he dabbed at the corner of an eye. "And that's what they did," he said, his voice suddenly soft. "Fact is, I wasted my life, Bobby, and I got no one to blame but me. But you, you still got a chance not to."

Bobby was touched. Gone, at least for now, was Paulie's arrogance, his playing-the-dozens obsession to come up with the best walk-away line, the insult to top all insults. For a moment, Paulie was sincere, subdued, reflective—traits not often seen.

"I hope so," Bobby said, as he gently put his hand on his brother's shoulder.

"I shoulda been more like you," Paulie continued. "Kind, polite, studious . . ."

"Ah, come on, man," Bobby interrupted. Even in a dream, he could feel himself blush.

". . . wantin' Dorothy."

"Huh?" Bobby removed his hand. He sensed a trap.

"Yeah, you was eight, nine maybe," Paulie said, smiling now. "Dad was sleepin', Mom was out. And you was by yourself in front of the TV, locked in like a zombie. Then the girl starts singin' that rainbow song and you start up, too. Next you pull your little thing out and start playin' with it right there on the floor. You wuz so into it, you didn't even hear me when I snuck up on you and shouted, 'Stop that, you weird little shit.'

"Man, I scared you so bad you wet yourself," he said, as he—eyes now watering, head now bobbing—bent over to slap his knee. "I kinda felt sorry after a while, but mostly it was after I was tireda laughin'. I was thinkin' maybe I shoulda said somethin' to you."

Bobby was blushing again, this time for a different reason. He worshipped his brother, his best ally. Paulie's ridicule—and his embarrassment—wounded him in an unspeakably painful way. But he never let on.

Once he calmed down, he began practicing the Alec Guinness stiff upper lip on prominent display in *The Bridge on the River Kwai*. But the truth was it was all for appearance, a fake. Bobby would have rather taken a punch to his solar plexus than to hear—or remember—Paulie's derisive laughter.

He had tried hard to forget what happened that day, telling himself over time that it was all imagined, a dream. He didn't really do what he'd done and, more importantly, Paulie hadn't caught him in the act and laughed at him. He had mostly succeeded until now.

"Why didn't you?" Bobby asked quietly.

Paulie took a deep breath to compose himself. "Why didn't I what?"

"Say something?"

Paulie shrugged. "I dunno, just got caught up in life in the projects, probably checkin' out some lady, you know how it goes."

In the dream, Bobby saw himself glare at his brother, a look so intense that Paulie turned away. "No, I don't know how it goes," he said calmly.

"Ah, come on, man, that was years ago." Paulie asked. "You ain't still mad?"

He gestured with both hands as he spoke, reserving the most emphatic gestures for the question posed.

Bobby refused to give his brother the easy way out. "I wasn't until I remembered what you did to me," he replied. "You should have said something."

Paulie's eyes bounced left to right, then back again. He was having a difficult time looking Bobby in the eye. "Yeah, I shoulda," he was finally able to say.

Bobby nodded. "You should have," he said, as his brother turned to walk away, vanishing slowly with each step taken.

He was finally alone in his dream, standing by the goalpost, his hands buried in his pockets. It was near sundown and the field lights had switched on. He was kicking absentmindedly at a clump of grass—a rare spot of green on the hard dirt field—as if repetitive motion would trigger something else.

In the distance, Bobby could see someone approaching. A man, judging by his outline, but frail and doll-like, not very tall. He was waddling side to side, possibly because he was carrying what appeared to be a suitcase.

The man suddenly stopped as if surprised. He looked at Bobby and took a few steps forward before stopping again.

Eyes squinting, Bobby calmly stared at him. The odd little man put down his suitcase and started dancing a funny little jig, spinning around and hopping from one foot to the other. He then began waving and staring back.

His slick black hair was held in place by what must have been half a jar of pomade. The man seemed vaguely familiar, although Bobby couldn't place him—at least not yet.

But the longer Bobby stared, the more convinced he was that he knew him, or had at least met him once upon a time. He closed his eyes and began to recall fragments of settings, snippets of time.

Sure, the little man looked harmless enough, comical even. But the longer Bobby stared, the faster his guts began to tighten and churn. He didn't understand why.

The man then did a quick about-face and, suitcase in hand, began waddling away. He turned and paused to wave once more before leaving the entrance to the playfield.

At first, Bobby wanted to shout and ask him what he was doing in his dream. He didn't, it wouldn't have done any good. This, he suspected, was the prelude, not the final act. He watched the man leave as he, alone once more, resumed kicking at the stubborn clump of grass.

Chapter Twelve

Maybe cold water would help, Bobby thought, as he squinted at himself in the bathroom mirror.

"Man," he whispered.

His reflection—pale, bloodless, exhausted—didn't look like him. What he saw was a young man who looked like he had no business being out of bed.

Bobby had managed to sleep, but fitfully, as his mind played and replayed the image of a strange little man dancing a jig. During the night, he would awaken then fall back to sleep—greeted on each occasion by the dancing little man. Bobby nodded his head and sighed, confident he'd figure out who he was, what role he'd played—just not right now. He had other, more pressing concerns.

Bobby turned on the tap, then gingerly massaged his face with a cold, wet cloth. He immediately felt better and looked again at his image. The reddish bruise around his eye had evolved into a full-blown shiner, running from the eyelid to just below his cheek bone.

No surprise, really, because the point of an elbow can cause that kind of damage. But that wasn't all. The undertrained muscles in his calves, back, neck, and arms were now silently screaming at what had transpired over two rounds—six minutes—a blip of time, unless it was spent trying to hurt someone badly. His only consolation was knowing that a measure of relief was just a long hot shower away, as hot as he could stand.

A black eye, though, was different. A little ice to tamp down the swelling, then later apply some heat. Standard procedure. He'd seen Paulie do it countless times. But he also knew from watching his brother that the process of healing would take days, if not longer.

That wasn't a problem for Paulie. He liked walking around Yesler and looking like a post-fight poster boy. Paulie had had plenty of black eyes as well as a couple of broken noses, a chipped tooth, and a full array of other battle marks. He figured it added to his reputation in the projects. When he would pass, some folks would nod knowingly, others would smile, still others would say, "Yeah, but you should've seen the other dude."

But Bobby wasn't Paulie. He didn't want that kind of attention. Besides, he didn't have his brother's blood-chilling rep. He imagined those he knew seeing him like this. He could picture them wincing, envisioning the fierce thrashing he'd never received.

He didn't want the misplaced pity of neighbors, acquaintances, and friends. He didn't want their condolences— *Poor, poor Bobby . . . Well, what do you expect? He sure as hell ain't Paulie. Now that was a fighter; that was a man. But this boy's anything but; he's so damn soft.*

Mostly, though, Bobby didn't want to explain. It would be better, he figured, to avoid the topic altogether. Better yet, to stay inside until his eye had fully healed. But that was impossible, maybe even dangerous. With the GED looming, he needed just a few more Deena-free days.

This morning before rising, he did a Deena check. Yes, he missed her, but the ache didn't seem as bad as yesterday's. He had high hopes as he rose from his bed that he could at least fake it through the day.

Deena, he concluded, rhymed—or at least kind of rhymed—with *incognita*, as in *terra incognita*, as in *unexplored land*. It was why he'd acted so badly, why a tailspin had become normal movement, why Virgil had paid the price.

He knew it wasn't entirely her fault. He just wasn't strong enough, mature enough, wise enough. Still, he should have tried harder not to lash out. Paulie, for once, was right. What he'd done to poor Virgil was immoral—there was no way around it. There was also no way he could take it back.

Bobby was calm now, remorseful and centered, but that could change in a second. She might call; he might answer, waste time, meet her, get upset, get confused, pick another fight, get arrested, flunk the test, get drafted, blow his life. That meant he'd have to go out, probably to the downtown library to review math equations, the Articles of Confederation, the causes of the Great Depression, and everything else he wasn't sure of.

Sunglasses could help. He bought a pair of knock-off wire-framed aviators last summer and wore them once. Bobby wearing shades—the look was so cool, a statement. Angie and a few other girls from the neighborhood told him so. Two of them smiled, one oohed and aahed as she twirled a few strands of his hair.

Could love be far behind?

Yes, it could.

He took the sunglasses off, convinced they were too cool for him. But he'd have to wear them today, even though the forecast was for rain by the buckets. It would start mid-morning, the weatherman joked, until it was time to coax the critters onto the ark.

Some joke. Bobby, who could already hear heavy drops bombing the rooftop, glanced at the tiny windup clock on the bathroom window sill. Twenty to eight and the deluge had already started, dashing any hope that his hike to the library would be pleasant and dry.

Bobby left the bathroom and returned a minute later wearing his once-worn sunglasses. Not bad, he thought, as he studied himself in the mirror. They looked manly, stylish, and, more importantly, the right lens covered some of the damage.

But wearing shades was so out of season. Ray Charles and Little Stevie Wonder were the only two he could think of who could wear them in a downpour. If anyone asked him or even stared for a second or more, he was ready with a deadpan reply.

Sure, of course it makes sense, he would say. *These are rain glasses, the latest trend—from Britain, no less. I'm so surprised you didn't know that. And besides, I play the piano.*

*   *   *

At first, the rain didn't bother Bobby as much as it should have. Part of the reason was that he was bundled up well, complete with winter coat, upturned collar, and baseball cap. The other part was that he was preoccupied with something else.

Before Bobby left the apartment, his father, already dressed, told him never mind dinner, just eat outside. He then reached into his pants pocket and pulled out a money clip holding together an eye-popping wad of twenties and fifties—maybe even bigger denominations, Bobby couldn't tell.

Bobby was puzzled; Dad had always been understated, never the type to flash cash, at least until today. The old man smiled and handed him ten crisp twenty-dollar bills.

"That should take care of you," he said.

"Thanks, Dad," Bobby said slowly, as he searched for the right words. "Ah, you look good."

Antonio was dressed to the nines, wearing his best suit—dark blue with broad lapels. A pressed white shirt, black silk tie, polished black Florsheims, and a sporty, perfectly formed black felt Borsalino, its front brim bent just right, completed his attire. The only accessory missing was a pair of white spats.

Bobby stepped back, folded his arms and stared at his father who'd turned overnight into Sky Masterson. He nodded. Impressive, he thought, but Sky never looked this good.

Dad explained that he was going to catch a ride with one of his other Pinoy pals to visit Manong Magno—*you remember, the one with the farm near Renton*—and was planning to stay a few days.

"He's sick," Dad said. "Not doin' so well."

"What's wrong with him?"

"Old mostly, I guess," Dad said sadly. "He lost his wife, an Indian girl, I think three years ago, so, mebbe he's lonely, too. But who knows? We come here together forty years ago, same town, same boat. Could be we're related."

"Why are you so dressed up?"

His father shrugged. "Oh, I dunno, your mom really like this suit. I figure why not. Besides, tha's what me and Magno useta do way back then when we work on the farm. After work, we shower, then dress up, go to town, have fun.

"I figure I take 'im out, have dinner, find 'im a girlfriend, that sorta thing. Back then, he useta like blondes. Mebbe I can find 'im one and cheer 'im up and he get better, who knows."

Bobby shrugged. "Sounds good," he mumbled, as he began gathering his books. Antonio then smiled, possibly at the thought of finding a blonde.

*　*　*

The rain had stopped by the time Bobby was nearing the library. By then, he was soaked to the bone and irritated with himself for being so impatient. He could have waited the squall out; forty-five minutes would have done the trick. But no, he had told himself that he had too much to review and too little time.

Then seeing his father like that—it had made him sad. Bobby didn't know why. He just knew he had to leave the apartment.

The story of Magno—sure, that was true, as far as it went. But there was something else, what Antonio was holding back, that bothered him so.

He felt a circle nearing completion. How Dad once was and what he'd become again—dapper, handsome, full of himself, when life in the new land was still brand new.

This is how I was, Son, he seemed to be saying. *This is how I want you to remember me.*

Outside the library, Bobby shook like a water dog, sending drops flying. He continued to shake, as if vigorous motion could somehow shake the ache in his heart.

It didn't. He dabbed at an eye as he entered the building and spotted the corner table, the same one he'd used yesterday. It was empty. A good thing, too. He didn't want anyone near him just in case he started to cry.

*　*　*

The sweat felt good. Under Mariano's watchful eye, Bobby was losing himself in a fast-flowing stream of rhythm and sound. His trip to the gym had been a spur-of-the-moment choice—no change of clothes, no towel, no problem. His loose-fitting khakis and Converse low-cuts would do. Besides, he wanted—needed—a hard workout to make his body scream loud enough to drown out everything else.

"Jab, jab," the old trainer barked, as a laser-like right twice found its mark on the taped and retaped leather heavy bag. Mariano smiled. Bobby wasn't just quick; he was a lot more powerful than he looked. In Mariano's long years in a hard business, he'd known a lot of skinny guys who were quick and clever, tricky to fight. But they couldn't punch.

Bobby was different. He was a stick man with pop—hard to imagine, easy to underestimate. In Mariano's line of work, deception was an advantage.

"Jab, jab," he repeated. "Left cross, hook, jab."

Five punches, each following the other, seamlessly and without flaw, each blow popping the bag hard.

By golly, Mariano thought, impressive; he has a knack for power, a God-given gift.

"Thirty seconds, Bobby," Mariano said. "Steal the round." The command, immediately heeded, unleashed a volley of jabs and crosses, hooks, double hooks, and uppercuts—each punch thrown with speed, power and malice.

Mariano counted down the seconds. "Ten," he said, which meant pick it up, pick it up, *faster*, kid, *faster*, lose your mind, *faster*, don't dance, *faster*, don't pause, *faster*, just throw, *faster*, *faster*, *faster*. And that's what Bobby did as he unleashed a blur of punches, his high-amp outburst mocking exhaustion, ignoring pain.

"Time."

Mariano nodded and smiled as Bobby, breathing deeply, stepped back and slowly stretched his arms and neck. He glanced at the clock on the far wall—2:00, almost two hours—then took off his bag gloves and unwrapped his hands.

"Look okay," Mariano mumbled, as he toweled him down. His word choice suggested he wasn't big on compliments—at least not in English.

This time, though, he'd made an exception. "Fast, strong," the old man added.

"Thanks, Manong," Bobby replied, as he took the towel and draped it over his head, before walking over to a tattered tan couch by the far wall. He wanted to sit for a moment and enjoy the rare silence. It was still early as gym hours go. Most of the fighters were regular working stiffs; others took a day or two off. The earliest birds would start trickling in in half an hour, maybe longer.

No doubt, he was tired and he'd probably pay the price tonight, but the sweat felt good. And that's what he needed and would never have gotten at the library, where he'd studied math, a little grammar, and the Great Depression. No wonder Mom and Dad loved FDR so.

Bobby then covered his eyes with the towel, leaned back, and kicked up his feet. Was there anything left to do today? What the heck. Dad wasn't home, he didn't have to cook, he'd already studied and liked his odds; a couple of eyes-closed minutes wouldn't hurt.

"Bobby."

A woman's voice, dream or real-time he couldn't tell.

"Bobby," the voice repeated, this time closer.

A hand touching his shoulder answered the question. He removed the towel and opened one eye, then the other.

"Deena," Bobby whispered, as he picked up the towel and draped it over his eyes. He wasn't sure how to feel. Yes, he had missed her, but the Deena-less time meant routine and discipline—getting essential things done. It also allowed him to postpone questions he didn't want to ask, much less have answered.

"How did you find me?" he mumbled through the towel.

"I called your house and . . ."

"Dad."

"Yeah, he said you might be here and that he wanted us to work things out. From what he knew, he thought we were good for each other."

Deena paused. "I'm hoping you feel the same way."

Bobby sighed and didn't answer. He should have been irritated at his father and at her—but he wasn't. The truth was he was thrilled to see her, overjoyed, in fact. Answers to questions—Did he love her? How should he love her? Did she love him?—these could wait till tomorrow, or whenever he got around to it. Forget what happened, he wanted to scream, it doesn't matter. Let's start again.

Besides, he knew he'd eventually have to visit this uncomfortable place, this heart of his heart. A few days early wouldn't change a thing. He removed the towel. It was time, he figured, to fully rejoin his world.

"Your eye," Deena gasped, as she seated herself on the edge of the sofa.

Bobby—his eyes blinking, adjusting to the light—scooted over to make more room. "Occupational hazard," Bobby said casually. "In this game, eyes have been known to punch elbows—but, surprise, the eye always loses."

He then shyly extended his hand, which she held and caressed, then placed on her lap. "Hi," he said softly.

"Hi yourself," she replied, as Bobby gazed at her face, unadorned by makeup. Still lovely, he thought, even with the dark lines under her large brown eyes, now reddish and swollen.

"I didn't know you boxed," she said.

"I was kind of surprised myself."

Deena was silent for a moment as she quickly looked away and back. She furrowed her brow, all the while holding his hand snugly on her lap, as if keeping it there was a life and death thing.

"I want to explain," she finally said.

"I know, but you can do that later," Bobby said, as he sat up, stroked her hair and kissed her gently on both cheeks. "First, you should get some sleep."

"I look that bad?"

Bobby paused, not wanting to be harsh. "Yes," he finally said. "You really do need to sleep."

"I know."

Bobby nodded and drew nearer to her. "With me," he whispered, almost as an afterthought.

* * *

In Bobby's bedroom, they were snuggled together like kittens on a comforter. Bobby's nagging aches and soreness had somehow disappeared. No doubt a hot shower had helped, but the main remedy, he guessed, was Deena lying beside him.

Earlier that evening, they had laughed and kissed; they had spoken of love and longing, of them together. They had spoken of making love—but had chosen not to. Emotional overload, Bobby said. Too much, too soon.

To his surprise, Deena agreed. "Just hold me," she said, which is what he did—his face to the back of her neck, his arms around her waist, their legs and feet intertwined.

Before falling asleep, Bobby whispered, "No dreams, no visits, Paulie, come on, please, not tonight."

"Pardon?" a sleepy-eyed Deena asked.

"Oh, nothing," Bobby replied. "Just a little prayer that I say every night."

"That's nice," she said, as she adjusted his grip, moving his hands to her breasts. "I love you, Bobby."

"I love you, too," he replied. Never mind he wasn't sure what kind of love—the way God loves or otherwise—he was referring to. All he knew was that holding Deena felt so right. For Bobby, a proper definition wasn't needed right now.

In the corner of the room, two men forming the oddest of odd couples were holding a conversation.

"Damn, Poly," Paulie said excitedly, as he jumped from his chair. He was clapping his hands for emphasis. "Man, didja hear that? Bobby was prayin' to me. To me. That kinda makes me a saint—or somethin'."

The old bishop rolled his eyes and smiled. "Well, it's all relative. You weren't as bad as some of the people who didn't make it here."

"I could get my own church, my own statue, feast day, even a halo. Ooh, check it out, on this side, won't even need no stick to hold it up. Call the Vatican. Get me the Pope."

"All things are possible," Polycarp said evenly.

"Man, I ain't been this excited since I nailed Julie Tavares in the back of . . ." Paulie stopped himself and looked at his friend. "Sorry, pal, I guess that ain't very saintly."

"Not particularly."

"Phew," Paulie said, as he sat back down. "About Bobby, whatcha think. I was gonna finish showin' 'im somethin' tonight. Some of the stuff he needs to see, but he prayed to me'n all and with me bein' a saint . . ."

"Let the boy sleep, you can show him tomorrow," Polycarp said firmly. "You're right, he's a very good boy—kind, thoughtful."

"Yeah, man, kinda like me."

Polycarp smiled. "He's kind and thoughtful, which reminds me," he said, as he reached into his robe, retrieved a cigar, and turned it over to Paulie.

"A Bolivar, as you requested," the bishop said. "You've won the bet and I've lost, and I'm very happy about that."

Paulie smiled. "Poly, my man, you never cease to amaze me. Where'd you get it?"

"Oh, a Cuban," Polycarp replied. "There are a lot of them here, especially since Fidel took over."

"Got a match?"

"No, not really," Polycarp answered with a frown. "Fire, as you know, isn't my favorite element."

"Oh, sorry, Bishop," Paulie said, wincing. "Ooh, ouch, ouch, ouch, I forgot." He then checked his pockets and, after a moment, hit paydirt in the form of a long-forgotten, presumed-lost lighter.

"Bingo," he said, as his thumb's downward thrust produced a tiny flame.

Bobby's nose twitched, then his eyes opened to the scent of cigar smoke. He stretched his neck and could see the cigar's lit end in the corner of the bedroom. It would move on occasion, seemingly suspended in mid-air.

He resumed his position—his face and lips to the back of Deena's neck. "Paulie, not tonight," he whispered. "Please."

Bobby heard, or thought he did, a reply: "That's *Saint* Paulie, chump."

Chapter Thirteen

Northwest weather is full of surprises, and this morning was no exception. Last night, the weatherman said to expect rain through the weekend and most of Monday—bet the house on it. But instead of the rat-a-tat-tat of raindrops, Bobby awakened to silence and to sunlight pouring through his bedroom window.

He yawned, then turned to glance at his watch on the bedstand—7:00, late for him, but no problem. Today, he had no pressing plans, no set schedule. Maybe he'd fix breakfast. Or maybe he'd just grab his books and stay where he was.

He smiled as he gazed at Deena, who was still asleep. She was beautiful, no doubt about that. Lying next to her wasn't such a bad fate.

This morning was special—their first shared dawn, a celebratory time. Bobby thought of Eula and Antonio and wondered what they'd felt on their first morning. It must have been powerful enough to keep them going for thousands of mornings more, through good times and bad. And, wonder of wonders, the end matched the beginning—his parents were still in love.

Maybe he and Deena would be lucky enough to last that long. He hoped so, but there was a caveat, a minor one. The answer would be known only over time and, yes, that meant taking chances. But what the heck. What other choice did he have? He wasn't leaving any time soon, and he didn't think she was either.

Bobby slipped quietly out of bed and tip-toed to the door. His immediate goal, a fresh pot of coffee to greet the dawn. He was content, happy, the only snag, a snippet of film that was playing in his mind.

In it, four old Pinoys were seated at a table playing poker. The room was jammed with Filipinos, just standing around or playing cards at other tables. He could also see the overly dressed, high-heeled women, most of them blondes, whether born that way or not. They liked the Pinoys, especially if there was money on the table. The scene was so real Bobby could hear the mix of dialects and broken-English conversations; he could smell the thick mix of smoke, perfume, chewed tobacco and spilled whiskey.

Bobby thought he knew the joint—a basement parlor just off King Street in Chinatown. Never mind the cops, the owner, Manong what's-his-name, had paid them well.

The corny picture on the wall depicting dogs in suits and ties playing cards was the giveaway. Dad had taken him and Paulie there years ago, while he'd sit and laugh and play a couple of hands. Bobby liked being with the old guys, who dutifully patted him and his brother on their heads and always slipped them cash—mostly ones, but sometimes fives and tens depending on the haul.

No, it wasn't Disneyland. But Bobby wouldn't have traded the card room for Mickey, Minnie, or even Annette.

"She got more than ears," Paulie had once said of the most famous Mouseketeer. His tone was reverential.

"She does?" Bobby replied at the time.

The boys' card room visits abruptly ended after one of the gamblers pulled out a snub-nose .22 revolver and shot another patron. He then bolted out the door, the story went, and immediately hopped a Greyhound for Stockton. The victim, a tough, stocky Ilocano named Chris, survived his wound but wouldn't press charges.

"Jimmy, he's my first cousin and sometimes he goes crazy," Chris explained to Antonio a few weeks later at the card room, where he was seated at his usual chair at his usual table. Antonio was standing nearby.

As Chris waited for the cards to be shuffled and dealt, he casually added that he'd stabbed his cousin once over a woman a long time ago. But they were young, they'd been drinking—as if either factor, or both—made stabbing poor Jimmy okay.

"I jus' poke 'im in his hand," Chris said, before reenacting the gentlest, most restrained knife thrust in recorded history.

Antonio nodded, but said nothing.

"Right there," he said, pointing to the flesh between his thumb and index finger. "Goodness sake, is not an eye or nothin' serious. Like a flu shot, tha's it. Like a flu shot, nothin' more. And it only take five stitches to fix."

Antonio winced. "No, is not an eye."

Chris smiled, perhaps impressed by his long-ago act of kindness.

He then glanced at his cards—a pair of treys—and studied the deadpan faces of the other players, all of whom took their poker seriously. One of them grunted and tossed in a twenty; the others matched it.

Not Chris. He threw down his cards and turned toward Antonio, who was standing nearby.

"Good to see you, old friend," he said, as he took a healthy swig from a small silver flask.

"Likewise."

"I guess Jimmy don' forget that," he said with a sigh. "Oh well, blood's thicker than water, you know. He's still my cousin. That means we gotta show up at Christmas and family gatherings and things like that."

Chris sighed. "Mebbe we're even."

"Mebbe," Antonio replied.

Bobby smiled at the memory—a fond one, oddly enough—before turning his attention to the details of his dream. He thought he recognized the poker players, but it was impossible to tell. The combination of cigar and cigarette smoke and the room's dim lighting clouded their faces.

It wasn't at all like normal dreams—those had always been clear, technicolor, fully developed wonders, at least since Paulie died. Bobby always got the point. Like an old newsreel, this one was grainy. The action went to mid-scene then stopped, as if someone had turned off the projector.

Eyes shut, Bobby sat at the kitchen table, trying his best to focus, to remember. There must have been more, he told himself, something he'd seen but for some reason wasn't remembering. Concentrate, concentrate.

He then opened his eyes to the plop-plop-plop of coffee brewing. No luck now, maybe later, he thought, as he pushed back his chair, stood up and grabbed two cups from the sink.

He was smiling as he walked toward the stove. Fresh, hot java in a warm bed with the woman he loved—now that was an idea.

* * *

There on the bedstand sat two cups of coffee, their contents barely touched and quickly cooling—hot to lukewarm to "Honey, a fresh cup, please." Not that Bobby or Deena cared a lick, their licks reserved only for each other after Bobby suggested—and Deena agreed—that abstinence was overrated.

It took no time at all for the room to heat up, its contours filling swiftly with sounds and sweet scents, with passion and murmurs, the surrender of hearts. They kissed a last deep kiss before uncoupling—Deena breathing heavily, smiling dreamily, and Bobby thinking forget coffee, this was a much better way to greet the dawn.

"I love you," she whispered.

"Ditto."

"Ditto?" she said, as an eyebrow slowly arched. "Is that the most you can say?"

It wasn't Deena's fault, really. In her experience, her lovers had always been wordy, even the wayward Jesuit pledging the world—here and hereafter—especially after sex.

In her mind, she was a magnificent lover, legendary. She was a goddess or queen, a consort of kings—or so her lovers told her. Verbal extravagance, even corny sonnets honoring the moment—that's what she expected. *Ditto* was so inadequate, puny even.

Bobby smiled, his eyes focused on the ceiling. As he lay there, he could almost feel her eyebrow ascending.

When they were making love, Bobby could feel her. He now knew her essence—that mysterious word—her needs and fears, her flaws and expectations. He knew her beauty and sexuality defined her, probably more than was healthy or wise.

Deena had stopped being a stranger; it was as if they'd been together for years. He didn't wonder how his insight came to be, but it was no big deal. After Paulie's beyond-the-grave visits, nothing any longer seemed strange.

Yes, Bobby loved her. But love was one thing—it could take a number of forms, shapes, expressions. Worship was another. In this case, "ditto" would do.

"Okay, you're right," Bobby finally said, trying hard not to chuckle. "Double ditto."

It was only a joke, and a weak one at that. But try telling that to Deena, who abruptly turned her back, acting like a woman in a marriage that had lasted too long. Yet even as she was turning away, she was already missing him, realizing then that petulance, like abstinence, can be hugely overrated. She knew that she wanted this man—or man child, manling, whatever he was. For her, it was a first-time feeling, something she'd have to get used to.

She was safe with him, secure, unlike the past when she preferred men of power, intelligence and ego. Big bad men, trophy men—the bigger, the badder, the better. Almost to a lover, they thought that they had seduced her, but the truth was just the opposite, each conquest confirming who she was, who she thought she was, her essence.

She had watched her mother do the same thing after her father had died, parlaying her good looks into a stately home near the bay and European vacations on a whim. Deena, after she discovered boys noticing her, even men sometimes, thought she'd give it a try, the only difference being that the mother had the common sense and discretion so lacking in the daughter.

That led her to a string of affairs, charges of infidelity (most of which were true), and less-than-graceful exits, the last one involving death threats and a gun and Deena running barefoot through the night. She didn't stop until she reached Seattle, where her former lover, Andrew, a fast-rising police lieutenant, had no jurisdiction.

Bobby, she knew, was different, not typical of the men she'd been with. He was gentle and had an innocence, a rare purity—sans guile or obvious angle. What he said he was, he was.

At that moment, Deena yearned to hold him, to feel his skin next to hers. But how could she turn around without seeming so shallow and silly?

The answer was provided by Bobby, who caressed her neck and bit her lightly on the ear.

"I love you," Bobby said softly.

"Ditto" was her whispered reply.

* * *

"Hey, Bishop, it's daylight and Bobby's still asleep," Paulie said. "Maybe it's time for the show."

Polycarp shrugged. "Why not?"

"Cool," Paulie said as he cupped both hands around his mouth. "Quiet on the set. Lights, camera, action."

Paulie then pulled out a Cuban cigar and lit it. "Damn, I've always wanted to say that," he said smugly. "Whatcha think, man, I'd look good in a beret?"

"No."

"Why not?"

"My son," Polycarp explained patiently. "You're not French."

"Oh."

"Let's watch the film."

As the bishop spoke, the old gambling parlor came into view. At first, the scene was mostly forms and conversations because of the smoke, which lessened somewhat after a door opened slightly and someone turned on a fan.

If the air in the room had improved, the four old Pinoys at the table didn't take notice. They were focused on other, more important matters.

One of them, a bent little man named George, solemnly studied his cards, then looked at the other players. Satisfied— three fours, a good hand—he threw down two twenties and a ten onto a pile worth more than eight hundred dollars. As each player knew, this was big money, especially for Filipinos—more than two months' wages for most of them.

"Raise fifty," George mumbled, surprised and somewhat troubled he was going this deep. In truth, he had no choice. His youngest sister in Mandaue—his only surviving sibling— had just written him. She had to go to Manila for an operation. She had to go soon. *Cataracts, please, older brother,* the letter asked, *could you please help?*

Never mind he was getting by on Social Security and a small pension from the fish cannery on the waterfront. Never mind the last time he'd seen her was in 1925. He had to do something.

Perhaps it was guilt that moved him. Maybe he hadn't done enough to try to bring her—or their other brothers and sisters—here, to America, the fantasized land of Filipino dreams. People didn't die here, the legend went, at least not from war or starvation.

Perhaps they would have done well; maybe most of them would still be alive. It was far too late for should have and could have now, but never too late for regret.

Then again, maybe it was all much simpler—a heartstring pull from a slender and pretty ten-year-old girl in the black-and-white photograph he'd kept after all these years. As George waited for the other gamblers to react, he could see the photo in his mind. He could see her on the dock as she waved goodbye.

His sister going blind? Not if he could help it.

"Too rich," muttered Sam, the player to George's right. He cursed quietly in a mix of Ilocano and English before tossing down his cards.

Fil, the player to George's left, smiled wanly. He raised a Salem Menthol to his lips then slowly rose before tossing his cards one-by-one face down onto the table.

Fil shrugged. "Sometimes you win," he said, as he wandered away, not bothering to finish his sentence.

Now it was a showdown, one-on-one. "Hoy, compadre," George began. "Is jus' you and me."

"Seems to be," he said, as he glanced at his cards.

"We go back a long way," George said. "Good times."

"Plenny," he said, as he his pulled out his money clip and put a crisp fifty-dollar bill on the table.

George gulped. What were the odds of topping three-of-a-kind? Not good. He should relax, he told himself, but to no avail. Tiny sweat beads began forming on the bridge of his nose.

The other gambler, dapper and unflappable, smiled. Holding his cards in one hand, he casually adjusted his tie with the other. He then cleared his throat and looked at George. "I call," he said.

George sighed and slowly put his trio of fours on the table, evincing a wince and a curse from his opponent.

"Sonamabits," he said, as he threw down his hand, the cards, landing scattered, face down and mixed in with Fil's. That way no one would know that three of the cards were jacks, the other two deuces—a winner on this and most other days.

He shook his head slowly before standing up and extending his hand. The two men shook.

"Everything else okay?" Antonio asked.

"Sure, why not, jus' like always," George lied. "Antonio, you comin' back?"

"Nah," Antonio replied. "You play cards too damn good. Jus' like Vegas. Besides, me and Magno got places to go."

Upon hearing his name, Magno bid a reluctant goodbye to his companion of the moment, a white woman named Lulu, a tall, busty forty-something blonde wearing a white dress with red flowers and a gold boa. She towered over him; if they had been boxers, they'd have fought in different divisions.

He said that perhaps he had had the pleasure of making her acquaintance. On second thought, he was quite certain he had. Was it ten years ago? Twenty? She was less sure. Like the great MacArthur, Magno then promised to return to help resolve the issue. History, he declared, demanded an answer.

And by the way, he added, would she still be here? He certainly hoped so.

She smiled demurely—maybe yes, maybe no, the smile said. For Magno, back in the hunt after so many years, that was promise enough. To the surprise of those who were watching, he suddenly bowed, lifted her hand and kissed it—just like he'd seen in the movies.

He was grinning, quite pleased with himself, as he made his way toward Antonio. Who said old dogs can't learn new tricks?

Hell, today at least one old dog did. He had even been tempted to sing—just like in the movies—but he remembered in time he couldn't carry a note.

Goodbyes finally over, Antonio and Magno slowly made their way up the stairs. "Hoy, compadre," Magno said quietly, then paused. "I saw your cards."

"Boy, I sure coulda used it a lotta other times," Antonio said breezily. "Pretty good hand, huh?"

"The bes'," Magno said. He turned toward his friend; he had a question to ask. "Why?"

Antonio shrugged. "Me and George, we been friends a long time," he began. "Then you tol' me 'bout his sister. Remember? That George, though, he's too proud for donations."

"Oh, tha's right, I did," Magno said, his smile returning. It now made perfect sense. "Merry Christmas, George."

"Mebbe happy birthday," Antonio added.

"Mebbe both."

"Well, now that I done that, I think I'm gonna fill up that old Mercury of yours and go for a ride," Antonio said, as he glanced at the sky. It was still light, the rain clouds having floated away. According to Northwest standards, it was a perfect day for a long ride.

"Where?"

"Way out in the country," Antonio replied. "North Bend."

"Why?"

Antonio smiled. "You can jus' drop me off there," he said. "I got a date."

* * *

"I got a date," Bobby mumbled, as he, half awake, snuggled closer to Deena.

"I'm more than a date, Hon," she replied softly, as she guided his arm across her waist.

The unexpected sound of Deena's voice lifted Bobby's personal fog. "Huh?" he asked sheepishly. "Sorry, did I wake you? I must have been dreaming."

"About me, I hope," she said, in her best fishing-for-a-compliment voice.

"No," Bobby answered, missing the hint.

"Oh," she said, as she bit her lip.

Deena didn't want to be this way, but she couldn't help it. For the first time ever, she was in love. She had thought long ago she'd figured out what made men tick, what made them act like imbeciles to prove their love, but this one was different—an odd, intoxicating mix of passion and distance.

But what if this strange, sweet-tempered and beautiful man got tired or bored? What if he decided to leave her? Deena had never thought about such questions before; in fact, she couldn't even have imagined putting the words together to form the question. It bothered her to think about them now.

Despite her fears, she felt he was well worth the risk, a once-in-a-lifetime chance. Miss this boat, Sweetheart, a little voice told her, return to the village and stay there. Keep doing the same dreary things you do so often and so well; keep making the same mistakes. Repeat them until the end of days.

"It involved my father," Bobby said. "He and his friend Magno were getting ready to go for a ride. In the dream, Dad was smiling, carefree." Bobby didn't share the mood.

"You're close to him, aren't you," she said. It was more statement than question.

"Yes, I am."

"Can I meet him?"

Before answering, Bobby rolled on his back and covered his eyes with his hands. "No," he said, in a voice that sounded far away. "It's not going to happen, at least not in this life."

*   *   *

"It's hard to explain," Bobby said, as he, now sitting up, told Deena about his world of ghosts and dreams. He knocked on the wall and then, fingers and thumbs raised, extended his hands, as if touching some invisible thing.

"They're both real," he said.

And no, he hadn't always been this way. It started with Paulie dying in the war and his deciding not to go away, at least not immediately. Up until then, he'd been pretty normal, or as normal as any poor young man from the projects who idolized Fred Astaire, loved *The Wizard of Oz,* ignored Angie, and whacked off to Dorothy.

Then came the first dream, followed by other dreams, then visits from Paulie and his mother, remembrances of the past, hints about the future, like the one about his father getting ready to die. To Bobby, it was no longer a question of if but when—whether Antonio's time on this planet had shrunk to days or hours.

"Your father's going to die?" Deena asked, her voice full of alarm. "Can't you do something?"

"No."

"Why?"

"He's happy; he's made up his mind," Bobby said evenly. "He's done what he could for me. He misses my mom; he misses my brother Paulie."

Bobby studied her, searching for clues and answers to questions. Did she think he was crazy? Did she believe him? Even if she did, was it all too weird for her or anyone else to accept? He sighed. He loved her, no doubt. She deserved a way out.

"Look," he began. "I'll understand if you think, 'Ooh, I'm so sorry. I thought you were Bobby Vincente, not Norman Bates. Stupid desk clerk with her bad hair, worse English, fresh-off-the-boat self. Wrong room, it won't happen again.'"

"Bobby, what're you saying?"

"Just that . . ."

"Just that . . . nothin'," Deena blurted in a tone so fierce she was surprised. In her mind a boat was leaving the dock without her. "I'm not going anywhere."

Sure, it was hard to accept what Bobby was saying, but Deena knew one thing—he didn't lie. A world of ghosts? Why not? She could—and had—done worse.

Deena's response also surprised Bobby, touching him and leaving him—at least for the moment—without words. He leaned over and gently kissed her.

"So, blame Paulie," he said. "I live in two worlds."

"Why not tell him to leave you alone?"

Bobby laughed. No problem, he thought. No sweat and, while you're at it, hey, why not tell cows to stop farting?

"You don't know Paulie," he finally said. "He's my older brother and he takes his role—and himself—very seriously. He'll leave when he's ready."

"Are they nice?"

"Who?"

"The ghosts."

Bobby paused, thinking about the time Paulie and his pals spied on Deena and him when they first got together. He was steamed at the time, less so now. All in all, it was a pretty good story and he'd tell her about it—later.

"Um, they have a sense of humor," he said.

*   *   *

As Deena sat at the kitchen table sipping a fresh cup of coffee, she discovered she was hungry, famished even. The growl in her gut surprised her. Not thirty minutes earlier, she had wanted to stay in bed—for today and maybe for the rest of her life. Only Bobby's time-to-eat declaration—so sudden and out of the blue—and his quick kitchen-bound exit convinced her that nap time was over.

She watched her lover as he worked, deftly flipping an oh-so-light omelet in one pan before sliding smoothly to his right to season pepper, onion, and mushroom slices in another. One more surprise. She'd never slept with a man who cooked. That task was always for someone else—girlfriends, wives, kitchen staff.

Deena was relaxed, content. And it wasn't just the wonderful aromas filling the small kitchen or the sight of the man she loved preparing a meal. Earlier, they'd traded secrets, his ghost stories for one of her own.

"That night with Leonard . . . ," Deena began. She'd felt nervous, tentative at the start.

"Shhhh," Bobby had said. He knew the story, retelling it wasn't necessary.

"How do you know?" she'd asked.

"I saw it, felt it when we made love," he'd replied.

"But how?"

"I don't know, but I know what happened."

Deena was skeptical, at least at first. But then Bobby described it scene by detailed scene. How she'd waited in the club for him to return.

"Why didn't you return?" she asked.

"I knew what he was doing," he said evenly. "I didn't want to kill him."

Then, after the show, Bobby continued, the sly, smooth Leonard said he would hail a cab and take her home. How, once in the cab, he'd suggested a slight change—a brief, hotel room detour. How she'd whispered what the hell and to hell with Bobby—one nightcap won't hurt. How she'd thought she was a big girl and could handle herself. How she'd cried the next morning and wondered if dying would be better.

"Not unless it's your time," Bobby had added, slowly shaking his head.

"To what?"

"To die," he'd replied solemnly. "And we have decades together."

As Deena sat in the kitchen, she smiled as she heard those words in her head—"And we have decades together"—almost forgetting how hungry she was. That changed when Bobby served her breakfast. The omelet was fluffy, perfectly shaped; she could smell the melted cheese, the bacon and caramelized onions. The vegetables glistened hot and flavorful, not overcooked.

"It's lovely, Bobby," she said.

Bobby smiled. "Go ahead, I'll fix myself a plate."

Deena needed no further encouragement as she lifted a fork to her mouth, savoring first the aroma then the taste—a winner on both counts.

"You know, you could do this professionally in a high-end restaurant," Deena said. "I know the money's pretty good." As she spoke, she recalled the many fancy meals in swanky white-linen joints courtesy of suitors seeking to impress. More times than not the food was fine, the men less so.

In those days, she'd played her role to the hilt—the perfect date, the stylishly dressed *accoutrement*. In all those pre-legal years, bartenders and waiters had never asked for proof of her age—another sign that beauty had its perks. For Deena, at least, it was a bucket of laughs, all good fun.

How ironic, Deena thought, to be sitting at the table in day-old panties and tee-shirt in a housing project apartment. She chuckled, wondering for a moment what those who had known her in her high-flying days would think of her now. So what? If given a choice, there'd be no choice: she'd take old panties, a good man, a good meal, and subsidized housing any day.

"Sure, I've thought about that—I heard Central's program's pretty good—so maybe I'll even do it," Bobby said, as he joined her. "But for me, cooking is personal. It's an art and one of the best ways I know to express love."

He paused. "For now, I'll just keep it that way."

Deena smiled.

"I used to cook for Dad," he said softly between mouthfuls. "I think I'm down to one."

"What's that?"

Bobby put down his fork and looked at Deena. "People on this planet that I love," he said.

*   *   *

It was a good day to be young and unemployed. After breakfast, Deena and Bobby just lay around, Bobby taking some of the time to study, but closing the books after an hour. He was now confident, convinced he'd pass the GED. Besides, rereading chapters on this president or that era was starting to bore him.

For her part, Deena relaxed in a hot bath that almost didn't happen. She had put her hand on the faucet then paused, reluctant to lose his scent—that reluctance another first.

With other men, their scents had always been the first to go, washed away at the first opportunity. Back then, she couldn't bathe quickly enough, using the shower or the tub to say, *It was nice, maybe I'll call you later.*

Deena finally turned on the water after reminding herself of the obvious: there would be other times, other chances for Bobby to mark her. Maybe as soon as tonight, she thought, perhaps even sooner if it was left up to her. After an hour— Deena thought it was less—her lovely bath and even lovelier plans for an erotic afternoon were suddenly interrupted.

"May I come in?" Bobby asked from the hall.

Her new man was so unfailingly polite—yes sir, no sir, three bags full sir—and used proper grammar. He loved complete sentences, frowned on contractions and, Deena guessed, even knew when to use "who" and "whom." She smiled; she would have to get used to it.

"Of course, Honey," she said, as he opened the door and stepped inside.

To her disappointment, Bobby was dressed—jeans, tee-shirt, tennis shoes—and, Deena figured, not headed for the bedroom anytime soon. "It's sunny outside, maybe it's a good time to go for a walk," he said.

"To where?" she asked, trying her best to sound chipper.

"Oh, I figured we'd go on a little tour."

"Of what?"

"My world," he said.

*   *   *

Eventually, Bobby and Deena found themselves seated on a bench on the waterfront. It was such a glorious day, such a stunning view of snow-capped mountains and sea that Deena forgot, if just for a moment, where she would much rather be.

"It's gorgeous," she said as she snuggled against Bobby seeking warmth against a breeze that had suddenly picked up. "I didn't realize it until today."

"Yes, it is," he said quietly. "I always thought this was a special place. I think that maybe the natives must have prayed here. It makes sense."

Bobby pointed to a nearby pier. "Paulie and I used to fish on that dock when we were kids," he said quietly. "I came here after Mom and Paulie died."

Bobby paused and took a deep breath. "And I came here when I thought it was over between you and me."

"Why?"

"To say a prayer."

"What did you pray for?" she asked.

"That you be well, that you be happy."

"That's it? Nothing more?"

"No, nothing more," he replied, as he gazed at the Olympics. One of these days, he promised himself, he would go there, stand at the base of the tallest peak and stare straight up.

"Why?"

"It wouldn't have been a prayer of love. Maybe one of need, my need, but not love," he replied. "Honey, they're just not the same."

Deena was amazed. Sure, she'd heard it before, but fully accepting his high-sounding definition was something else. Now she knew and she knew as well why, at the center of his soul, he was so different—and why she loved him so. He was such an innocent, already canonized or at least beatified.

Phew, she thought, a saint who loved sex, or at least was very good at it. Thank God for that. And she loved him, too. Okay, so maybe her love wasn't love at its purest, but it surely was the best she could ever have imagined herself giving. By her standards, she was doing pretty darn well. Deena smiled, wondering how she'd look in a halo.

"It was hard," Bobby continued.

"What?"

"Not praying that you come back to me," he said, as he closed his eyes.

Deena was relieved. Her saint was human after all. "What are you doing now?" she asked.

He smiled. "I'm just saying thanks that you came back to me," he said.

* * *

Bobby and Deena were heading home, walking arm in arm along the waterfront, not saying much, not having to. Bobby's head was slightly bowed. Deena wondered if he was still praying.

"Hi Bishop, hi Paulie," Bobby mumbled, as they walked by a vacant warehouse. A few steps earlier, he'd heard the strike of a match and, glancing up, noticed the vague outline of two human forms standing by the old building's padlocked door. The giveaway was the lit end of a cigar, seemingly suspended about where Paulie's mouth would be.

Deena, surprised, looked around. The closest pedestrian was at least a block away.

She pulled on his arm. "Honey, there's no one here," she said.

"Oh that's right, I'm sorry," he said sheepishly, as they continued walking.

Deena sighed. This world of ghosts thing would take awhile for her to get used to. Still, she was willing to accept what he said was real at face value.

"Who's this bishop?" she asked. By then, they were standing on the corner next to the ferry terminal, waiting for the light to change.

"Polycarp," he said, as they walked onto the street. "He's my brother's best friend."

"Well, that sure says a lot."

"Actually, I did a little research," he said, as they reached the other side. "He was the bishop of Smyrna and an early martyr of the Church."

"And he and Paulie are friends?"

Bobby shrugged. "Sure, why not?" he replied. "My brother admires courage and old Polycarp was a very brave man. Plus, there's the name thing, Poly and Paulie. So, tell me, what are the odds on that?"

"I guess," she said.

"Believe it or not, he does have a sense of humor," Bobby continued. "It may be odd, sometimes offensive and completely unacceptable, but it's still there."

Bobby paused, the corners of his mouth turning ever-so-slightly upward. "You'll get used to it," he said. "I did."

They continued walking, soon passing under the viaduct, the massive concrete throughway, where the unbroken roar from speeding cars and the thump-kathump-thump of interstate trucks made conversation impossible. The absence of chatter gave Deena time to think.

How did Bobby become the way he was? Good parents, maybe even great ones—that had to count. But then Paulie had the same mother and father—and he was so different. According to Bobby, his brother gloried in violence and his bloody reputation as a chest-pounding brute.

Maybe it was the parish school. Earlier in the day, she and Bobby had stopped by St. James. Morning mass was over and several youngsters had suddenly appeared to reclaim their turf from scores of car-parking parishioners. As children everywhere do, they flew around the yard; they screamed, they laughed, they threw balls. Bobby was smiling, maybe remembering himself at that age on this playground.

He'd pointed to several black, brown, and mixed-race youngsters. "Some of them are from the projects," he'd told her. "If they make it through here, they'll at least have a chance."

The frenetic activity had lured one of the nuns to the yard; she was in a far corner refereeing a fast-moving game of dodge ball. Bobby blinked; she looked familiar.

"Time out," the nun suddenly shrieked, after the ball had hit a red-headed boy in the face, stunning him and knocking him to the ground. She bent over and gently tended to the child, whose lack of coordination and quickness strongly suggested that he try another activity.

"Sister Victor," Bobby had whispered, his voice tinged with awe, affection, and not a little fear. He was her favorite student, he explained, an attentive, polite audience to her endless warnings on the evils of premarital sex. Sister was heartbroken when Bobby had dropped out of St. James. She'd even called the apartment, begging Eula and Antonio to please let Bobby stay—to no avail.

To Deena, Bobby had seemed wistful in the telling, seemingly lost in thought, like he'd wished Sister Victor had carried the day. "Better go," he'd suddenly said, nodding at the nun, now standing and looking in their direction.

"Why?"

"You don't understand," he'd explained. "That's Sister Victor. She'll want to know when we got married."

"Marriage," Deena thought, as they reached First Avenue and turned right toward Yesler. How ironic. She used to think it was for suckers and chumps—the weak. But that was then. Now, if it happened to her—to her and Bobby, to be exact— she wouldn't object.

They continued walking, mostly in silence, Deena concluding that Bobby wasn't much for words, at least not the chit-chat kind. At First and Cherry, they stopped, with Bobby suddenly veering toward the boxing gym entrance.

"I just want to talk to Mariano," he explained. "Come with me. We won't be too long."

Inside the still-empty gym, the old trainer was sitting on the shop-worn sofa, reading the sports section and casually smoking a cigarette. As always, he was impeccably dressed, right down to the spit-polish shine of his brown wingtips.

"Hoy, Manong," Bobby said.

Mariano lowered the newspaper and smiled broadly as he recognized his latest protégé. He glanced at Deena; she looked familiar. His eyes narrowed. A looker, he thought, bad news, a potential roadblock to his fighter's—and his own—aspirations. That's what happened to another of his boys, Marcus, a top-notch prospect he'd trained for over a year. After a string of wins, he'd found a doe-eyed, caramel-colored, sweet and sweet-talking girl who'd found the Lord, with Jesus telling him through her that boxing was the devil's work. So he hung up the gloves, picked up the Bible, and started spreading the Word in the south end of town.

Mariano shuddered at the memory. Losing Marcus had been tough, tougher than losing girlfriends and even spouses. He then straightened his tie and cleared his throat, all the while hoping that this girl wasn't religious.

"Hoy, Bobby, you gonna train today?" Mariano asked.

"No, Manong," Bobby replied. "I'm getting ready for a test Tuesday at school, but I promise I'll be back after that. I'll be ready to go." Bobby paused. "Oh, and this is Deena."

"Nice to meet you," Mariano said, as he tried to smile and to sound polite.

Deena wasn't buying. "Nice to meet you," she mumbled, as she squeezed Bobby's arm. Boxing, she thought, was such a strange world. A few of her ex-boyfriends' wives had been less hostile to her than this old coot.

"Actually, Manong," Bobby said, as he slid onto the couch. Three, Deena figured, was a crowd; she remained standing. "I want you to tell me about Dad."

"Whatcha mean?"

"Oh, how he was as a fighter," he said. "You saw him in his prime, right?"

The old man closed his eyes and nodded. "Oh, lotsa times," he said softly. "Lotsa times."

"And?"

"Ah, lemme see," Mariano began. "He always go right at the guy and hit 'im hard, no matter the guy hit 'im back. Antonio win lotsa fights that way. Crowds always cheer 'im. He was an action guy, a headliner, tough, strong with lotsa heart."

Mariano paused, as if reluctant to move too soon from a string of faded, cherished memories, this day's unexpected treat. For a man his age, he knew there weren't many treats left.

"Those were good days, Bobby," he finally said.

Bobby smiled, then surveyed the gym, pinpointing the chair where his father had sat and watched him box.

"I know," Bobby said.

"How's Antonio?"

Bobby looked away and bit his lip. "Okay," he said, unable to say anything more.

"Tell 'im hello for me," Mariano said.

Bobby nodded but said nothing.

Mariano then pointed a gnarled index finger at his fighter. "You got heart, same as Antonio. Talent, too," he said. "Your talent's jus' so different from your dad. By gosh, sometimes is hard to believe how you fight, not at all like father and son."

Bobby smiled, stood up and shook the old man's hand. "Thank you for your confidence, Manong."

"Jus' tellin' the truth," Mariano said, as he raised the paper and resumed reading the sports section. He fished in his jacket pocket for a cigarette.

"I been aroun' a lotta fighters," he said, as he clicked his lighter. "And you could be good, a real good one."

"Thanks, and oh, by the way, I think it's easy to believe."

"Wha's that?"

"That we're father and son," Bobby said, as he and Deena turned and walked away.

"Where to now?" she asked, as they stepped onto First Avenue.

They were soon standing on the corner, waiting for the light to change. "We go Chinatown," Bobby said, imitating the way old Pinoys talked. "Noodles and barbecue pork, Honey. Oh so good, my gosh, the bes'."

*   *   *

For Bobby, noodles and pork were just one of the reasons to go to King Street, the heart of Chinatown. He loved this neighborhood. It was a place full of memories, especially those of Dad and Mom taking Paulie and him to eat at different cafes or to visit old friends in their hot-plate rooms. He loved the sights, sounds, and smells—even the stench of the live chicken shop up the street.

Deena marveled as Bobby would walk a few yards up King, then stop in front of a pool room, a barbershop, a residential hotel—wherever old Pinoys gathered—to say hi and shoot the breeze.

Deena could see that he was enjoying himself—and showing her another corner, an important corner, of his world. At each destination, he would introduce her to Manong so-and-so. "He and Dad are from the same village." "He and Dad worked in the same cannery." The oldtimers would politely tip their fedoras or caps, nod approvingly, and say "please to meet you," then fill in the blank—"Dinah," "Deena," "Miss," "Honey," "Baby," "Sweetheart" and "oh, you beautiful, beautiful girl."

At each stop Bobby also made sure to ask if his father had been here. And inevitably someone would say, *yeah, sure, just the other day at the gambling joint. Antonio was with Magno. Your dad was playing cards, but losing big.*

But how did he seem? Bobby would ask. *What do you mean?* Was he happy? *Oh yeah, smiling, plenty happy for someone losing a lot of money. I don't get it.*

I get it, Bobby thought, as he sighed and squeezed Deena's hand. By mid-block, he had confirmation; the dream had been accurate. The only piece missing was how, when, and where his father had died.

"What're you thinking?" Deena asked.

Bobby looked at Deena and forced a smile. "That we're here," he said, pointing to a drab-looking restaurant across the street. A handful of steps and less than a minute later, they were seated in a booth, menus in hand.

Deena had never been here before. She squirmed and glanced around at the grungy surroundings, closing her eyes and feeling the grime seep into her pores.

"Okay," Bobby said, without looking up, "never mind the décor—the peeling wallpaper, the scuffed and dirty formica floor, the sticky tables with ancient mounds of discarded gum underneath—and, while you're at it, try to ignore the cigarette plume wafting from the crowded counter. The same goes for the occasional scurrying bug."

"You're spooky," she said.

Bobby lowered the menu and shrugged. The bottom line, he said, was that all the Pinoys he knew loved this joint. Just look at who was sitting at the counter—all Filipinos, not an empty seat.

"The food's always cheap," he explained. "And, if you get the right cook and know how to order, it's also pretty good."

"Hi, Bobby," said their waiter, a boyish young immigrant from Hong Kong.

"Hi, Slim," he replied, as he looked up. Of course, it wasn't his real name—the real one, in all likelihood, was a Cantonese tongue-twister he and other Filipinos and anyone who wasn't Chinese couldn't pronounce.

But two years ago, he'd heard one of the other customers call him that and, for Bobby, he's been "Slim" ever since.

Slim didn't mind because one evening he and Paulie had taken care of some boorish, out-of-town customers who were amusing themselves by calling poor Slim *ching-chong Chinaman* names. Paulie, of course, had started the brawl and did most of the fighting, but Bobby had pitched in by breaking a plate over a fellow who lacked the sense to stay down.

Slim never forgot that. When Paulie was buried, he was at the funeral. He cried, and he stayed 'til the end.

"The usual?" Slim asked, without bothering to take out a pen to write down the order.

"Sure," Bobby replied. "Is Sam cooking today?" Sam—also not his real name—was Slim's older brother.

"Yes."

Bobby smiled a just hit-the-jackpot smile. "In that case, I want something off the Chinese menu, none of this fried rice, chop suey, sweet and sour, tourist stuff."

He paused and winked at Deena. "I have a date to impress. You know how these high-class private-school girls are."

Deena stuck out her tongue. "I'm more than a date," she hissed.

Slim laughed. "Sure, no problem. Sam, he'll take care of you. What're you thinking?"

"Sea bass," Bobby said. "Is it fresh?"

"This morning."

"Whole?"

"Yes."

"In that case, my friend," Bobby began, "a whole steamed bass in oyster sauce, please. And tell your brother it's for me."

"Nice pick," Slim said approvingly, before turning and walking to the kitchen.

Bobby then took a deep breath and leaned back, lacing his fingers behind his head. He was clearly delighted, seeming already to savor the meal.

*   *   *

Dinner was even better than Bobby had expected, the proof being the suspension of conversation after the first bite. For her part, Deena deftly darted her fork among the dishes, each mouthful joined to a satisfying "mmm." At the end, only two fish eyes were left.

"Watch," Bobby said. He then extended his fork, poked out an eye and popped it in his mouth.

"Not bad," he said, as Deena scrunched up her nose and made a face. One eye to go, but Deena beat him to it before he could move.

"You're right, not too bad at all." She then put down her fork, rubbed her belly and, Bobby thought, looked pleased enough to purr. Before today, she hadn't given much thought to food, or specifically, food as both art form and symbol of love. But here it was—a spectacular breakfast and spectacular dinner—gifts of love from Bobby to her and from Slim and Sam to Bobby.

For some reason, Deena had felt famished all day. A one-day quirk or the start of something new? She didn't know. What she did know was that the young man seated across the table loved her; she hoped he loved her fat.

Deena burped, then blushed. "Excuse me," she said.

Bobby chuckled. "Must've been the eye," he said, as he rose and started walking to the rear of the restaurant. "Bathroom stop. I'll be right back."

He would have, too, but for a slurred "Hoy, Bobby" coming from the last booth. He turned toward the speaker, Manong Magno, who was cuddled next to a busty, boa-wearing, forty-something white woman, currently a blonde.

Bobby slid onto the bench facing them. Both were four of the required three sheets to the wind.

"This is Lulu," Magno said. "She's my, ah . . . , Sweetheart, what are you anyway?"

Lulu smiled. "Girlfriend, Honey."

He laughed. "Tha's right, she's . . ."

Bobby, normally the politest of souls, cut right to the point. "My dad, where is he?"

"Gonna be my wife," Magno said, completing his sentence. He chuckled as he turned to Lulu and kissed her on the cheek. "Yeah, we decide that today, didn't we, Sweetheart?"

"Magno," Bobby said sharply. "My father, where is he?"

"Antonio?"

"Yesss," Bobby said, trying hard to stay calm.

"Oh, yesterday we gamble, then after that we go for a ride," the old man began.

"And then?"

"I drop 'im off," Magno said, before reaching into his jacket pocket to pull out a flask.

"Where?"

"North Bend, South Bend, oh, I dunno, one of those Bends," he said, as he took a swig then passed the flask to Lulu. "Save some for the boy."

"Sure, Honey."

"That's okay," Bobby said. "Ah, no, no thank you."

"He says he has a date," he added, too drunk to see—or to grasp—the impact of his words.

Bobby's shoulders sagged and he lowered his head. "Thanks, Manong," he mumbled, as he started to rise.

"Oh, one other thing, Bobby," Magno said. "Your dad says you should go to his closet. He's got a red shoe box. He make me promise I tell you."

"Ooh, new shoes," Lulu said. "Lucky boy. I need some new shoes. Honey, you can take care of that, won't you?"

"Oh, Sweetheart, don' worry, I'll get you some tomorrow, first class all the way," Magno said, as Bobby, unnoticed, turned and walked quietly to his booth.

*　　*　　*

At first, the brisk night breeze was a welcome change from the dead, smoke-filled air of the restaurant. But not a block later, the wind picked up, causing Deena to shiver and Bobby to raise his collar and bury himself in his jacket. Arm in arm they walked, wordless, just as before. But for Deena, this time seemed different. She hadn't seen him enter Magno's booth, but when he emerged he looked different—pale and withdrawn.

They stopped at the corner of Jackson and Sixth, waiting for the light. There, Deena nudged his arm with her nose. Bobby turned and kissed her gently on the cheek.

"He's gone," Bobby said quietly. "Back in the restaurant, I saw Manong Magno. He was with Dad."

"Did he say how he died?"

Bobby shook his head. "No, he didn't have to. What he talked about I saw in my dream," he said, as the light changed and traffic stopped. They stepped onto the street. "Right down to the last detail," he added glumly, then paused. "I guess there's a difference between knowing something and *really* knowing something."

Chapter Fourteen

That night, Bobby knew he would dream and had told Deena that if he started to talk or thrash about, don't wake him, please. Let the dream run its course, he'd said. It's the family's way of reaching him, the last son, the last one standing.

And don't be afraid, he'd added, trying his best to reassure her. It's just a dream.

Sure, sure, Deena had said, as she stripped off her clothes and hopped into bed. He then turned off the light and wrapped his arms around her waist. Don't be afraid, he'd repeated.

She wasn't, she'd said. But a shiver—almost imperceptible— told him otherwise.

The main feature started within minutes of Bobby closing his eyes. At first, he was surprised. His father was nowhere in sight.

It was just him at eight, maybe nine, standing in the living room with the television on. His pants were sopping wet, his cheeks bright red. Paulie was in the hall, laughing hysterically, calling him hurtful names he didn't want to hear.

In the dream, Bobby then dashed to his room and grabbed some clean clothes before hurrying to the bathroom for a quick shower and change. He was driven, a boy on a mission.

It was early Saturday afternoon. Confessions at St. James started at two, or in about thirty minutes. If he hurried, he could be the first one in line.

*　*　*

Inside the confessional, Bobby was about to report the heart of the matter. He closed his eyes, took a deep breath and braced himself. "Father, I think I did something bad, maybe a mortal sin," he said in a small voice.

"And so, my son, wha's that?"

Odd, Bobby thought. He sounded different from the regular priests—more like Dad and the other old Pinoys.

"Father, are you from the Philippines?" Bobby asked. "My father's Filipino."

The priest laughed. "Why yes, I'm visiting from Cebu City. I run an orphanage. But enough about me; tell me your sin."

Bobby hesitated, embarrassed by his act. "Father, I, ah . . ."

"Go on, my son," the priest urged. "Remember you're a child of God and He's always willing to forgive his children."

Bobby had always liked confession, especially the sense of relief he had when walking out of church. Absolution was insurance against a premature death—a safeguard strong enough to keep the fires of purgatory and even hell indefinitely at bay. All of that for three Hail Marys and two Our Fathers—a painless penance, not a bad deal, Bobby thought.

But the earlier sins he'd confessed were ordinary offenses—an occasional lie, an unkind thought or word. Today was different.

"I played with myself," Bobby managed to blurt.

The priest, at first, didn't respond.

Bobby tried hard not to panic. "Father, is that a sin? Is it a mortal sin?"

"That depends," the priest said, his tone now more serious.

"Father?"

"What's your name, my son?"

Bobby was surprised and slightly uncomfortable; no confessor had ever asked his name before. Maybe it's how they did it in the islands. Still, the inquiry must be for his own spiritual good. "Bobby," he finally said.

"Well, Bobby, the question of whether or not you committed a sin depends."

"On what, Father?"

"On whether you touched yourself in the presence of someone you love."

"Father, I'm not sure what you mean."

"God loves you, He also loves me," the priest began. "He commands us all to love each other. Tha's why I love you." He paused. "Do you love me?"

"I guess," he replied, unsure what the priest was getting at.

"Bobby, do you love me?"

"Yes, Father, I do, I do," he said.

"Good, now is there anyone else in the church besides us?"

"No, Father."

"Ah, tha's very good, my son," the priest said, as his breathing quickened. "So very, very good. My name is Father Veronico, but since we're friends, please call me 'Father Ronnie.' I prefer it that way."

*   *   *

Next in the dream came a series of scenes, more slide-show images than film: of Bobby and Veronico walking together and holding hands; of Bobby and the priest together in the chapel, kneeling before the altar in prayer; of Bobby removing his shirt while Veronico, smiling, looked on.

But for Eula's watchful eye, Bobby's ordeal would have gone on longer than a handful of days. In the dream, she was standing on the edge of the St. James campus, waiting to pick up her son. When he appeared, he was walking with a priest, judging by his cassock, with his arm draped around Bobby's shoulder. It struck her as odd. Most of the priests she knew— Father Williams, Father Marsh, Father Norris, and one or two others—kept their distance from children, perhaps guarding their authority against unnecessary chumminess.

He was also such a tiny fellow, not much taller than her boy. When Bobby noticed his mother, he began waving excitedly, hoping to draw her attention, while tugging on Veronico's sleeve.

"It's my mom, Father Ronnie," Bobby exclaimed. "I want you to meet her."

"Perhaps tomorrow, Bobby," Veronico replied, as he freed his arm and patted the boy on the head. He then waved at Eula and turned toward the school.

"I have so much work to do," Veronico explained.

Eula waited as Bobby raced toward her and, as he always did, stopped suddenly and gave her a big hug.

"Who's that?" Eula asked.

"Oh, that's my friend, Father Ronnie," he replied.

"Is that his last name?"

"No, it's his first."

Another oddity, Eula thought. She'd always addressed priests as "Father," then added the last name.

Bobby grabbed his mother's hand and pulled her toward home. Cartoons, he knew, would be starting in half an hour and he didn't want to be late.

"'Father Ronnie,'" Bobby explained. "It's what the kids in the orphanage call him in the Philippines."

*   *   *

As Bobby was staring at Bugs and his pals, Eula was staring at Bobby. Just a few minutes earlier, her son had removed half of his uniform—sweater and starched white shirt—before plopping down not six inches from the television screen.

"Move back, Bobby," Eula said from the hall. "Bein' that close is bad for your eyes."

The boy moved a little but not much—a half inch at best. Eula sighed. It was like this every day after school. She walked into the living room and stood next to her son.

"Scoot back, Mister," she said. This time the distance was more than six inches. "More," she said. "More," she continued to repeat until Bobby was at the foot of the sofa across the room. All the while, his eyes stayed glued to the television screen.

"Good boy," Eula said.

As she leaned to pat his head, she noticed for the first time a dark splotch at the base of his neck. She knew immediately what it was, having received her fair share of love bites and nibbles in her heyday. She blinked and looked again, staring at the discoloration in the afternoon light. No, she thought, it can't be. He's too young, too innocent, not interested in girls.

Eula gasped, as she thought the unthinkable and her heart started to race. Maybe it was a sign of something malignant, an incurable cancer perhaps. For her, a life without Bobby meant no life at all. Somehow, she managed to calm herself.

"Bobby," Eula said, trying to sound calm. She wiped the moisture from her palms on the sides of her dress.

"Yes, Mom," he responded, without looking up.

"What's that on your neck?" she asked, as she gently touched the spot.

"Oh, Mom, it's nothing," he said.

"How did you get it?" she asked, her voice still calm as her palms again became clammy.

"I can't say," he replied. He was still more interested in Bugs than this conversation.

"Why?"

This time Bobby turned toward his mother, his right index finger touching his lips. "Shhh, it's a secret," he said, before turning back toward the television screen. Just in time, too. Something Bugs had done had caught his fancy and he giggled with delight.

"How did it happen then?"

Bobby turned again toward his mother. "I can't say. It's a secret," he said. "If I tell, Father Ronnie won't be my friend."

Eula just stood there, stunned at first, then furious, imagining how she would track down that little creep and dismember him. She understood better than anyone that Bobby was sensitive and very fragile. Unlike Paulie, he was also extremely naive, her overprotected child. He may even be unaware that he'd even been victimized. Maybe he thought it was a game? She certainly hoped so; in the future, that trait—his innocence—might save him a lot of sorrow.

Eula then took a deep breath, instinctively knowing that her best course for now was to play it down, play along and pretend the secret had been kept.

"Okay, Honey, I won't ask anymore, I promise," she finally said. "You did a really good job of keeping the secret."

"Thanks, Mom," he said, pleased with himself. He wondered what the always resourceful Bugs would do next.

*   *   *

Any doubts about what had happened to Bobby were erased later that day when he was in the bath tub and Eula, as she always did, brought him clean underwear and his pajamas. This time, though, she sat on the edge of the tub as the boy laughed, splashed water, and played with his plastic boat and other toys.

Hers was a heart-wrenching task. Eula was looking for and finding similar marks all over his body—near his nipples and on his belly, back and upper chest. She stifled an urge to vomit.

Eula suddenly rose and left, not wanting to search any further. In the hallway, Antonio was peering through a crack in the door, seeing what his wife saw. As she—tears streaming down her face—passed her husband, he grabbed her by the arm.

"I'll fix that sonamabits tomorrow," he snarled, sliding the edge of his hand swiftly across his throat.

*   *   *

The plan to kill Father Ronnie was carried out the next day. It started with a late-afternoon phone call to the parish rectory. Eula had planned to use an alias, just in case the receptionist or another priest answered. Instead, Veronico picked up the phone.

"Halooo," he said, in a thick Filipino accent.

Eula, who couldn't believe her luck, got right to the point.

"Father Veronico?" she asked.

"Yes."

"I know what you did to my boy," she began. "You a dead man."

The object, of course, was to flush him out—a goal achieved not fifteen minutes later when Veronico walked out of the rectory, suitcase in hand. He glanced around nervously before heading west, toward downtown, intending to catch a Greyhound or board a train.

Two blocks away, Veronico began feeling better about his chances. He even started humming a show tune and moving his head side to side. This was soon followed by a dance step or two.

Sure, he felt bad about Bobby and might even miss him, but this was the first time anyone had threatened him over his preference for young, hairless boys. Who could blame him? They were so perfect, he thought, like Sistene Chapel cherubs.

In Cebu, church officials had heard disturbing rumors; they tsk-tsked, then counseled him and heard his confession—but otherwise did nothing more. Of course, family members of the children at the orphanage had no say in the matter. The kids were orphans, for goodness sake, abandoned collectibles, like baseballs that flew out of the park.

He stopped at the corner, took a deep breath and smiled, reveling in the beauty of the late afternoon sun and his own good fortune. Sure, he'd miss Seattle—just look at those snow-capped peaks and that shimmering bay. But home is where his heart now was—and it would be safer, too.

Oh well, he told himself, at least he had some time left. Before going back to Cebu, he thought he might ride the bus or train all the way to Disneyland, where he imagined cute and young, sun-kissed boys growing on palm trees.

He was so entranced by this happy moment and his future plans, he wasn't aware that a black Mercury had crept up behind him, that a door was quietly opening, that a dark, fierce-looking man was about to jump out.

* * *

In a sense, Veronico was lucky: it took him less than two minutes to die. Antonio had knocked the priest out with a straight right hand to the temple, before dragging his limp body to the car. In the back seat, he hit him twice between the eyes for good measure, then wrapped his hands around his throat, listening closely for pops and gurgles, strangling what little life remained out of him.

All the while, Magno was driving and trying his best to look casual, trying not to attract attention. He turned on the radio and cracked the window just a little. Although he was trying to cut back on smokes, he lit one up anyway. For Magno, smoking and listening to music while cruising around in a huge V-8 looked and sounded normal.

"You done?" Magno asked, as they came to a stop sign. He snuffed out the cigarette in the ash tray.

"Yes," Antonio replied. "Anyone watching?"

"No."

"Good," Antonio said, as clambered over the front seat, settled in and wiped his brow.

"Where should we go now?"

"Oh, I dunno, mebbe out in the country," Antonio said. "Find some woods, dig a hole, dump 'im there."

Magno smiled as he turned right on Rainier Avenue heading south toward Renton and home. "I got a better idea," he said. "Mebbe we go to my place."

"The farm?"

"Sure," Magno answered.

"You wanna bury 'im on your farm."

"Not bury, compadre."

"Then what?"

Magno laughed. "Pigs," he said. "They're big ones, real mean and always hungry."

* * *

For the sake of appearances, Eula and Antonio allowed Bobby to continue at St. James until the end of the term. To the priests and nuns, Veronico had seemed to vanish into thin air. One of the priests had filed a missing person's report, but without any sign of foul play or a body, there wasn't much the cops could do.

Then, with the coast seemingly clear, Eula and Antonio pulled Bobby out and sent him to the public school his brother was already attending. Can't afford it, Eula explained to Sister Victor, who didn't take the news well.

Eula, who knew how much her son loved St. James, almost wavered. But in the end, she held firm, remembering the pain Veronico had caused. What if there were others—monsters and devils masquerading in black and white? She couldn't—wouldn't—take the chance. At least this way, Paulie would always be able to keep an eye on his gullible brother.

When Eula broke the news to Bobby, he at first resisted, pouting and telling her he'd miss his friends and the nuns and priests and that public school kids were like Paulie—too rough.

Eula then folded her arms and glared at her son. "Can't afford it no more, Mister," she said seriously. "That's the end of this conversation."

Bobby knew better than to mess with his mother when she got that way. "Okay, Mom," he said meekly.

"Oh, by the way," she added, making sure her tone was casual. "Remember that little secret you'd had with your friend, Father Ronnie? I heard that he'd gotten suddenly homesick and went back to the Philippines." She also recalled that he and the good priest had a little secret and here's what he should do to always protect it.

Bobby looked up. "What?" he asked.

"You should close your eyes and forget whatever happened that you ain't supposed to talk about," she said. "My mom taught me this when I was your age."

"Oh, okay," he said, as he dutifully closed his eyes. "Why?"

Eula smiled and looked lovingly at her son. "Honey, you can't never break a secret you can't even remember." As she gazed at Bobby with his eyes still closed, she blinked, then blinked again at a tingle in her spine. She could have sworn she felt him start to forget.

* * *

"My, that was rather severe," Polycarp said, wincing at the memory of what he'd just seen. "Oh, and what happened on that farm, it was so ghastly."

"I know," Paulie said casually, as he lit a cigar. They were standing by the wall in Bobby's darkened bedroom. "Damn, my last stogie. Gotta find me some more dead Cubans." He paused. "Hey, Poly, you know if Fidel killed anyone lately?"

The old bishop shrugged. "So, why did you show it to the boy?"

"Dad," he said, as he leaned back and blew several O-rings. He smiled as he watched them float upward then disappear.

"Your father?"

"Yeah, sure," Paulie replied. "He wanted Bobby to know everything, good and bad, the entire picture, dig? Mom and him, knowing he was such a weak little chump, tried to protect 'im by always hidin' shit. But all that did was make 'im confused and an even bigger chump. Dad figured he's man enough now to handle it."

"And that priest, what happened to him?"

Paulie chuckled. "Oh, the little freak's around here somewhere, but I know one thing," he said.

"And what's that?"

"He ain't gonna be nowhere near Antonio," Paulie replied, before repeatedly poking the air with an index finger. "Ooh, ooh, make that two things."

"What's the second one?"

"He won't be eatin' bacon with his eggs," Paulie said, in his best deadpan voice. "Anyways, not any time soon."

Paulie glanced at his friend, hoping he'd get the joke. As usual, he didn't. It might be an age or language or culture gap. Was comedy big in Smyrna? Maybe it was his delivery?

"I don't see why," the old bishop began.

"Never mind, Poly," Paulie said, as he began walking away. "Man, you a tough audience."

"Pardon me?"

"Never mind."

"Where are you going?" the bishop asked.

"I'm goin' on a mission," he explained. "I did what I was asked. Finished. Done. Now, I gotta go find me some dead Cubans."

The two friends left the room, unaware that only one of the bed's occupants was asleep. Deena had been awakened by the aroma of cigar smoke. A Bolivar, she'd correctly guessed, the same swanky brand her abusive cop lover favored. She froze at first, figuring that somehow he'd tracked her here, intent on reclaiming what he thought was his.

She'd quickly concluded that wasn't so after sneaking a peek above the covers, her eyes slowly adjusting to see what looked like the lit end of cigar floating through the darkness. She then closed her eyes and moved closer to Bobby. Something was going on. Whatever it was, she wasn't sure whether she should welcome it or be frightened out of her mind.

Chapter Fifteen

Deena had never been an early-morning girl. But today, dawn couldn't come soon enough.

The early rays of sunlight allowed her to sit up and scan the room, making sure whatever or whoever had been here was no longer present. She had thought about turning on the lamp but decided against it, reasoning that if what she saw was real—and not some mind-twisting mirage—whoever or whatever it was might become irritated enough to do her harm.

So, for several hours, Deena had cowered under the covers, hugging Bobby and reciting barely remembered prayers over and over. She had taken great care not to breathe too heavily, chatter too loudly, or make some other ghost-attracting sound.

Eventually, she told herself, she would get used to it. She'd have to; this was her man's strange world. But making it all seem as normal as buying a bottle of milk at the neighborhood IGA was for later, maybe much later. For now, all she felt was relief. Dawn had come and she'd made it through the night.

Deena then turned toward Bobby. During the night, she had heard him mumble and felt him toss about. As she gazed at him, she wondered how he'd fared. Deena didn't have to wait long for an answer.

"Man," he mumbled, as he started to stir.

"Honey," she said, as she gently stroked his hair.

Bobby opened his eyes and sat up, drawing his knees in and wrapping his arms around them.

"Want to talk about it?" she asked softly.

He smiled and kissed her, then took a deep breath, exhaling through his mouth. "Wow," he said, shaking his head slowly. "That was some dream. It was good, though, cleared me out."

"Why?"

"It answered a lot of questions," he replied. "It filled in a lot of gaps I'd thought about but couldn't figure out, like this funny little man I'd dreamed about earlier."

"What happened?"

"Well," he said slowly. "For starters, Dad killed him."

"In the war?" she asked.

"No, right here in Seattle," he said calmly.

Deena knew she loved Bobby, felt it in every corner and crevice of her heart. But his answer—that her lover's father had murdered another human being—unnerved her, shooting an unexpected shiver up her spine. The soles of her feet dampened ever so slightly.

Like father, like son? Was homicide a genetic trait? It was too late to wonder about that now.

"Who?" she finally asked.

"A priest named Father Veronico," Bobby said, his face impassive.

He then started describing in graphic detail what he'd seen in the dream from beginning 'til end. He spoke throughout in a "just-the-facts" monotone, offering no hint of what he was thinking or, more importantly, feeling.

"And the pigs, they . . . ," she began, the horror of the image making her sputter, then rendering her speechless. At this moment, she wanted him to feel the revulsion that she felt.

Bobby, though, was revulsion-free. "Yes," he said evenly. "Right there on Manong Magno's farm."

"Magno, Magno, wasn't he . . ."

"Yes," Bobby said, interrupting her. "He was the old man in the restaurant."

Deena, a pained look on her face, started to squirm. Bobby's casual demeanor in reciting such gruesome details was getting to her. If she had been watching, she would have seen Bobby's face relax, this time in the form of the tiniest of smiles.

"It kind of makes you rethink your views," he said.

Okay, she thought, now he's finally serious. Boy, it's about time.

"On Porky Pig, for example," he said drolly.

"Bobby," she scolded.

"Now, I'm wondering what he does outside the studio."

"Bobby!" she screamed, and turned away.

For a moment, he'd thought about not saying what he'd said. But the Porky Pig joke was too funny, the timing too good to resist. Now he had to focus on soothing the feelings bruised by this blowout, disagreement, or whatever other couples called it.

He was new at making up. Maybe—or maybe not—he should start with a kiss.

A semblance of harmony was eventually restored, but only after several minutes of Deena's cold-staring, arms-folded silence and a bucket full of Bobby's kisses and murmured apologies. Even then, they were walking gingerly on an emotional surface covered by black ice.

"Well, how do you feel?" she finally asked, realizing immediately it was a lame, open-ended question; it was also the only one she could think of at the moment. His response was almost predictable.

"About what?" he answered quietly, which she took to mean, *Ask another question, silly white girl, with your trust fund*

parachute and your uptown sensibilities. If the plane goes down,
you can always jump out and pull the cord.

"About your father, about what he did," she blurted.

He took a deep breath. "Dad did. Mom did, too," he
quietly began. "Knowing what happened doesn't change at all
what I feel about them. My parents were trying to protect me.
They did what they believed they had to do."

"Wasn't there another way?"

Sure, Bobby thought. Don't feed the pigs, pretend it didn't
happen, let the white cops pretend they care about a one-drop-
of-blood black boy and whatever-else-he-is projects' kid, get on
your knees and pray to Jesus, just look the other way and let
the little freak go free. This time, though, he kept his thoughts
to himself.

"Maybe," he finally said, as he searched for the right
words, at first not wanting to shake Deena more than she had
already been shaken. He sighed—but truth is truth. He had to
tell her.

"I guess I look at it this way," he began. "If something like
that should ever happen to our child, I would probably do the
same thing."

Deena heard all the words, the violent message, the somber
tone. Perhaps she should have been more troubled—Bobby
had never shown her this darker, more dangerous side. This
time, though, she wasn't.

Our child, she thought, focusing on the term. Funny, she'd
been thinking that way, too.

"My parents, Paulie," Bobby continued, "they were all in
their own way very fierce people. Actually, a lot of folks who
live here are like that. Life is a struggle; we adapt."

"It seems so," she said, gently touching his hand.

"I used to think, maybe even hoped, I was different from the others in my family, especially Paulie," he said softly. "Maybe I'm more like them than I know."

"And maybe that's not such a bad thing," she said, as she pulled on his arm, coaxing him to lie down. She wanted to rest her head. What better place than his chest.

As she lay there, thoughts and emotions swirled like dust devils through her mind. He was such an odd mix—a loving and kind soul capable of violence. She'd never encountered the breed.

For now, Deena was calm, content, reassured—surprisingly so. Not much else seemed to matter—except a nagging memory from the night before.

"Honey," she said softly. "I saw something when you were sleeping. I can't explain it."

Bobby was on the edge of dozing off. "What?" he mumbled groggily.

"It looked like the lit end of a cigar," she said. "First, it was just hanging there, then it moved through the air. I could smell it, too."

Bobby chuckled. "Oh, that's just Paulie," he said, stifling a yawn. "My brother's recently taken up smoking cigars."

"But what does it mean?"

With a smile, Bobby turned toward Deena and kissed the top of her head. "That he's given up cigarettes."

"Bobby."

"Welcome to the family," he said. "That's what it means."

* * *

The clinking of two coffee cups signaled the start of breakfast. "Let me propose a toast," Bobby said. "To the late, unlamented Father Veronico and our pig friends who ate him."

To her surprise, Deena giggled and joined in. "To our pig friends," she added, as her cup passed over this morning's meal—ham and eggs over easy.

Deena was amazed by her change in attitude. She had never disrespected the dead. Ever. She was afraid to, in fact.

She wasn't sure ghosts were real but she wasn't taking any chances, either. Her father's unexpected death had spooked her. She missed him, sure, although she didn't know him too well and made fun of his thick accent behind his back.

He was a nice enough man. But what if he came back? Daddy floating through the house scaring the pee out of Mom and her would have been even worse.

Later, when some other relative or even the friend of a friend died, she would dress up and make several visits to a nearby church. There, she would light candles, close her eyes and whisper, "Don't visit me, please."

Her ritual must have worked. Until recently, she'd lived a ghost-free life—her preferred way of being. So what was she doing living with a man who got regular updates from the other side?

But Bobby had told her not to worry, at least not in this case. Living or dead, Veronico deserved their ridicule and abuse—if not worse. She'd decided to take his word for it.

'You know," Deena said casually, as she sipped apple juice, "it did make me rethink my views."

"About what?" Bobby said, without looking up. He wasn't paying attention, so focused was he on delicately placing a whole egg on a thick slice of ham.

"About Porky," she said, in her best deadpan tone.

Bobby smiled and looked up. "Yes, I'd hoped it would."

*   *   *

A good late-morning cup of coffee sounded right. That's what brought Bobby and Deena to the coffee shop near the college where Bobby said she had seduced him. It was mutual, she insisted, as they both nibbled pastries, thumbed through different sections of the morning newspaper, and sipped coffee, so rich and strong, so different from the domestic brands sold in grocery stores. No gulping allowed, Bobby thought, as even the smallest amount warmed, then jolted, his insides.

Bobby smiled. It was such a perfect moment, or maybe *pluperfect* would be a more fitting modifier. He'd stumbled across the word earlier this week in his English text while reviewing for the GED. One of the meanings—"more than perfect"—caught his eye, and he'd been looking for a chance to use it ever since.

Never mind the word was illogical. After all, what could be more than perfect?

Yes, but so what? Logic aside, it described how he was feeling—about Deena, their future, his hopes for a degree and beyond, a decent and productive life away from Yesler. Bobby figured he might as well use it. He was just a test away from going to college, where he promised himself he would continuously strive for *pluperfection*. Eula and Antonio would expect him to do no less.

Was there even such a word? Who cares? Language changes and grows; it doesn't stay the same. Just listen to all those white kids trying their best to sound black. Besides, he was determined to say it some day without sounding like a fool.

As he sorted through the sports section, an AP story on the Boston Celtics caught his eye. Somehow, the proud and aging Celtics were defying the critics and driving hard to the bucket against Father Time. They had beaten the Knicks last night, the second of back-to-back wins on the road. As usual, the great Bill Russell led the way with 20 points and 18 rebounds.

Impressive, Bobby thought, for a player who was supposed to be nearing the end of the line. On second thought, Russell's performance was much better than that.

"Pluperfect," he mumbled, saying the word for the first time. He liked it so much he said it again. "Pluperfect."

"Pardon me?" Deena asked.

"Oh, nothing," Bobby said.

* * *

After coffee, Bobby and Deena strolled up and down Broadway, taking advantage of the weather—overcast but mild, with not a raindrop in sight. They dawdled and window shopped, no schedule or destination in mind. To Bobby, Deena, usually the chatty one, seemed quiet, unusually so.

Eventually, they ended up a block away from Broadway on a bench looking out on a large city reservoir. There, several large, well-fed gulls were having a grand and raucous time, swooping and diving, a few seeming to delight in turd-bombing the water.

"Ooh, look at that," Bobby said, feigning a frown. "And we have to drink it."

Actually, he thought the scene was quite funny. In his mind he was seeing the city's best restaurants, where mysterious clumps would suddenly appear, bobbing in soups and floating in sauces.

He shook his head. Juvenile humor—he was hoping to outgrow it soon.

To Bobby's comment, Deena finally nodded and frowned, but otherwise said nothing and looked straight ahead. Maybe she wasn't feeling well? Sensing something was wrong, he moved closer and draped his arm around her shoulder.

"I'm a little worried," she whispered. "It's a feeling I haven't been able to shake."

"What is it?"

Deena then turned toward him, her eyes starting to redden. "What if I'm pregnant?"

Deena then lay her head on Bobby's shoulder, wondering how she could have messed up so badly. She said she'd been on birth control since fifteen—enjoying years of all-play, no-pay, one-pill-a-day keeping baby away. Taking the pill was a daily ritual, like morning communion for the heaven bound.

It was one she had sworn by and observed faithfully—until last month, when her prescription ran out. No big deal, she'd told herself. A little abstinence wouldn't hurt her; and besides, she hadn't been in the mood—couldn't even imagine being in the mood—not with the philosophy and literary types she'd started hanging out with.

But then Bobby came along and her mood had suddenly roared back—caution be damned. She was worried, and for good reason. Now, she might be paying the price—and perhaps this relationship, too, would pay a price.

"Bobby . . . ," she began, not sure what more she wanted to say.

"Ssssh," he said, as he nuzzled her cheek and held her more closely. "We'll make it through."

He hoped he'd sounded reassuring and confident—more confident than he felt. Just a few minutes earlier, seagull turds had greatly amused him—and now this. Welcome to the not-so-fun world of adults.

Hope for the best, Bobby thought, but get ready for the worst. He figured that some part-time work would help. There were also loans and grants through the college. Maybe he'd ask Mariano to skip the amateur bouts, take him straight to the pros, where he'd don the small gloves and risk life and limb. It would be worth it if he needed the cash.

Then there was the matter of medical care. The family doctor, Dr. Templeton, had delivered him and his brother. Over the years, she had also made house calls all over town and accepted payments over time from his parents and other poor patients. He would call her tomorrow, confident that Deena would be in good hands.

Bobby figured that these details could all be settled later. For now, he was focused on telling Deena how much he loved her, how he wouldn't be joining the Navy to see the world—and avoid responsibility. And, by the way, he added, shouldn't they be sizing rings and thinking about marriage just in case?

"If you're pregnant, the child should carry my name," Bobby said.

Deena looked at him sadly. "That's just it," she said. "I don't know if it's yours."

"Leonard's?"

"I don't know."

Deena closed her eyes, unsure what to expect. Would Bobby scream and call her names? Would he strike her? Would he stand up and walk away?

What she hadn't considered was what happened next. Bobby was still for a moment, seeming to digest the information, unsure what to make of it or how to respond. He then folded his arms across his chest, leaned back and sighed.

"Irony can be such a bitch," he finally said, but didn't elaborate.

Deena was surprised; it was the first time she'd heard him curse. She also wasn't sure what he meant, but she didn't ask.

Bobby then glanced at his watch and sat up. "It's almost two-thirty," he said. "And that means . . ."

"What?"

"It's noodles and pork time, silly," he said, as he stood, then reached to help her up. He then held Deena and kissed her on her lips.

Noodles and pork meant walking to Chinatown, a healthy stretch from where they were. "But it's only two-thirty," she said, trying not to whine.

"So what?" he said. "It's probably dinner time in China or someplace in the world where there are a lot of Chinese people who, just this second, are eating noodles and pork. And you want us to miss out on that? I don't think so."

Actually she did. Deena was feeling tired, overwhelmed. At the moment, her preferred destination was Bobby's bedroom, where she could take off her clothes and climb under the covers.

"And just how're we getting there?" she asked, already knowing the answer.

"Well, you don't see a limo, do you?" Bobby replied. "That means we walk."

"But it's more than two miles," she whined, this time not caring what she sounded like.

"Oh, Honey, think of the pioneers crossing the plains, think of the Israelites fleeing Egypt, think of John the Baptist in the desert," he began. "They got to where they were going by doing what? Walking, that's what."

"John, as I recall, didn't end up so well," she grumped.

"Okay, he had one bad day," he said, grabbing her hand as they began walking south toward Chinatown. "But he's been doing just fine since."

*   *   *

It was ten after three when they reached their destination, the same restaurant from last night. Deena, declaring she was tired, slid into the booth closest to the door. Bobby scooted in next to her.

During their hike, Bobby had been unusually talkative, telling her stories about Paulie and their parents, the old Pinoys he knew, his neighborhood and friends. She'd walked mostly in silence, occasionally smiling at a pun or comment, all the while wondering why he was doing this, filling the air with words.

The answer suddenly dawned on her as they neared their destination.

Deena knew that between men and women, silence could be deadly—the harbinger of a heartbreak to come. In the past, she would often stop speaking to a lover days before leaving him. It was over, Rover. Why bother to explain?

That wasn't happening here. In her mind, she saw an image of words tumbling into a mortar, gathering there to be ground into paste—a glue to hold her, and them, together. She paused, checking herself for metaphorical purity.

One of her former boyfriends, an older, self-described intellectual with one quarter at Berkeley, used to drone on about his friendship with student activist Mario Savio. They were on the frontlines, he said proudly, pointing to a photo of him getting whacked by the cops. He and his comrades were in the vanguard protecting free speech and leading the revolution—and he hoped she appreciated it.

Savio's pal would also mix leading horses to water with teaching them new tricks, especially when he was loaded, which was far too often, even for Deena. The boyfriend took the value of his hard-earned wisdom seriously; she took it and him much less so.

They'd been together about a month. He'd been talking about making it permanent. He had started to bore her. "You should've stayed in school" were Deena's parting words.

Fortunately, Bobby didn't bother much with metaphors, mixed or otherwise, or pretensions of self–import. She'd glanced at him and smiled as they entered the restaurant. He certainly was an odd one, she'd thought, but kind, loving and lovable—very, very lovable.

Those thoughts still lingered even as Deena scanned the menu. As it turned out, coming to the restaurant was an excellent idea. She was suddenly hungry, famished, in fact.

Bobby nudged her. "Sam's not in the kitchen and I don't know who's cooking," he said quietly. "That means ordering on the safe side, picking easy dishes they can't screw up."

They eventually settled on noodles and pork, fried rice, and garlic fried chicken wings—not too elaborate, but filling and not too bad, either. Somewhere between the second-to-the-last wing and the last spoonful of noodles, Deena suddenly learned about irony and its being such a bitch.

"Leonard's my father," Bobby said, after carefully wiping the grease from his fingers.

Deena, her mouth full of noodles, almost gagged, as Bobby gently patted her on the back.

"Here's some water," he said, handing her a glass.

"He's what?" she finally managed to ask.

"Yeah, we're related," Bobby said evenly, as he recounted what he knew of his mother's one-night affair.

"That means you're not Antonio's . . ."

"So what?" Bobby said, interrupting her. "Leonard did nothing for me or Mom. That's why I didn't come back to the club that night."

"Why?"

"I knew what he was doing," he said calmly, as he opened and clenched his fist. "And I probably would have hurt that worthless piece of shit."

Deena winced but said nothing. She was already aware that Bobby had a harder, more jagged edge, but unlike some of the men she knew, it was one he kept in check, at least as to her. She'd known a lot of outsized male egos, but his was different. He kept his fangs hidden and didn't prey on the weak; his ego didn't depend on it. Bobby may, on occasion, unnerve her, but she knew in her heart she was safe.

It was also the second time Deena had heard Bobby curse and she hoped the change wasn't permanent. She liked his old, more careful way of talking better.

"Antonio did everything else, all the heavy lifting," he continued. "He was always there when I needed him. In my book, that makes him my father and that makes me his son. 'Vincente,' it's the name on my birth certificate. Period. No asterisk needed."

As Deena listened, she found herself becoming both amazed and deeply touched. She didn't really know her dad and wasn't especially close to her mom.

But she could feel how deeply Bobby loved Antonio—an emotion so rare and pure, raw and powerful, especially under the circumstances. As she imagined the closeness of this mix-and-match family, she felt a passing pang of envy.

"How did your parents survive . . ."

"My mother's betrayal?"

Deena winced, recalling her own affair. "It's not the word I would've used," she said, her eyes downcast. *But if the shoe fits*, she thought sadly.

Bobby shrugged. "Antonio loved Eula," he said. "He understood that even good people make mistakes. For Dad, Mom was better than good. She was the best thing to ever happen to him. And he was decent enough and smart enough to understand that."

As he cleared his throat, he paused and glanced at the ceiling. "He was a wonderful man," he finally said.

Deena sighed. Bobby, she knew, was blessed, even now, in the absence of those he loved. Her ex-boyfriends seldom talked about their fathers and, when one of them did, the words were brief and bloodless, mere biography fillers mentioned only in passing. "Oh, Dad?" the fallen Jesuit had said. "He's retired and spends his winters in Phoenix."

"I wish I had known him, Bobby," Deena said softly.

Bobby nodded. "You know, Dad also had a feeling about you, a good one," he began. "When we weren't seeing each other, he kept prodding me. 'She seem like a nice girl, mebbe make you happy,' he said. And then you called and he told you I might be at the gym, even though I asked him not to, and . . ."

"The rest is history," Deena said softly, as she kissed his cheek. "Any regrets?"

Bobby smiled and wrapped both arms around her. "Not one," he whispered.

"Why do you suppose your father liked me?"

"I can't say for sure," Bobby replied. "But maybe you reminded him of someone."

"Eula?"

"Maybe."

*　　*　　*

Hand in hand, Deena and Bobby stood outside the restaurant. Their bellies were full, their hearts fuller. He was running low on cash. With Antonio gone, he'd also have to give up the apartment, the only home he'd known, and then what? Deena's place? He'd worry about the rest of his life tomorrow. Now was all he could manage.

A final splurge was in order and he decided to hail a cab. The apartment wasn't that far away but getting there was mostly uphill. Deena, he figured, had done enough walking for today.

He spotted one coming their way but before he could raise his arm, he felt a tug at his elbow.

"Hoy, Bobby," a familiar voice said.

Bobby turned toward the voice. "Manong Magno," he said, surprised to see him two days in a row. His farm near Renton was a long way from Chinatown.

"I got somethin' to tell you," Magno said in a loud whisper. "Is important."

Bobby was uneasy, not sure how to respond. He wasn't that fond or surprises. "This is Deena," he said.

Magno smiled, nodding toward her and tipping his hat. He said a quick "How you doin', Honey," before refocusing his attention on Bobby.

"Manong, Deena and I are together," Bobby said slowly, trying not to exclude her without offending the old man. "I'm sure it will be fine to tell both of us."

Magno paused, a forefinger to his cheek, and briefly pondered the change in plan. "Okay, I guess is okay," he began. "I saw Antonio this morning?"

"What?"

"Yeah," the old man continued. "He was sitting at the kitchen table when I got up. 'I didn't hear you come in,' I says. 'I go fix us some coffee. You had a good time?' Then I go to the stove and heat some water and Antonio says, 'Hoy, Magno, remind Bobby about the shoebox in my closet. That boy, he's good, but sometimes he forget.' When I turn around to say something back he wasn't there no more."

The old man shook his head. "The strangest thing, huh?"

"Not so strange, Manong," Bobby said softly.

Chapter Sixteen

The shoebox was in a corner of Dad's closet, atop which was a note addressed to "My Sons." Bobby knew the message was from Eula; Antonio had never learned to write.

Bobby bent down and reached for the note before hesitating, then withdrew his hand. It was all too strange, too final and sad, his parents' last act.

He glanced at Deena. "I don't know," he said.

"Antonio and Eula wanted it this way," she said quietly. "Whatever's in there they want you to have."

Bobby nodded. He then took a deep breath before plucking the note and carrying it to the bed where the light was better.

"I'm not long for the world and neither is Dad," the note began. Bobby, his eyes welling up, couldn't continue. He put the onion skin sheet down. It wasn't just the message, it was the script—squiggly and imprecise, so untypical of a woman proud of her elegant handwriting.

Over the years and on Antonio's behalf, she had written letters on other onion skin sheets to his relatives in the Philippines. They always responded. A young nephew, Inocencio, had even lavishly praised the eye-pleasing style before adding, oh, by the way, could Tio Antonio send fifty dollars, please? Inocencio stopped receiving letters.

Good penmanship, she'd once told Bobby, was a sign of the writer's respect for beauty and order. It was a lesson she'd learned from Midori, her closest childhood friend. Eula would

247

visit Midori's home, where the two girls would giggle and spend hours practicing the intricate brush strokes to create Japanese characters, each character a work of exquisite beauty.

Midori had given Eula one of the reasons she'd liked St. James, where good penmanship ranked just below godliness and chastity and was almost equal to cleanliness. She was confident that Bobby would learn, as she did, to properly dot each "i" and to correctly cross each "t"—every dot an identical bullet, every cross an identical horizontal line.

Bobby wondered what effort it had taken Eula—weakened and in her last days, possibly hours—to scrawl her final message of love? She wouldn't have liked the note's messy appearance.

"I can't go on right now," he said, in a voice choked by emotion.

He handed Deena the note. "Please read it to me," he managed to say. "Please."

"Bobby, I shouldn't."

"Please."

Deena looked at him, then reluctantly raised the note to the light. "'Your father and I have saved for you both,'" she began slowly. "'Some of the money comes from my odd jobs; some comes from Dad's poker winnings over the years. The final amount surprised us—it wasn't bad. Dad and I only wish it could have been more. As parents, we count our blessings. In your own distinct ways, you were the very best of sons. We only ask that you continue to love each other as deeply as Antonio and I have loved you.'"

Deena sighed and dabbed at her eyes. She gently placed the note on a pillow then rested her head on Bobby's shoulder.

Opening the shoebox, she knew, would have to wait. For now, though, not another word would be said; not another word would be needed.

*   *   *

Poylcarp was smiling; he enjoyed being a bishop bearing gifts, in this case a box of Bolivars, Paulie's favorite brand. He'd looked for Paulie at the pier and his other favorite haunts before finding him seated in a corner of Antonio's bedroom.

"Paulie," the bishop said. "I brought you something."

The younger man looked up, eyes blinking, trying to smile. "Thanks, Poly," he whispered hoarsely. "That's real kind."

Polycarp was both surprised and concerned. Normally, Paulie was such a free spirit, upbeat, a source of constant amusement. It was one of the reasons the old bishop was so fond of him. In death as in life, opposites do attract.

"What happened?"

"You know, Bishop, I seen a lot of beauty here," Paulie began. "But what I just seen and heard in this room . . ."

"What was it, my son?"

Paulie shook his head slowly. "Where we're at's so sweet that sometimes you forget about the beauty you left behind," he said softly. "Damn, Poly, there's still a lot of it there."

*   *   *

Bobby was sitting at the kitchen table and staring at the wall. On occasion he would sip from a tall glass of Jack on the rocks, courtesy of Antonio who always kept a bottle handy.

He wasn't much of a drinker and wasn't too fond of Jack Daniels, either. But none of that mattered, at least not tonight. This evening, all he planned to do was to sit and sip, sit and sip, until the bottle was empty—or he felt numb—whichever came first.

Deena had joined him at the start when the fifth was full—it was half that now. She drank ice water, aware she might be carrying a child. After half a glass, she said that was it. She was tired, her feet hurt, stay up if you like, she told him, but she was going to bed. Bobby then said she should open the shoebox and count the cash.

At first, she frowned and hesitated. He insisted. "You'd be doing me a favor," he said.

Bobby didn't want to think or remember. He didn't want to count money. Mostly, though, he didn't want to feel, as he sat and sipped, sipped and sat.

So focused was Bobby on his task that he had failed to notice that Deena had entered the kitchen and was standing beside him, gently coaxing him to stand. He was vaguely aware he was on his feet and moving, but he couldn't feel his arm draped over her shoulder or the slow and clumsy shuffle to his room.

"I stopped counting at ten," Deena said, as she sat him down on the bed.

Bobby was momentarily upright but not for long. "Dollars?" he said, as his upper body plopped over, his head landing on a pillow.

Deena then completed the job by lifting his legs onto the bed and removing his tennis shoes. "Thousand," she replied, before reaching over to turn off the light.

*   *   *

There have been better, more appreciative audiences than Bobby Vincente, who tonight was stuck in the deepest valley of a thoroughly pickled sleep. No matter, the show must go on, in this case, a lushly colored dream of the day his father died.

In the dream, Antonio was as Bobby remembered him—dressed to kill, relaxed and happy. He was in a clearing in the woods, sitting on a mound of grass and resting his back against the thick trunk of a century-old evergreen. Bobby could also hear, but couldn't see, the sound of moving water, possibly a creek or a small stream nearby. It was an isolated, idyllic scene, Bobby thought, straight out of *National Geographic*—the perfect spot for a lovers' picnic.

The day was sunny, unseasonably warm, and the old man had removed his jacket and loosened his tie. He seemed to be waiting for someone, as he plucked nearby dandelions and clovers, flicking them into the air and watching then rise and fall.

Suddenly his eyes darted toward the sound of movement in the underbrush, of twigs and leaves cracking. He smiled, the smile seeming to say it wouldn't be long now.

Bobby could see the back of a woman wearing a dark dress that was narrow at the waist. He recognized it from the old black-and-white photo of his mom. From her right arm dangled a small basket full of sandwiches and fruits.

"Hi, Honey," the woman said.

Antonio, eyes glistening, turned toward her and smiled. "Eula, I miss you, Sweetheart," he said softly.

"You remember this spot?"

Antonio nodded. "Of course," he said. "North Bend, how can I forget? We visit it when? I don' remember. But is beautiful here, jus' like you, Honey."

"Bobby's taken care of?" she asked.

"Yes," he replied.

Eula smiled. "Shall we go?" she said, as she extended her hand.

In the dream, Bobby then saw his father reach to grasp Eula's hand, then slowly begin to rise—to rise out of his body and to stand facing her. Bobby gasped at first, not believing what he'd seen.

Dad's essence, he thought. That's what it had to be.

"Now, that wasn't so hard, was it?" Eula asked.

"No, not so hard," Antonio said.

They both glanced at Antonio's body resting against the tree. "You look peaceful," Eula said.

Antonio nodded. "Yes."

For a moment, they stood facing each other, just smiling and holding hands. As they did, the wrinkles around Eula's eyes began to disappear, the same with the white in Antonio's hair. At the end, they'd become who they were on that night in San Francisco, so many years ago.

"If we want to, we can do that," Eula explained, as they began walking toward their picnic spot, rounding a bend and soon disappearing from sight.

"By golly," Bobby heard Antonio say giddily. "Oh, my goodness, Sweetheart, I think I'm gonna like it here."

* * *

In the dream, part two, the scene shifted to an opening wide-screen shot of Bobby standing in the middle of a movie set. The camera suddenly zoomed in to focus on the only other person present. Paulie was sitting on a director's chair and smoking a cigar. He was dressed in a blue blazer and black beret and seemed pleased with this, his latest reincarnation—former street thug as artist.

On his lap was a small dog with bristly fur, some kind of terrier, Bobby guessed. The dog looked vaguely familiar.

"Pretty slick, huh?" Paulie said. "Little brother, what you saw was my last film. But I'm all done now, gonna split while I'm on top, gonna hang up my beret and leave my many fans beggin' for more."

Paulie then bowed and waved his hand to an imaginary audience. "'That's all, folks.'"

He chuckled and took a puff from his cigar. "Figured I'd go out in style. Know what I mean?"

Bobby shrugged. He actually thought the beret was a size too small and looked downright silly flopped over a side of his brother's big head. But that was just Paulie being Paulie. He was never shy; he was always looking for a stage.

"Good to see you," Bobby said. "So, Dad's okay?"

"Yeah, it was how he wanted to go."

"I'm glad."

Paulie then said that Antonio wanted Bobby to take care of some important business for him, so listen close. First, he had to call the sheriff's department to recover the body. Make up a story, Paulie advised, that maybe he got lost, disoriented, and wandered in the woods down by the river—old people do it all the time. Keep it simple—something even blockhead deputies can understand.

Then contact a funeral home—Antonio didn't have a preference—and, most importantly, go to Chinatown and tell all his pals that there's free food and booze afterward. Dad wants a crowd, a party. Use some of the shoebox money and don't be cheap, he added; there's plenty of cash to go around.

"Dad's already got a plot picked out and paid for," Paulie added. "So, no need to worry about that."

Bobby was surprised. This was news to him. "He does? Where?"

"Right next to Mom," Paulie replied.

He then picked up the dog, cradled it like an infant and rubbed its belly. "Ooh, you so cute, so cute," he cooed. "Ooh, Poochie, don't be scared of Filipinos. I promise not to eat you."

Paulie smiled and looked up. "Oh, I almost forgot," he said. "You should get started on it Wednesday after the exam."

"That's kind of late, isn't it?"

"Nah," he said dismissively. "Dad's dead and he'll stay dead. Trust me, I know these things. A few more days ain't gonna kill him, so to speak. And besides, he didn't wanna mess your head. So, after the exam, Schoolboy, got it? Dad's orders."

Bobby nodded. "Got it," he said, and started to walk away. He would have continued walking but there was something about the dog that tweaked his curiosity and turned him around.

"Paulie, isn't that . . ."

His brother smiled. "I was wonderin' when you'd notice."

Paulie was now holding the dog upright facing Bobby, his thumb and forefinger grasping the animal's right paw. Their up-and-down movement mimicked a wave.

"Toto, say hi to Uncle Bobby," Paulie said. "He promises he won't eat you either."

Bobby was flabbergasted. "Wow, Toto" was all he managed to say.

Paulie lowered Toto to the floor, where it wagged its tail and barked once before jumping onto his lap. "I'da brought you Dorothy, too, but she just ain't dead enough yet," he began. "That's changin' real soon, though."

"How do you know?"

"Man, bein' dead, I can find out anything."

"Like?" he asked, as several tantalizing questions floated through his mind.

Paulie was already where Bobby was going. "Like the exam? Hey, no sweat," he began. "Like you and Deena? Same thing. Kids. Marriage, grandkids, happy and long lives. Ward and June Cleaver, the whole boring bit."

"Well, is Deena . . ."

"Uh-huh."

"And . . ."

"It's a boy," Paulie replied.

"And . . ."

Paulie again put Toto on the floor, where again the dog stayed for a second or two before clambering back up. "Well, I guess Toto loves Pinoys," he muttered. "Not sure if that's good or bad."

He then stared at Bobby. "You sure you want the answer to that?" he said.

Bobby shrugged but otherwise didn't reply.

"You love her, right?" Paulie asked.

"Yes, of course," Bobby said.

"You gonna raise him, right?" Paulie said evenly.

"Yes."

"You gonna give him our name and love him like me and Dad loved you, right?"

Bobby could feel himself getting warm. "Yes, of course, I . . ."

"So, what the hell does it matter anyways?" Paulie said. "Either way—brother, son—hey, check this out: A *broson*. Man, now that's a cool word. Made it up myself, right here and now, I might add. Man, I got this gift for language."

Paulie laughed and clapped his hands, clearly pleased with himself. "Ooh, sometimes I could just kiss myself."

He then cleared his throat and looked his younger brother in the eye. "Whatever the kid is, he's gonna need your love," Paulie said solemnly. "It's that damn simple and it ain't that hard to understand."

Ashamed, Bobby looked down. "You're right," he mumbled.

"Oh, yeah, one other thing," Paulie said. "Dad says you need a haircut."

"Huh?"

"He's tired of you lookin' like a Beatle or somethin'," Paulie said.

Reflexively, Bobby reached up and touched the hair on his neck. "It's not that long," he said.

Paulie, though, was in no mood for an argument. "Three tomorrow, at Mama's in Chinatown, be there," he ordered. "You know the place. I'ma show up and my little dog, too."

"Sure," Bobby said, as he nodded and turned to walk away.

"Toto, say goodbye to Uncle Bobby," he heard Paulie say, as the dream, part two, slowly faded, the last sound that of a small dog barking.

Chapter Seventeen

When Bobby opened his eyes, he had one thought only: So this is what a hangover feels like. Sure, he'd had a sense of it from Paulie and his pals, who incessantly bragged of their overlong, heavily liquored nights—sometimes, but not always, involving female companions.

Up until last night, Bobby had avoided such misadventures—vomiting through his mouth and nose and falling dead drunk on the floor weren't his idea of fun. And now, he was paying the price in the form of aching muscles, a rumbling gut, and creaky, old-before-their-time bones. Even his kneecaps hurt.

But he didn't have a headache, which Paulie swore showed up sure as sunrise on every morning after. It was a blessing after a fashion, one for which he was thankful.

Just to be sure, he slowly shook his head and no, there was no headache, although his stiff neck and shoulders made him think twice about ever shaking his head again. Without moving his head and while looking straight at the ceiling, he slowly extended his left arm, then his right. He felt nothing but sheets and blankets.

Where the heck is she? he wondered. The question was followed by a groan. Of course, Deena could have been anywhere—an errand, perhaps, or out for a walk if the morning was pleasant. But a freshly pickled brain can often miss the most obvious details in its effort to grasp a narrowed version of reality.

Wherever she had gone, Bobby figured he was to blame. He couldn't help thinking this way—too many nuns, too much original sin. It started with the drinking—a sin, he'd once been told by Sister Victor. He shouldn't have done it; actions have consequences. Losing her was his punishment.

His current Deena-less predicament all made Baltimore Catechism sense. Guilt, he was gobbling it by the can—skip the cream, no sugar, please.

Right now, a less drastic explanation for Deena's absence wouldn't do.

He thought he must have done or said something stupid enough to drive her away, to make her think that he and his nosy and intrusive family of ghosts were too much for any sensible woman to take.

He didn't puke or smack her—at least he didn't think he did. But what if he had? What if he'd been an unforgivable ass? He'd seen his brother and his friends act that way.

Maybe sometime in the night Deena had just thrown up her hands and taken the first bus back to Frisco. Would she even send him a postcard?

This time, Bobby filled the room with a louder groan, followed by an eyes-closed, fists-clenched attempt to piece it all together, moment by moment. He cursed himself; he cursed the night, as if such outbursts would help him remember. The overall effort was futile—any veteran drunk could have told him that.

Despite his soreness, Bobby summoned enough will to ignore the pain and to prop himself up. *Think*, he told himself, as tiny sweat beads formed on his brow. *Concentrate*. He did remember sitting at the table and drinking, he did remember flopping into bed. Also recalled was the dream, not all of it, but enough—of Dad's last hours, of Paulie and Toto, of a haircut at Mama's later today. But beyond that were too many question marks, too many blanks.

Bobby was so focused, so distressed, he almost didn't hear the creak of a door slowly opening.

"Hi, Honey," Deena chirped, as she brought him a tall glass of bubbling water. "I went to the store and got you something," she said. "Pop, pop, fizz, fizz—I figured you'd need it."

As she handed him the glass, Bobby sighed heavily. "Thanks," he mumbled.

Deena smiled, then turned and walked toward the door. "I'll be running you a nice, hot tub, as hot as you can stand," she said from the hallway. "You're gonna need it, and I gotta get you ready."

"Why?"

"Pardon?" she asked, as she poked her head into the room.

Bobby raised an index finger as he drained the glass. He wrinkled his nose as he downed the last gulp before wiping his lips with the back of his hand.

"Why?" he repeated.

"Oh, I don't know," she said, as she stepped back into the hall. "I heard you're getting a haircut. Three at Mama's, right?"

* * *

Bobby and Deena were sitting close together in the back seat of the cab, destination Mama's. She was quietly explaining—almost whispering—what had happened to her during the night. It was very strange, but she found that by being with

Bobby, her tolerance for, ahem, odd things happening had significantly increased.

"It used to scare me," she admitted. "Not so much now. I guess it's an acquired taste."

Bobby smiled. "It is."

Deena said she was soundly asleep when she suddenly found herself on what looked like a movie set. From where she stood, she could see and even hear Bobby and Paulie and the little dog that looked like a terrier.

"You didn't see my father?" Bobby asked, referring to the first part of the dream.

"No," she said.

The response troubled him. He wasn't sure at first what to make of the omission. "So, that's Paulie," he finally said. "What do you think?"

"You two don't look at all alike," she replied, as she reached to hold his hand. "If you ask me, I got the pick of the litter. Besides, he looked kinda silly in that beret."

"He'd be crushed to hear you say that," Bobby said, as he glanced out the window and gazed at the landscape—the old brick buildings and the familiar brown faces. A great place immersed in memories, he thought sadly. But wandering through Chinatown will never be the same without Eula, Antonio—and even Paulie.

The cab soon turned onto King Street, just a few blocks away from their destination. "I think he wore it just for you," Bobby said quietly.

Deena squeezed his hand. "But I'm with you. I know your brother's type. Maybe in the past, but no more."

"Paulie's always been that way," Bobby said. "He's always had a hard time with limits."

"We're here," the driver announced, as the cab slowed to a halt in front of a white storefront barbershop, where the shades had been drawn. Bobby peered out the window—no light inside, it looked closed. He knew otherwise.

"Maybe it's a good thing, then," Deena mumbled, as Bobby handed the driver a five for a two-dollar fare.

"Keep the change," Bobby said, as he stepped out of the cab. He then turned toward Deena, who had joined him on the sidewalk.

"Honey, I'm sorry," he said. "I didn't hear what you said."

Deena's cheeks reddened. That's the problem with talking to yourself, she thought. Someone's bound to overhear you giving voice to random, careless thoughts. She hesitated, wondering if she should repeat what she'd thought and had partly spoken. She sighed and rolled the dice.

"Maybe it's a good thing Paulie's dead," Deena finally said.

Bobby blinked, uncertain how to reply. Sure, his brother had his faults, many of them major, and if he'd lived, trying to steal Deena might have been one of them.

But Paulie had been his protector, his childhood hero, always with him through thick and thin. There might have been friction had he lived, maybe even a fistfight, but Bobby knew—or at least believed—they would have somehow worked it out.

In the end it boiled down to Paulie causing problems or Paulie being gone. No sweat, Bobby thought, he would pick the first one every time.

He then glanced at Deena, whose uncertain look revealed what she was thinking. Had she crossed a line? Maybe she had, but so what? Be kind, Bobby told himself. She's a newcomer and doesn't fully understand the blood rules of the small tribe he'd once been part of—and perhaps still was.

"No," he said softly, as he took her hand, caressing it. "It's not a good thing, not a good thing at all."

*   *   *

It took just a turn of the knob and an opening door to visit a chapter of Bobby's past. In the filtered light of the afternoon sun, Bobby scanned the old barbershop. It was as he remembered—spotless, the way Mama liked it—with two big chairs in the middle and two rows of tall, wall-length mirrors facing each other. He was pleased to know it hadn't changed.

Mama, who lived in the back room of the barbershop. was gone. Why, he didn't know. Paulie, Bobby was sure, would be able to provide an explanation.

Bobby smiled. He liked being once again in this warm, familiar place. Antonio used to bring the boys to Mama's when they were young. But their trips abruptly ended when one of his long-time friends, Manong Teo, set up shop three blocks away.

Never mind that Teo was nearsighted and not very good at cutting hair, something that became evident after their first visit to the new barbershop. Over the years, the boys' heads would sometimes look a tad lopsided; one time, he stabbed Bobby's ear with the scissors; on several occasions, Bobby and Paulie would whine that they missed Mama's gentle, expert touch.

Bobby and his brother weren't alone. The sons of other old Pinoys would join them at Teo's, where they'd sit, sullen and mute, awaiting their fate.

For Antonio, none of that had mattered; long friendships counted almost as much as family ties. In Teo's case, the old man had shown his respect for their decades-old bond by paying cash for his sons' bad haircuts. After three years of operation, Teo had saved enough to go to the Philippines and return with a new—and very young—bride from the countryside.

A young Paulie had once taken a stab at trying to explain their father's loyalty to his friend. They were still in the apartment, a few minutes before a scheduled trip to Teo's.

"It's an old Filipino deal," Paulie said *sotto voce*—Antonio was just down the hall. "And Dad's a . . ."

"Old Filipino?" Bobby replied.

"Yup, they're funny that way," his brother continued. "That means more crummy haircuts cuz him and Teo's so close. And guess what? We'll probably be the same way with our own kids."

That conversation and other memories came rushing back as Bobby stood quietly in the middle of the room, gazing at his image endlessly reflected in a mirror. As a little boy, he would stare in awe, wondering where the end of forever was. He was wondering the same thing now.

His dalliance with fond childhood memories was brief. A familiar voice quickly carried him back to the present.

"Bobby," Deena said. "What're you thinking?"

She was seated on a small couch away from the door. Bobby shrugged as he walked over to join her.

"Ah, nothing, really," he said. "Just remembering this place, that's all. It's been a long time."

He smiled as he sat next to Deena, savoring her beauty, her face illuminated by the soft afternoon light. He wondered how she would look ten, thirty, fifty years from now. Still lovely, no doubt. He knew Antonio had felt the same way about Eula, his only love. The feeling made sense to him.

"What do you think'll happen next?" she asked.

"I guess we'll just have to see," he said.

They didn't have long to wait. First came the movements—Deena's eyes fluttering, her head turning slightly—then the sound. "Honey, your brother's here," she said.

"You can see him?"

She nodded. "Yes," she replied. "He's wearing a beret and sports jacket, same as in the dream. I can also see Toto and this old guy with a long beard."

"Polycarp," Bobby mumbled, as he turned toward the center of the room.

"Poly who?"

"Remember, I told you about him," Bobby began. "He was a bishop and an early Christian martyr. But mostly, he's my brother's friend."

"Oh, yeah," she said. "Now I remember."

"Hey, man," Paulie said. "It's wrap-up time, you know, the point where Roy Rogers sings 'Happy Trails' and be sure to tune in next week, li'l buckaroos, unless you do somethin' stupid, like die before the next show, or somethin'."

Paulie was perched on one of the red barber's chairs, with Toto nestled happily on his lap and Polycarp, staff in hand, standing next to him.

"Today, we got a little travelin' to do and my pal here," he said, nodding to Polycarp, "he's gonna show us the way. Ain't that right, Bishop?"

Polycarp nodded and snapped his fingers. "Ooh, my bruthaa, you got that right."

Bobby and Deena looked at each other, surprised by the bishop's demeanor and choice of words.

Paulie smiled. "The night before, we went and checked out James Brown," he said. "Live at the Apollo. That's right, New York City. Hey, when you're dead you can be anywhere you wanna be. And after all that, Polycarp here just ain't been the same."

Upon hearing his name, the old bishop smiled and thrust his fist skyward. "Power to the people," he said.

Paulie shook his head. "Now he wants to be a Famous Flame or maybe a Panther or maybe both, who knows? But I says, 'Whoa, my man, wrong race, wrong century. We gotta go one step at a time, starting with the sandals.'"

Paulie paused. "Man, try skatin' across the floor on them," he said. "No way, they just too funky; it can't be done, uh-uh. It's tricky when a white dude goes black—and don't never go back."

He then turned his attention to Deena. With a dramatic flourish, he doffed his ill-fitting beret, then bowed slightly before speaking.

"We haven't formally met," he began with a burst of eye flutters and the slyest of smiles. Why not bring out the big guns from his overstocked arsenal of charm?

"I'm Paulie," he continued. "I know my baby brother's told you about me—and ooh, good God, you just the sweetest young thang, if you don't mind me sayin' so. And I'm hopin' you don't."

"Oh, geeze," Bobby muttered to no one in particular.

Actually, Deena did mind, but she held her tongue. She blushed as Bobby, fighting a growing irritation, rolled his eyes. Paulie was just being Paulie; he's family, a blood tie, he kept reminding himself.

"Hi," Deena said meekly.

"Where's Mama," Bobby asked, hoping to change the subject and Paulie's focus. He could almost hear his brother's heart thumping; he blinked, thinking he could see the blood on his teeth. For Paulie, the chase was on. For Bobby, it was embarrassing.

"She's out in Kent hangin' with one of her farmer cousins or somethin'," Paulie said, without looking at him. "A couple days ago I sent her a dream that maybe she should go do that and, oh, forget lockin' the door while she was at it."

"Are Mom and Dad coming?" Bobby asked.

"Yeah," Paulie said, still smiling, still gazing his overly fond gaze at Deena.

"When?" Bobby asked evenly, hoping that a series of bing-bang questions would finally distract him.

He knew it wasn't anything personal his brother was doing. He was on automatic pilot and couldn't help himself. Forget the booze, the dope. His big addiction was insufferable ego, the ongoing need to affirm himself, to be unforgettable—number one in the street, number one in the hearts and minds and the bedrooms of the ladies, any lady for that matter. Dying hadn't changed his attitude.

Bobby sighed. Being brothers wasn't easy. He closed his eyes, knowing what would happen next, praying that Paulie wouldn't cross a line he couldn't forgive.

Paulie turned and looked at Bobby, the look a barely concealed scowl. "Man, I don't keep their schedules," he spat, before turning back to Deena.

Bobby looked away, determined to stay calm. The scene would have to run its course.

"Like I was sayin'. . . ," Paulie began.

Deena fidgeted, her eyes darting left to right, then back again. Paulie made her nervous. She knew she was watching a two-legged canine, an alpha dog used to getting his way. Andrew, her ex-boyfriend cop in Frisco, was a little like that, but even he had his limits, such as a fear of losing his job should someone catch him going too far. She didn't believe Bobby's older brother had any idea what "too far" was. Had the two met, she had no doubt that Paulie would have beaten Andrew up and then shot him with his department-issued revolver—the latter just for fun.

Suddenly, Deena became very still, as she focused her gaze on Paulie. "It's nice to meet you and become a member of this family," she said quietly.

She then turned to Bobby and kissed him gently on his lips. "I'm in love with your brother."

For a moment, Paulie was speechless, surprised by her rejection. Bobby and Deena glanced at each other, nervous and unsure what would happen next.

A trace of a smile appeared on Paulie's face, which was followed by laughter, the sound of which soon filled the room. "Sometimes I amaze myself," he said. "I was just playin'."

He leaned back in the barber's chair and stared at the overhead light. "Oh man, mackin' when a super fine lady's on the scene," he began. "It's a hard habit to break, almost like instinct, you know? And I was good, too, the best. My brother can tell you how I useta be when I useta run the streets. Even bein' dead, I still got caught up in the game, that's all."

He paused and looked first at Deena then at his brother. "I didn't mean no harm," he said softly.

Bobby was relieved. "It's not a big deal," he said with a shrug. "We're brothers. Your dying didn't change it, and that's what matters in the end."

Paulie smiled, then turned away. He didn't want anyone to see his eyes start to water.

Bobby noticed and stared at the floor, waiting for his brother to compose himself. He then cleared his throat. "So, what happens next?" he finally asked.

"Honey, this is what happens next." It was Eula's voice. But where, Bobby wondered, as he quickly scanned the room.

"Over here," Paulie said, pointing to one of the wall mirrors.

Bobby stood up and extended his hand toward Deena, who remained seated. She took it, but hesitated at first, leading him to believe she was overwhelmed, emotionally exhausted by his world of intrusive and challenging spirits. And who could blame her?

For him, the surreal—the erasure of the line between life and death—had become as normal as December rain. The unknown had become known, even intimate and sometimes welcome. Besides, what was happening was a family affair. There was no way he could have avoided Paulie, Eula, and Antonio even if he'd wanted to.

But for others, especially an outsider, the challenge of redefining reality—and discarding the comfort of memorized rules and predictability—can be daunting. He knew that Deena deserved a boatload of credit for holding steady so far, accepting one strange, brain-rattling experience after another. It was, he concluded, a matter of will—she was here, suspending disbelief, because she wanted to be, because she loved him.

He felt blessed by this woman. Anyone else would have run screaming from Dodge a long time ago.

"It'll be okay," he whispered, wishing he could somehow come up with the right words, powerful *abra-cadabra* words, to magically erase her fears.

She looked up, her smile tiny, uncertain. "I know," she managed to say, as she took Bobby's hand.

"It's the last act," Bobby added.

She nodded but otherwise said nothing as they walked toward the mirror, standing to the right of the chair Paulie was occupying.

"Check it out, man," Paulie said, nodding toward the mirror.

"I don't see anything," Bobby replied.

"Look closer."

Bobby blinked and squinted. In the distance, he could see two tiny spots, not much bigger than the miniature plastic soldiers he'd played with as a child. At first, he couldn't see movement—they were too far away. Then, after a minute, he could see arms and legs moving as they walked toward him, growing larger by the step, eventually becoming the Eula and Antonio he'd seen in his dream—young again, happy, deeply in love.

Holding hands, his parents—Dad in his suit, Mom in her elegant dark dress—stepped out of the mirror and entered the room, flashing the brightest smiles at Paulie and Polycarp, Bobby and Deena. Bobby wanted to say something, a greeting, anything, but couldn't, at least not at first. His stomach churned and growled as he glanced around the room, picturing in his mind a final curtain call, then the theater going silent and the stage turning black. Of the four people he loved, three would soon be gone.

He felt a lump in his throat. "Mom, Dad," he said softly, only to be met by Eula's index finger raised to her lips.

"Shhh, Honey, there's no need to say anything," Eula said. "Your father and I can read your heart. We can feel your love. And your sadness, but there's no need to be that way."

Eula paused, still smiling. She fixed her gaze on Bobby. "Baby Boy, we, Dad and I, Honey, we love you, too. And that's why your father stuck around, we all did, to make sure that you could take care of yourself. We wanted to be sure you'd be fine, and now you are."

She nodded at Deena. "You got yourself a good girl," Eula continued. "You'll take care of each other. You—both of you—you gonna have a good life."

"Yeah, man," Paulie added. "Me and Dad here, we got ya'll together and damn, you still almost messed it up." His brother, smug as usual, reached into his inside jacket pocket, pulling out a Bolivar and lighting it. He then took a puff, smiling and taking a moment to savor the taste before crossing his legs and leaning back.

"Man, you owe me and Dad big thanks," he said between puffs and an occasional chuckle. Bobby knew his brother had recovered. He recognized the tone, full of smugness and smirk. It was a set-up. A hammer was about to be dropped. There was nothing he could do now but brace for the impact.

"If it hadn't been for me and him," Paulie began, "you'd still be solo, sittin' in your room and playin' with that teeny little weenie of yours."

Bobby grimaced and could feel his cheeks quickly redden. Despite his embarrassment, he kept his anger in check, choosing instead to say nothing, wondering why his brother was doing this. He didn't understand. In the old days, Paulie was protective of him, sometimes even gentle.

But his attitude had changed. Was it jealousy—as in, *Punk, if I was alive, Deena'd be mine*—or was it something more complex? Maybe just being with a beautiful woman meant Bobby'd grown up and joined the ranks of other young men—for Paulie, potential rivals in the pack to smack down and be kept in their place.

Whatever the reason, Bobby figured it was too close now to reply in kind and mess things up even more. His parents deserved better. All he wanted now was the most graceful end that all of them—finally together as a family—could muster.

At that moment, it didn't look promising. Antonio, who had a pained look on his face, glanced first at his oldest son, then at Eula. She took the cue. "Paulie, hush up! That's enough," she said sharply, pointing her finger at him.

Paulie shrugged and turned toward Polycarp. "Hey, Bishop, what I say wrong?"

Polycarp wasn't paying attention. The old bishop was too busy staring in the mirror, primping himself, seeing how he looked in a top-of-the-line pair of Ray-Bans.

"Ooh, I'm just too sharp, so cool I could almost kiss myself," he mumbled, before turning toward Paulie. "Hey, man, you say somethin'?"

"Never mind," Paulie said, irritated that his mother had scolded him and that his friend had tuned him out. Eula, God bless her, had also taken Bobby's side.

It had happened in the past, like the time years ago when a thoroughly bored Paulie had to babysit his brother, then five. Bobby had fallen asleep on the couch. Just for laughs, Paulie had tied the boy's shoelaces together and tip-toed from the room. He then called him from the hall.

The ensuing stumble and head-long fall struck him as hilarious. He couldn't stop laughing. Eula, though, wasn't amused after Bobby snitched on him. Paulie's prank had cost him a hard smack upside his head and, even worse, a long lecture from his mother on what being a big brother meant.

Paulie sighed as he replayed the incident, still sharp and fresh after so many years. It was tough being the oldest, especially with Bobby, so different from him, so soft and fragile and always on the verge of breaking apart. His folks had made clear, Eula especially, that his job was to keep that from happening—or else.

Who then, he remembered thinking at the time, had the job of protecting *him*?

Paulie hadn't planned to be tough—at least not that tough—but he had to be, for himself, of course, but also for the brother he was charged with protecting. His first win was over an older boy who'd been picking on Bobby. He recalled the thrill he felt as his opponent surrendered, such a potent adrenalin high. He remembered at that moment thinking about Eula and whether she'd be proud of him.

Over the years, he'd found he was good with his hands, perhaps too good, and what had started out as a front—the fierce, never-give-in attitude—had become part of his identity, central to who Paulie Vincente was, or thought he was. Any chance of change had been squashed by his pals, who cheered him and praised him and helped spread his legend.

Over time, the legend grew teeth and claws; it breathed fire. In the end, it held him captive. He couldn't escape even if he'd wanted to.

As Paulie sat in the barber's chair, he began to slowly rub his forehead and temples. He wondered what would have happened if he'd been more cautious or reflective, even occasionally fearful? Would he still be alive today?

What the hell, Paulie thought, answering that question was useless. It was water under the bridge. He stared solemnly at the mirror, taking another slow drag before shifting his attention to Polycarp, who was standing in front of him and ready to resume the conversation.

"Well, whatever it was and whatever you said," Polycarp began, as he reached inside his robe and pulled out an identical pair of Ray-Bans, "this'll li'l thing'll cheer you right up. Besides, where we goin' there's a whole lotta light. You gonna need 'em."

Paulie's face brightened as he took the shades and tried them on. "Thanks, Brother," he said.

Nice fit, the image in the mirror told Paulie, who smiled and nodded approvingly, reassured he was once more the fairest in the land. His sulk, just recently so pronounced and off-putting, quickly vanished, suddenly becoming a thing of the past.

"Uh, Poly, man, where'd you get 'em?" Paulie asked.

"Man, dead rock stars, movie stars, and groupies, livin' fast, dyin' young," Polycarp explained. He glanced at the mirror and ran his fingers through his hair, mugging and making sure the part was just right.

"They all over this place," he continued. "Man, premature death, this just gotta be a sixties thang."

"Maybe."

Further discussion on this topic was interrupted by a speaker who'd been silent so far. "Is time to go," Antonio said abruptly, as he held his Borsalino in front of him, shaping and reshaping the front brim until it bent just right. "We got a long way to go."

Antonio, the hat now perched jauntily on his head, turned toward Eula. "Hey, Honey, this look okay?"

She straightened his tie, then nodded and kissed her husband on his lips. "Ooh, Baby, you lookin' so good."

Bobby smiled. He'd been a witness to this scene—and had heard those very words many times before. He took comfort in knowing that nothing had changed.

"Bishop," Antonio said. "You been there before; mebbe you should lead the way."

"Cool," Polycarp answered, as he, followed by Toto, walked toward the mirror. Without breaking stride, they stepped in, going a few yards farther before turning around to face those still in the room. The Bishop was smiling and shrugging—Toto, tail feverishly wagging, was scurrying about—both man and dog seeming to say it was all so easy, no sweat at all.

Antonio smiled and squeezed Eula's hand. He turned toward Paulie and nodded, his wordless message telling his oldest son it was now time to go.

"Aw, man," Paulie grumbled, as he took another puff and looked around the room for an ashtray—none in sight. He then tossed the still-lit Bolivar at the mirror. The stogie passed through the glass and landed on the other side, where Toto greeted it by racing frenetically in circles before stopping for a sniff, then raising a hind leg and extinguishing the light.

"That stupid mutt ain't got no respect for fine tobacco," Paulie mumbled, as he left the chair to join his parents.

"Hold my hand," Antonio said, as Paulie approached. "We goin' where we goin' as a family."

Paulie looked up, surprised. He hadn't held Antonio's or anyone else's hand—other than the ladies around whom he'd loved to prowl—since he was nine, maybe even younger. He frowned. Holding hands was, well, unmanly; it's what little children did—and he'd stopped being a child a long time ago. For Paulie, Dad's idea was too cute by half.

Eula put an end to any further resistance. "Boy, grab Dad's hand," she said sharply. "I'm not playin' now."

Paulie glanced at his mother, her frown, her furrowed brow, and her beady-eyed stare confirming her words. It had always been that way. Antonio, whose English was limited, preferred to have Eula do the talking—and threatening—to their English-only boys.

Paulie sighed and surrendered. Just as in life, there was no escaping his mother. Reluctantly, he grabbed Antonio's hand.

"That's better," Eula said, nodding in approval.

"Yes," Antonio said, as he pivoted slowly, the movement eventually turning the three of them—Eula on his right, Paulie on his left—to face Bobby and Deena.

"Well, I guess this is it," Antonio began. He turned, looking wistfully at his wife. "I think mebbe we should say somethin' now."

He paused. "Honey, you wanna go first?"

"Okay," she said, as she cleared her throat, gazed at Bobby and seemed to force the tiniest of smiles.

"Baby Boy, you know how much you mean to me, how much I love you," she said, with each succeeding word becoming softer, slower, less audible. She then turned away and placed her head on Antonio's shoulder.

"Nothing changes that," she managed to whisper, unable to continue.

"Mom," Bobby said, unable to say more.

Antonio turned his head just enough to kiss Eula on her tear-stained face. He wanted to comfort his wife, but he wasn't doing too well himself.

The old man took a moment to compose himself. "Bobby," he finally said. "I love you, you know that," he began in a steady voice. "Staying behind to help you out, to make sure you can take care of yourself— that was nice, special, you know?"

Bobby nodded, but said nothing. Dad had never been real good at expressing emotions.

"And then to see you in the ring against that boy," Antonio continued. "What's his name?"

"Alfonso," Bobby replied.

"Yeah, tha's the name," Antonio said. "I was so scared and then you done so good and I'm so proud, so very proud." He then stopped and looked away, then looked back again.

"I love you, Son," he whispered. "I missed your mom and your brother, but I'm glad I stayed."

"I love you, too, Dad," Bobby said, as he took a step forward, both arms inching upward. His brother's voice stopped him dead in his tracks.

"Hey, man," Paulie said. "Don't be comin' over here."

"Why?" Bobby asked.

"Man, you retarded or what?" Paulie said derisively. "You can't be huggin' no ghost. It ain't possible. Sure, we here but we ain't here—least not in the usual way."

"Oh, that's right," Bobby said sheepishly, as he took a step back. "I really hadn't thought about it that way."

He could feel Deena reach for his hand and hold it, the cool softness of her palm and the bottoms of her fingers feeling good to the touch.

So good, in fact, that his sorrow suddenly began to lift as he then glanced at Deena, amazed at how lucky he was. Lucky, too, that he had a chance to say a proper goodbye to Mom and Dad, even difficult and cantankerous Paulie—three of the four people he loved.

Bobby turned to face his brother, whose mien oozed indifference—*cut the sniffles and tears, this overlong drama*, he seemed to be saying. *Let's get this show on the road.*

Paulie had dug a moat and built a thick emotional wall—made up of machismo and anger, possibly resentment—that

Bobby intended to breach. Striking first, he recalled his brother telling him, was better than striking twice. It was now or never.

"I want you to know," Bobby said, checking himself for tone—steady, he thought—trying his best not to blink.

Paulie wasn't making it easy. He released Antonio's hand and pulled out a fresh Bolivar from his inside jacket pocket. He casually lit up, casually inhaled, and casually blew o-rings into the air.

Bobby was undeterred. Sure, reducing this goodbye to a couple of words and a quick wave would have been easier, certainly tidier. He could avoid abuse, implied and explicit, by keeping his thoughts unsaid and letting his older brother leave.

But for so much of Bobby's life, Paulie was the one constant, the young and reluctant surrogate parent who was there when Eula was working and Antonio was fighting his demons. That's why saying goodbye, without saying more, just wouldn't be right. If only Paulie would cooperate.

"I'm glad you're my brother," Bobby said. "I love you. I think you should know that. And I'm thankful for all the times you bailed me out and backed me up."

He then searched Paulie for a sign, an emotional response, a fissure in the wall. Nothing yet.

Paulie shrugged. "Yeah, man, there were enough of 'em," he said calmly, as he flicked the ashes on the floor. "And before you split, make sure you sweep this mess up."

He pointed to a broom and dust pan by the door. "Mama ain't so young no more," he said.

"Sure," Bobby said, irritated, as he struggled to stay on track. He was composing in his mind what he planned to say next.

"Well, man, I think it's time to go," Paulie said suddenly. He then took his father's hand once again and started leading Antonio and Eula toward the mirror.

"I'll see ya when I see ya," he said nonchalantly. He didn't even bother to turn around.

Bobby hadn't expected that. The scene was moving too fast; he had to somehow slow it down.

"Our boy," Bobby said, panic rising in his voice. "We're naming him after you."

That was news to Deena, who was still hoping her pregnancy was a suspicion, not confirmed fact. She pulled Bobby's hand to get his attention. "Huh?" she asked, but said nothing more.

"Paulie Vincente," Bobby replied, without hesitation.

Paulie suddenly stopped, releasing Antonio's hand and turning to face his brother. "You are?" he asked.

Bobby blinked, surprised his spur-of-the-moment gambit had worked. Steady now, he told himself.

"Yes, 'Paulo.' Deena and I like the sound," Bobby began. "And speaking for myself, I'll miss my friend and brother who carried this name."

There they were, ten simple words, starting with "I'll miss." He was suddenly very tired, drained. But not all of the words had missed, as evidenced by his brother's smile—faint, upward twitches at the corners of his mouth. It was smile enough, as far as Bobby was concerned.

"Thanks," Paulie said softly. "I'd like that." He then glanced down for a moment, causing Bobby to think that maybe he'd say something else, causing Bobby to close his eyes and hope for the best. Instead, he grabbed Antonio's hand, nodding at his father and at Eula, the nod saying that the conversation was over, he was ready to go.

The trio then walked through the mirror, Paulie first, then Antonio and Eula. Once on the other side, the three of them—their hands still joined—turned to face Bobby and Deena. Like a Broadway cast, they bowed as one as their two-person audience clapped and hooted and blew kisses for three lives that, under the circumstances, had been pretty well lived.

Polycarp tossed in a flourish by presenting each of them with a long-stemmed white rose. Task complete, the old bishop stepped back, his hand extended in presentation. Paulie, Antonio, and Eula, their faces beaming, then bowed once again—their final time, at least on this stage.

On Antonio's command, they began to move, executing a wheel turn to face the endless reflections of Mama's barbershop. Where they were going was somewhere down the road. Antonio took the first step, as the others fell in.

Bobby and Deena were holding hands and watching in silence, and not a little bit of awe, as Bobby's family plus two moved farther away, entering one smaller barbershop, then another and another, until, finally, Antonio, Eula, Paulie, Polycarp, and Toto were tiny dots in the distance.

Bobby turned toward Deena. "Did you hear that?" he asked.

"What?" Deena asked.

"Paulie's voice."

"No," she replied. "What he say?"

"'St. Paulie,'" he said. "'Make sure you tell your boy that's who I am.'"

She giggled. "Sounds just like him."

Bobby smiled. "Yes, it does," he said. "Must be a brother-to-brother thing."

Deena nodded. "Must be."

He sighed and then walked to the door to grab the broom and dust pan—a final task before they could go. As he was sweeping the ashes near the barber's chair where Paulie had so recently been sitting, his ears perked up. Bobby heard—or thought he heard—a man's clear baritone voice singing the opening line of "Let Me Call You Sweetheart." He stopped what he was doing.

Antonio, he thought.

As a child, he'd heard him croon it to Eula. There was nothing wrong with his father's voice; it was good, in fact. Antonio could carry a tune. But that never mattered to Bobby and Paulie, never stopping them from making faces and crying "ooh" and "corny" each time their father tried to serenade his wife with her favorite song.

He now regretted what he and his brother had done. Kids, he realized, can be so stupid.

Bobby had heard the song one last time at Eula's funeral, where his father had somehow gathered enough of himself to sing it again—his way of saying goodbye. Since that day, he had sometimes wished he could hear Antonio sing it one more time.

No such luck. For Antonio, forced to live a life without Eula, the song had stopped making sense.

"Wow, listen?" he said, as his skin started to tingle.

"Yes, I can hear it," Deena said, as the singing came to an end, followed by the sound of two hands clapping, which was followed by a train of girlish giggles.

"Dad," he said.

"I figured," she said softly.

Bobby resumed sweeping, fully intent on removing every last ash. Paulie was right. Mama was old; they had used her barbershop; she shouldn't have to clean up. He suddenly stopped sweeping, as the first notes of a familiar and beloved song began drifting into the room.

"Do you hear that?" Bobby asked.

Deena nodded, as a man's voice sang, "We're off to see the wizard . . . !"

"That's Paulie," Bobby said with a smile. He shook his head, surprised by his brother's choice of songs. "For all these years, I thought he hated the movie."

Paulie was soon joined by the voices of others, presumably his folks and Polycarp, and the non-stop yip-yipping of a smallish dog, presumably Toto. At the end, all they could hear were yips growing fainter and fainter.

Bobby sighed and dumped the ashes in a small garbage can. He then looked around the barbershop where so much had just happened. He allowed his gaze to linger on the barber's chair, the two mirrors, the sunlight filtering through the blinds. More than anything, he wanted to remember every detail, to absorb the memory of this special day.

"Well, a good goodbye," he finally said, as placed the broom and dust pan by the door. "What do you think?"

"I didn't like the song," she replied.

"Why?"

"That Dorothy," she sniffed. "She's still such a bitch."

*　　*　　*

Bobby and Deena walked east on King Street toward the restaurant, the young couple reveling in the beauty of a cloudless sky and a warm, late afternoon sun. Deena had told him she was hungry; he was, too, come to think of it.

In Chinatown, Tuesday was a great day to eat. Bobby knew that Slim and his brother worked Tuesday afternoons—a delicious off-the-menu meal for sure. Along the way, they passed the familiar haunts—the card rooms and bachelor hotels the old Pinoys favored and that he knew so well.

Sometimes, Bobby would stop and greet well-known faces—Manong so-and-so and Manong so-and-so—pals of his folks, taking time each time to shake hands and introduce Deena, to chit-chat and be polite. But when the old men turned the conversation to Antonio, he would smile, excuse himself, tug on Deena and resume walking. He figured the old-timers would find out soon enough that their numbers had grown smaller by one, just not today.

"You're eating for two now," Bobby said, as he and Deena neared the restaurant.

"How do you know?" She'd been hoping that all that talk about naming the baby after his brother had been just for show, nothing more—a graceful, feel-good end to a tense situation.

"I asked Paulie. He told me."

He stopped and gently patted her tummy. "We have to feed Paulie," he said.

Deena sighed. "Paulie, I guess we gotta get used to the name."

"Yeah, Paulie," he said, as he opened the restaurant door, releasing a mix of enticing aromas that moved them from hungry to ravenous. Slim glanced up from a table he was serving, his warm smile welcoming them as he pointed the way to an open booth.

"Good to see you, man," Slim said, shaking Bobby's hand and nodding at Deena.

"Same here, my friend," Bobby replied, as he and Deena slid onto opposite benches.

"Is your brother back there?"

"Yup."

Bobby beamed. "Then we're all set," he said. "He'll know the score. Off the menu, the best stuff Chinese folks eat. His pick."

Slim winked and turned toward the kitchen. "Gotcha covered," he said over his shoulder.

Bobby leaned back, suddenly aware he was very tired, almost exhausted. Today's events—out of the ordinary by any standard—were finally taking their toll. He picked up a chopstick and began tapping it on the table.

"So, Honey, that's my family and you haven't run away yet," he said with a smile. "I expect it'll be calmer now."

"Doesn't matter," she said with a shrug. She reached across the table and held his hand. "I worked hard to get you, something I've never done before with any man. After all that, what's a few ghosts anyway? No big deal, Baby. I'm not going anywhere."

"Kind of like Eula and Antonio," he said softly.

"Yeah," she replied. "Kinda."

She paused. "By the way, when you talked to Paulie, did he say anything else?"

"No."

Deena glanced away, a tad uneasy, not certain how far to probe. She ended up staring at the wall. Although Bobby had assured her that he'd buried the past, there was always "but then again"—the time-honored escape clause that men often took. For a few moments, all she could hear was the chopstick tap-tapping in her head.

But who was the father? Even thinking about the question made her cringe.

"Did you ask?" she forced herself to say.

"Kind of."

"And?"

Bobby shrugged. "We'll love him. It doesn't matter."

"Baby Paulie, then," Deena said, sighing. "Guess I'll just have to get used to it."

"Little broson," Bobby said with a smile—his smile, despite her reservations, triggered a smile of her own. "He's either my brother or my son."

"Hope he likes Chinese," she said, as Slim suddenly appeared, placing a tea pot and two cups on the table.

"The first dish will be right up," Slim assured them, before hustling off to take another order.

"Only if it's off the menu," Bobby began, as he picked up the tea pot and started to pour. "Standards, Honey. He's got to have them."

Bobby raised his cup as Deena did the same. "I propose a toast," he said.

He paused, making sure his gaze was fixed on Deena. "To little Paulie, our son," Bobby said solemnly, recalling, as he spoke, what Antonio had done for him. "We'll love and protect that child, we'll love each other and to hell with the rest of it."

His words touched her and erased all doubt. "To us, to our son," she managed to whisper, as she dabbed at an eye.

Deena stopped to gather herself. "To broson," she finally said.

About the Author

Peter Bacho has written several books during his career. His nonfiction book *Boxing in Black and White* (Holt) made the Children's Center for Books Best Books List in 1999. He has also won an American Book Award (for *Cebu*, 2006), a Washington Governor's Writers Award (for *A Dark Blue Suit*, 1998), and The Murray Morgan Prize (also for *A Dark Blue Suit*). *Cebu* was listed as one of the top 100 books written by a University of Washington (affiliated) writer over the past century. Bacho has been praised as a "major voice in contemporary literature" (Tom Howard) with a "strong, steady style" (Kathleen Alcala) and a "disarming . . . sense of humanity" (Thomas Keneally). Bacho teaches at The Evergreen State College (Tacoma Branch) in Olympia, Washington.

BOOKS FROM PLEASURE BOAT STUDIO: A LITERARY PRESS

(Note: Caravel Books is a new mystery imprint of Pleasure Boat Studio: A Literary Press. Caravel Books is the imprint for mysteries only. Aequitas Books is another imprint which includes non-fiction with philosophical and sociological themes. Empty Bowl Press is a Division of Pleasure Boat Studio.)

Lessons Learned ~ Finn Wilcox ~ $10 ~ an empty bowl book

Jew's Harp ~ Walter Hess ~ poems ~ $14

The Light on Our Faces ~ Lee Whitman-Raymond ~ poems ~ $13

Petroglyph Americana ~ Scott Ezell ~ poems ~ $15 ~ an empty bowl book

Swan Dive ~ Michael Burke ~ $15 ~ a caravel mystery

The Lord God Bird ~ Russell Hill ~ $15 ~ a caravel mystery

Island of the Naked Women ~ Inger Frimansson, trans. by Laura Wideburg ~ $18 ~ a caravel mystery

Crossing the Water: The Hawaii-Alaska Trilogies ~ Irving Warner ~ fiction ~ $16

Among Friends ~ Mary Lou Sanelli ~ $15 ~ an aequitas book

Unnecessary Talking: The Montesano Stories ~ Mike O'Connor ~ fiction ~ $16

God Is a Tree, and Other Middle-Age Prayers ~ Esther Cohen ~ poems ~ $10

Home & Away: The Old Town Poems ~ Kevin Miller ~ $15

Old Tale Road ~ Andrew Schelling ~ $15 ~ poems ~ an empty bowl book

Listening to the Rhino ~ Dr. Janet Dallett ~ $16 ~ an aequitas book

The Shadow in the Water ~ Inger Frimansson, trans. by Laura Wideburg ~ $18 ~ a caravel mystery

The Woman Who Wrote "King Lear," And Other Stories ~ Louis Phillips ~ $16

Working the Woods, Working the Sea ~ Eds. Finn Wilcox, Jerry Gorsline ~ $22 ~ an empty bowl book

Weinstock Among the Dying ~ Michael Blumenthal ~ fiction ~ $18

The War Journal of Lila Ann Smith ~ Irving Warner ~ historical fiction ~ $18

Dream of the Dragon Pool: A Daoist Quest ~ Albert A. Dalia ~ fantasy ~ $18

Good Night, My Darling ~ Inger Frimansson, trans. by Laura Wideburg ~ $16 ~ a caravel mystery

Falling Awake ~ Mary Lou Sanelli ~ $15 ~ an aequitas book

Way Out There: Lyrical Essays ~ Michael Daley ~ $16 ~ an aequitas book

The Case of Emily V. ~ Keith Oatley ~ $18 ~ a caravel mystery

Monique ~ Luisa Coehlo, trans. by Maria do Carmo de Vasconcelos and Dolores DeLuise ~ fiction ~ $14

The Blossoms Are Ghosts at the Wedding ~ Tom Jay ~ essays & poems ~ $15 ~ an empty bowl book

Against Romance ~ Michael Blumenthal ~ poetry ~ $14

Speak to the Mountain: The Tommie Waites Story ~ Dr. Bessie Blake ~ biography ~ $18/$26 ~ an aequitas book

Artrage ~ Everett Aison ~ fiction ~ $15

Days We Would Rather Know ~ Michael Blumenthal ~ poems ~ $14

Puget Sound: 15 Stories ~ C. C. Long ~ fiction ~ $14

Homicide My Own ~ Anne Argula ~ fiction (mystery) ~ $16

Craving Water ~ Mary Lou Sanelli ~ poems ~ $15

When the Tiger Weeps ~ Mike O'Connor ~ poetry and prose ~ 15

Wagner, Descending: The Wrath of the Salmon Queen ~ Irving Warner ~ fiction ~ $16

Concentricity ~ Sheila E. Murphy ~ poems ~ $13.95

Schilling, from a study in lost time ~ Terrell Guillory ~ fiction ~ $17

Rumours: A Memoir of a British POW in WWII ~ Chas Mayhead ~ nonfiction ~ $16

The Immigrant's Table ~ Mary Lou Sanelli ~ poems and recipes ~ $14

The Enduring Vision of Norman Mailer ~ Dr. Barry H. Leeds ~ criticism ~ $18

Women in the Garden ~ Mary Lou Sanelli ~ poems ~ $14

Pronoun Music ~ Richard Cohen ~ short stories ~ $16

If You Were With Me Everything Would Be All Right ~ Ken Harvey ~ short stories ~ $16

Our Chapbook Series:

From other publishers (in limited editions):

Orders: Pleasure Boat Studio books are available by order from your bookstore, directly from our website, or through the following:

SPD (Small Press Distribution) Tel. 800.869.7553, Fax 510.524.0852
Partners/West Tel. 425.227.8486, Fax 425.204.2448
Baker & Taylor Tel. 800.775.1100, Fax 800.775.7480
Ingram Tel. 615.793.5000, Fax 615.287.5429
Amazon.com or **Barnesandnoble.com**

Pleasure Boat Studio: A Literary Press
201 West 89th Street
New York, NY 10024
Tel/Fax: 888.810.5308
www.pleasureboatstudio.com / *pleasboat@nyc.rr.com*

How we got our name

. . . from *Pleasure Boat Studio*, an essay written by Ouyang Xiu, Song Dynasty poet, essayist, and scholar, on the twelfth day of the twelfth month in the renwu year (January 25, 1043):

> "I have heard of men of antiquity who fled from the world to distant rivers and lakes and refused to their dying day to return. They must have found some source of pleasure there. If one is not anxious for profit, even at the risk of danger, or is not convicted of a crime and forced to embark; rather, if one has a favorable breeze and gentle seas and is able to rest comfortably on a pillow and mat, sailing several hundred miles in a single day, then is boat travel not enjoyable? Of course, I have no time for such diversions. But since 'pleasure boat' is the designation of boats used for such pastimes, I have now adopted it as the name of my studio. Is there anything wrong with that?"

Translated by Ronald Egan